Past Lives

Past Lives

Ryan M. Williams

GLITTERING THRONG PRESS • RAINIER

*This book is dedicated to my grandparents,
for all their love and support. I miss you.*

Chapter 1

Olinda

I call my companion Drac, a joke and an insult that he doesn't understand. I can't pronounce his true name. My mostly human vocal cords can't make those sounds. I'll give Drac this, he moved as quietly as the bat he resembled.

Night on Olinda never gets entirely dark. Especially not when the planet's two moons, Hansel and Gretel, hung in the sky. Drac stuck to the shadows of the craggy rock face above me, his dark body hidden to normal human eyes.

Not mine. Brock Marsden, detective and a founding member of the Moreau Society. I've incorporated alien DNA into my body through the use of the Galactics' Moreau

Pod. I've remade myself. I see much better than normal humans. Even more than that, I saw all around us with my Euzebian scent-sight. An odor of rust and blood rose from Drac, that familiar smell of a Nosferan, but in my scent-sight, he glowed with a pearly sort of color.

The dark, craggy rocks sheltering Drac gave off little odor. A few ashy molecules hinting at the long-dormant volcanic activity that thrust up the shattered islands that made up most of the habitable land on Olinda.

Shadows might hide Drac from other eyes, but to my inner scent-sight, he was glowing as the molecules rose up and the wind snatched them away. The rust and blood smell of him blended with the salt spray of the ocean and the peppery smell of the pastel green coiled plants clinging to the rock face with us.

Twenty meters below us, the waves pounded against the rocks. Hardy organisms clung to the pockets and pits of the rock, nourished by the spray. No sandy beach here. Nothing but a long drop into waves that would smash us to bits.

Not that Drac had to worry. He could fly

away. He climbed to stay out of sight. I, on the other hand, despite my other enhanced abilities, wasn't so lucky. If I fell that'd be it and any hope of saving my lover and my best friend would die with me.

Muriel Reinhard, fellow detective, Moreau, and my lover, had disappeared into the past. She wasn't alone. Drac had brought proof of that. Our agency's intern and my friend, a massive Eyotan named Dyami was with her. Dyami was huge, black with orange stripes and looked like some sort of Halloween nightmare. Sweet guy, unless he got mad.

The key to saving them was above us, locked in Orlando Pike's fortress. He had a piece of Galactic tech which I needed to get them back.

"We must move, Esteemed One." Drac's whisper reached my sensitive ears.

"Brock. I've told you." The whole Esteemed One business brought up memories I didn't want to think about. Things I had thought safely buried almost a hundred years ago.

I reached up with my left hand, fifteen segmented, bright red tentacles reaching out and finding tiny cracks in the rock. The

C'lacktal hand wasn't my idea, even if it had proven useful. The tentacles were a lot stronger than they looked.

Anchored, I reached with my other hand. I relied on my scent-sight and feel to find the next handhold. I pulled myself up the narrow crack. Like Drac, with my dark coat, I was effectively hidden from most eyes. Unless an alien came along that saw infrared, no one would see us. Even then, it might not matter. Olinda's permissive laws regulated very little, so long as it didn't harm anyone else.

Climbing the rocks wasn't the problem. What we planned to do when we got to the top? That was something else.

Chuffing cries floated through the air behind me. I didn't see anything at first, but I recognized the sound. A second later I picked up a salty, musky smell, a blur in my scent-sight, streaking past a meter from my head.

Olindan diving bats. Bat-like, native animals, with a daredevil streak in them. They nested on the steep rock faces, like this one. The last thing I wanted to do was get close to their nesting ground. They had a long flexible mouth surrounded by a ring of sharp teeth.

Ordinarily used for plucking fish from the ocean, but they would try to take a bite out of us if we ventured too close.

Drac kept moving, kept climbing. If the diving bats bothered him, I couldn't tell. With humans, my scent-sight gives me emotional clues to what someone is feeling. With aliens, I don't have the wiring to understand what I'm picking up. When I focused on Drac, I picked up a faint sweetness beneath the more over-powering rust and blood smells.

Worry? Enjoyment? Fatigue? Who knew?

"You doing okay, Drac?"

"Yes. Climb."

Climb. Fingers and tentacles found pockets and pits in the rock. With my thin-soled boots, I found plenty of traction. Centimeter by centimeter we climbed higher up the rock face.

More diving bats flew past, chuffing loudly. The wind of their passage buffeted me.

A warning. They must have a nesting site above.

Drac hissed. His leg kicked out, dexterous clawed toes snatching at a passing diving bat.

He missed. The bat folded its wing, dropping beneath the leg.

Daredevils. Down on the roadways and crag-spanning bridges, the diving bats would fly in front of passing ground vehicles or flitters.

"They must have a nest above," I said.

"I don't care!"

Drac's wing snapped out. His four-fingered hand at the top of the wing, snatching a diving bat as it twisted and tried to rise above the wing. He caught it right behind its neck. The bat was almost half Drac's size, but its momentum lost, it flapped frantically in his grasp.

"No—"

The diving bat emitted a shrill cry of fright, cut off when Drac clenched his fingers closed. Bones snapped and cracked. He released it, and the corpse fell.

I pushed against the rocks as the black, hairless bat tumbled past and disappeared far below in the waves.

Agitated chuffing cries grew louder all around us. Diving bats are communal, social creatures, and Drac had just killed one of the colony.

In number, they could probably force us right off the rock face. What a way to start the day.

CHAPTER 2

Three months earlier...

One moment you're teetering on the edge of the precipice, the next falling in space.

Muriel clutched the chair as the lights failed. Artificial gravity was out. The restraints held her, but she still gripped the slick arms.

Space outside blurred. The alien ship that had moved to intercept Brock's escape pod, the teeming hive of Hansel below, and the stars all shifted.

Then the holographic view of the space in front of the Tretan's ship winked out.

Banging noises echoed through the ship. Metal screamed. A sharp electrical smell stung Muriel's nose.

"Dyami!"

A deep throbbing moan that vibrated

her bones, felt more than heard, came out of the dark.

Was his translation band off? Before the lights had failed, Dyami's massive black and orange striped body had been draped over the log-shaped couch at the front of the cabin.

"Pilot?" Muriel raised her voice. "Pilot!"

The Tretan's pilot, a cybernetic mnemonic clone, partially organic, partially non-organic, was in the forward compartment. If that was lost, if Pilot was lost, they might not have any way to regain control of the ship. Assuming the integrity of their compartment held, they'd have to wait for rescue from Hansel.

And what about Brock? The same alien ship that had fired on them had been moving to intercept Brock's escape pod. Was the ship working with Kelwyn? Part of the whole plan to ransom their way into the Galactics' Glittering Throng?

Muriel took a deep breath. Artificial gravity and power were out. Whatever the ship had fired at them, it had disabled the ship's systems. Given that the Tretans had once been part of the Glittering Throng, before being expelled, that was pretty impressive.

Brock was on his own until they could get power restored and assess the situation.

Running her hands down the restraints, Muriel found the emergency release and pressed the button. Three loud snaps and the restraints broke free.

Keeping a grip on the chair, Muriel pulled a comm tablet from her pocket. The screen lit up at her touch. The dim light filled the cabin.

Thin smoke clouded the air, but she could still see around the cabin. Dyami's eyes were screwed tightly shut, and his massive arms and legs clutched the log-shaped couch.

Muriel kicked off her chair and floated past the other chairs in the cabin to Dyami. She caught the end of the log and her feet swung around through the air toward the door to the forward compartment.

Being weightless was somewhat like swimming in the ocean, without the water around to push against. Muriel pulled her legs in and swung down to straddle Dyami's couch. She squeezed her thighs against the firm material and tucked her feet beneath.

Then she reached out and patted one of Dyami's thick fingers. Short bristles on his knuckles tickled her hand.

"Dyami? Hey, come on, I need your help."

One lemon-sized eye opened, his golden, green-flecked iris shrinking as his bi-lobed pupil expanded. His other eye opened and both focused on her for a second, then her comm tablet, before moving to take in the cabin. His fleshy lips parted as he spoke, a deep infrasound vibration that carried through the couch to her thighs.

On his right arm, his flexible translation band translated the sounds into standard speech.

"What happened? Feels like falling!"

"We're weightless. The artificial gravity and main power are out. Are you okay? Are you hurt?"

Dyami's head swung toward the forward wall. More vibrations and the translation band spoke up. "I am unharmed. The other vessel, it fired on us?"

"I think so. I don't know what it hit us with, but it knocked out our systems. I need your help to see if we can get to the Pilot."

Dyami pushed up with his thick arms. The automatic restraints held him down. He twisted around. "I am strapped down."

Muriel patted his arm. "There's an emergency release. Hang on, I'll help you with it."

She used his arm — thicker than her waist — as an anchor to pull herself back to the straps. She held on and pulled herself hand over hand down to the emergency release at the base of the couch. With his thick fingers, it would have been a challenge to do himself. Muriel shoved it down.

With a loud snap, the release came free. Muriel caught the couch to stop herself from drifting away.

Dyami sneezed a loud, explosive sound. Muriel automatically jerked away and lost her grip on the couch.

With the grace of a juggler, Dyami reached out and caught her around the waist with one massive hand. His big fingers nearly encircled her waist. He pulled her back to the couch.

"What do we do?" He asked.

Muriel pointed at the doors leading to the forward compartment. "Let's check the hatch. Maybe there is a manual release."

Once she had a grip back on the couch, Dyami released her. Muriel pulled herself along the couch, then kicked off toward the door.

She floated across the space between and carefully caught herself, damping her motion when she reached the doors. She hung in the air, her feet inches from the floor, while she studied the hatch, moving the comm tablet's light over the surface.

A thin line, much too small for even her fingers to gain purchase, traced the boundary of the hatch. When they had boarded, and Pilot had gone through, the hatch had slid to her right. The walls on both sides were featureless. Nothing that looked like an access point.

Dyami had pulled himself to the end of the couch, holding on with his long arms while his shorter legs floated out behind him.

"Do you see a manual release?" He asked.

"No." Muriel reached out and ran her fingers lightly across the hatch. Slick, frictionless material. Nothing on which to get a grip, and nothing nearby that she could use to brace herself. "Pilot? Hello? Pilot?"

A chirruping beep answered from the tablet. Muriel tapped the notification.

Pilot appeared on the tablet screen. Part of him, his metallic spider-like face scarred and scorched. His blue eyes pulsed. "Are you harmed?"

"We're both okay." Muriel coughed, the smoke irritating her throat. "No power, no artificial gravity, and there is smoke in the air. What's our status?"

"Primary systems are offline. Secondary systems are in safe mode while my remotes assess damage and make repairs."

"What did they hit us with?"

"Many of my systems are offline. The weapon struck as the Space-Time Coordinate drive engaged. Navigation systems lost lock. When power is restored, I will identify our coordinates."

Dyami's voice thrummed. His translator band spoke up. "Is the ship secure?"

"Remotes report venting and are attempting repairs."

Muriel looked around the cabin. "Venting? We're venting atmosphere? How long until those systems are patched?"

"Unknown-n-n." Pilot jerked and shook on the screen.

"Pilot?"

"Are you harmed?" Pilot asked.

"What? We're okay, I told you that. What's wrong?"

"Primary systems are offline. Secondary s-s-systems —" Pilot's eyes flickered and dimmed.

The screen went blank. Muriel looked at Dyami. "I've lost contact."

"He sounded damaged," Dyami said.

He did. And without the pilot, they didn't have any access to the ship systems. Their compartment could be losing atmosphere right now. They had to get some systems back online and at least make sure that they didn't both suffocate before rescue ships arrived from Hansel.

Chapter 3

Terran Exploration Vessel: Australia

Deep space exploration sounded exciting until each day the panel walls looked closer, the corridors longer and narrower. The sound of the scummers working in the walls took on the sound of a dentist's drill, growing more and more shrill as the days passed into weeks and then months in the nothingness.

Deep space. Dust and distant stars. Nothing for the xenology team to do.

Dr. Helen Shaw tapped the lock key on her system, triggering an automatic sync of the *Cristobel* data analysis. She was thirty-four, fit, with a figure that held up despite all of the time in space. She stayed in shape in anticipation of their destination. A whole new world to explore, still two months out.

CY-HC-2347, an Earth-sized world orbiting a super-giant in the Goldilocks zone along with several smaller, possibly habitable moons. A whole system, within a solar system to study. Forty light years from Earth, out on the fringe of explored space. Nothing at this point except a few key images and data provided by a fly-by interstellar probe.

She pushed the heels of her hands against her eyes.

The last thing, the very last thing, that they told you when shipping out was that you'd spend months reading reports of other teams, on other worlds. Knowing that they had gone through the monotony didn't help. Not one bit.

She groaned and dropped her hands.

"Problems, doctor?" Clay Yeager, fourth generation spacer and barely old enough to shave. Brilliant, but oh, so young. His unruly red hair stuck out in every direction as he lounged, safety belts unfastened, at his station.

They were the only two on duty in xenology right now. The bare minimum. Skeleton crew. The rest all out eating, exercising, fucking, or sleeping.

Helen said, "No."

She said. "Give me a nice chiller pod over this, next time. Okay?"

"Company doesn't like 'em," Clay said.

"Yeah, because they expect us to work off our passage. I think I'd rather take the unpaid leave instead of spending my time looking at other xenology teams exploring other worlds!"

Clay grinned brilliantly white teeth. "Isn't that how we learn—"

The ship lurched and shook.

Clay tumbled free from his chair. She saw him tossed into the air like a rag doll thrown by a dog. He yelled just before he hit the bulkhead with a thud, then fell to the floor. Her own straps held her secure and helpless to do anything.

What the hell happened? The *Australia* didn't move like that. Fluctuations in the artificial gravity generators? Caused by what?

Sirens sounded. The lighting changed, a red spot appeared in the heart of each panel and spread outward in a red pulse that spread to the edge, then repeated.

"All hands secure." That was Command

on comm. "All hands secure stations. More hard maneuvering."

"Clay! Strap in!"

Clay stirred and pushed up on hands and knees. He shook his head. "What?"

Over the comm. "All hands secure! All hands secure!"

"Clay! Move! Strap in!"

Clay scrambled across the floor. Helen held her breath. What the hell was going on? Hard maneuvering? What did that mean? Had they reached the system's Oort Cloud early? What were the odds that they might actually hit one of those space icebergs?

Clay grabbed his chair. He wasn't using his left arm. He held it tucked against his gut. His jaw clenched. Sweat beaded on his forehead.

With a sharp hiss of breath, he pulled himself up and dropped into the chair.

"Strap in!"

"I'm trying!" Clay fumbled with the belts one-handed.

The ship lurched again, throwing her against the straps. Clay hung onto his belts, slid in his seat, but didn't get thrown off this time.

"Shit. Shit. Shit!" He fumbled his arm through the belt. Got it over his chest and clicked the right side in place.

Come on, come on, Clay. Helen mouthed the words, clenching her own belts, her hand on the release. Not pressing it. Couldn't press it. Leaving her chair to try to help him with the all secure called would be crazy dangerous.

Grunting, biting his lip, Clay reached across and pulled the other strap over his left arm. He used his right arm to lift the left, panting in obvious pain, to get it through the straps. Clicked the belt in place. Snapped the center-piece closed with one hand.

His head fell back against the chair. He closed his eyes and cradled his left arm. Must be broken. "Oh, fuck. Fuck!"

"Hang on," Helen said. "When they call the all-clear we'll get that arm looked at."

Clay rolled his head. Opened his green eyes. "Yeah, and I spend the next two months with my arm in a cast."

"You don't know —"

The ship shook again. Massive thrust built, throwing her against the straps. What the hell were they doing in command? What was the situation?

Chapter 4

Olinda

A diving bat dove at my head, the ring-shaped mouth snapping sharp, hooked teeth at me. I hugged the rock. The wind of its passage swept over me, carrying that fishy and musky scent.

On the rocks above, Drac hissed a warning at the chuffing bats.

This plan wasn't working out how I'd expected. I reached up with my C'lacktal hand, finding a grip in the rock and pulled myself up. My scent-sight didn't help much, except it did give me a warning when the diving bats got close enough to smell. I didn't need to see more than their bluish blur to duck the swooping attacks.

Drac snarled again. His odor, the rust and blood stink of it, poured down over the rocks. It was a pearly color that almost made the Nosferan look angelic.

I concentrated on the traces he left, the odors forming an image in my mind. Without looking, I saw where he had grabbed, what hand and toe-holds he had used.

I climbed faster, following his route. Around us, the chuffing cries of the diving bats grew louder.

"Climb!"

Drac didn't move. His wing swept out, attempting to catch another diving bat. This time the bat swept its wings back, stalling its flight, and landed right on the tough membrane of Drac's wing. Scarlet vapors swirled out from his wing along with the sharp stinging scent of Nosferan blood.

I ducked another bat. At least a dozen of them swirled around us in an agitated cloud. I didn't want to hurt them, but they weren't giving me any choice.

Hanging on with my C'lacktal hand, I drew my Lottier 65 with the other. Firing nanoparalyzers coded for hundreds of species, along with shock darts to take down non-organics, it was an effective and mostly non-lethal weapon. Unless used up close against a fragile target. And if I missed, I might paralyze Drac, sending him to his death in the waves below.

More bats swept past. Their teeth barely missing me while the one still clung to Drac with sharp claws. He couldn't reach the bat on the backside of his wing.

I fired a single dart at the thickest part of the diving bat, that spot right between its shoulders at the base of the neck.

The dart hit right on target, severing the bat's spine. It fell bonelessly off Drac, tumbling past me and against the rocks below.

"Drac! Climb!"

Drac moved at last. He crawled up the rocks, finding places to grip faster than I could manage alone. I followed his scent trail upwards while the diving bats continued to sweep past, crying their chuffing agitated cries.

I followed Drac. A few meters further up we passed a series of ledges, cracks across the black rock. There, among the pale pastel green and blues of the vegetation clinging to the rock, were bowl-shaped nests made of bits of bone and dried fish skin. Each nest held a single dark, bumpy egg.

Which ones belonged to the diving bats we had killed? Would the others care for the eggs?

Drac kept climbing on past the nests. Diving bats swooped in and landed in front of the nests. Each spread wings a meter across and blew their chuffing cries at us. Glinting dark eyes watched each move we made.

After we climbed past their nests, the diving bats didn't pursue us. I put aside thinking about the bats and focused on our objective.

A fortress sat on top of this peak. No roads connected the peak to the main island. It was one of at least a hundred similar islands just off the coast, out past the scab district of Olinda. All along the equatorial island chain that made up most of the habitable land on the planet were similar islands carved by wind and wave. Some attached when the tides went out, others by rock arches, natural bridges carved out by wave beneath.

This peak sat alone within view of the main island but surrounded by water at all times. The fortress on top was biocrete, a gleaming white structure of spires and walls that melted right onto the supporting rock. The only way in was by air, and flitter traffic was closely watched. Armed defenses protected the fortress from the approach by air.

We'd chosen to make the unexpected approach by water to the base of the peak, and then climbing the exterior. Our observations had suggested that this approach would be the most likely way to get us up and inside without attracting attention.

The biocrete wall wasn't far above now. The walls were smooth, unscalable, and unbroken. Except for one opening.

A waterfall poured out of the fortress, above and to my left. Orbital scans showed the water came from a small, naturally occurring lake at the heart of the fortress. The water came from the frequent rainfall, collected in the caldera of this peak, and drained out through an opening in the side. When the fortress was grown the biocrete surrounded the opening but didn't block it.

That was our way in.

It'd be guarded, of course, by a variety of security measures. I figured I could deal with those.

Getting to the opening was another difficulty. It lay higher on the biocrete wall. No way to climb there. A flitter approaching that close would be detected and fired upon.

But with Drac's help, we had a chance.

Drac reached the end of the volcanic rock, right beneath the biocrete. I climbed up the rocks beside him. The walls above blocked the moonlight and gave us deep shadows at the base of the wall.

"Are you ready for this?" I asked Drac.

"Yes. I shall not fail you, Esteemed One."

I ignored the title. I didn't need reminding of my past right now. There'd be time for that later.

I took out an auto-anchor and placed it in a deep crevice in the rock face. I triggered it. There was a chance that the fortress would have seismic sensors to detect something like that, which is why we didn't use them while climbing. One might be overlooked. Bits of rock must flake off the peak all the time. Placing one anchor might not look all that different.

Next, I attached a line to the anchor and handed the spool over to Drac. He took the ring with his dexterous foot and launched himself out into the air. Massive wings beat, and I hugged the rock, turning my face from the wind. In my scent-sight Drac was a glowing pearly form, blurred and indistinct, rising above me along the biocrete wall.

The line played out beneath him as he flew. I was too big for Drac to carry me. A couple Nosferans working together could manage and had in the past, but more would have increased our chance of detection. And one was too much as it was.

The only reason I was working with Drac was to get Muriel and Dyami back home. If that was even possible. The answer to that question was above us, inside the fortress.

In moments Drac landed on the narrow edge beside the waterfall. A grate across the opening blocked the entrance. Drac was nearly invisible in the deep shadows above the waterfall.

He moved, securing the spool. The line in front of me went tight against the rocks, rising up to the waterfall above.

My turn. I took out two small magnetic grips and slipped them on over my hands. My C'lacktal tentacles twined around each other out of the way.

The line was almost impossible to see, even with my eyes. When the sun came up the light might catch the fiber, but we'd be gone by then.

I reached out with one grip. It snapped to the line. I snapped the second on and walked up the rocks onto the biocrete wall.

The line held. I walked right up to the waterfall, released the grip and grabbed onto the grating over the opening. The biocrete grew right over the rocks, but the uneven shapes around the waterfall provided some slick footing. The other side of the grating was a dark tunnel half filled with rushing water. Big enough for us, not by much,

Talking, over the sound of the waterfall, was impossible. And unnecessary. We both knew what came next. I took out chameleon charges. I passed a set to Drac before going to work on my side.

Each charge was a small gray rod in the case. I placed the first and pressed the arming spot. The material softened and flowed around the bar, shimmered and took on the matte black color of the bar itself. A close examination could reveal that the last few centimeters of the bar were fatter than the rest. No one would get a chance to check.

We finished placing the charges. This was

a tricky point. If it went wrong, I was going to be in trouble.

I stepped down into the water. *Cold!* Like ice running past my legs. The bottom of the bed was smooth, slicked by all that water running past. The water threatened to grab me and shove me right over the cliff.

Feeling as best I could with numbing feet, I found places on each side to brace my feet against the rock. I held onto the grate at the center.

I nodded to Drac. "Blow it."

Whether he heard me or not, he got the message. Drac clung to the biocrete with three limbs and reached over to the belts that ran around his body from shoulder to groin.

He carried the trigger in a pouch on his belts. His impossibly big eyes blinked. For a second a tiny pink tongue poked out of his wrinkled pug-like face past sharp fangs.

He pushed the button.

The chameleon charges went off with a sharp snap and an electrical flash. The grate came free in my hands. My foot slipped.

CHAPTER 5

Olinda

For a heart-hammering second, I teetered on the brink of the abyss. The waterfall thundered away beneath me, down into the waves smashing into the jagged rocks so far below.

In my hands, the metal grate threatened to pull me over the edge. I fell to one knee in the freezing water, hitting hard against the stone bottom. The stream splashed up my chest into my face. My Euzebian scent slits along my neck reflectively snapped closed.

Even as the water fought to shove me out, Drac's wing swept up against me from behind. Nosferans aren't all that strong, but it was enough to steady me. I braced myself against the stream.

Once I'd secured myself, I shoved the

grate forward into the tunnel, wedging it against the sides and the ends left poking out of the biocrete. Each charge had cut through the metal with a micron-thin slice.

Drac crawled over me, pulling himself into the tunnel. He moved into the tunnel making small whistling noises. *Happy?* It was his sort of place, after all.

I dragged myself up out of the water. I was completely drenched. The water wouldn't damage any of my equipment. I'd expected to get somewhat wet, but not completely drenched.

In the tunnel I braced myself. From one of my inner pockets, I took out a tube of Braxian glue, made from the shells of a carnivorous beetle. Difficult to harvest. Expensive, but an extremely effective adhesive.

A couple drops on the ends of the grating, then I lifted it up into place. The glue seized the metal and anchored the grating back into place as good as new. A detailed inspection might turn up what had happened, but I didn't expect anyone to look. Unless things went really bad, no one would know we'd been here.

Bracing my feet on the sides of the tunnel,

bent over thanks to the low ceiling, I followed Drac into the tunnel. He stopped a couple meters in, waving a small egg-shaped device in the air.

"Sensor fields!"

We'd expected that. Drac put away his detector and pulled out a light shimmery cloth from another pouch. The material hardly weighed anything at all. He spread it out, unfolding it into a large cloth.

"Closer!"

This was the part of the plan I didn't like. Unfortunately, I didn't have a better suggestion. I moved up close to Drac. I kept my Euzebian scent slits closed. It didn't entirely cut out the odor but damped it down.

Drac crawled up higher on the tunnel walls. I ducked lower and shivered as he moved and dropped onto my back.

The cloth drifted down over us both, covering us in the almost weightless folds. It was a scatter cloth designed to confuse sensor fields.

Drac's thin, bony body pressed against mine. He didn't weigh much at all. It was like being hugged by a leech. His breath smelled of carrion.

In the Human-Nosferan war, the Nosferans consumed the human dead. Carrion eaters, and creatures of nightmares hated across the Rim, and I had one clinging to my back.

"Esteemed One?" Drac whispered against my neck, as close as a lover.

That was a stomach-churning thought.

"Let's move."

The scatter cloth was essentially see-through, a thin veil between us and the darkening tunnel. My dark-adapted eyes let me see in much lower light levels than regular humans. Despite that, it wasn't long before there wasn't any reflected moonlight reaching us.

My Euzebian scent-sight isn't affected by darkness. It affords me a three-sixty view of everything around me, interpreting scents in such detail that I can see everything around me.

Except I had to open up my neck slits and let it all in, Drac's stink along with the rest. To my scent-sight, the world is ghostly, insubstantial at times and always dissolving.

Both Drac and I were strong sources of light. His pearly and white, my own a more golden color. Scents rendered a visual image in my mind. It had been like this when I first came out of the Moreau Pod after the Euzebian modifications. It had taken time for my eyes and the scent-sight to learn to work together. For a short time, I went about blind-folded, relying entirely on the scent-sight to find my way.

I moved forward down the narrow tunnel. The water rushed beneath us. Drac clung to my back. The scattering cloth clung to us, wrapping itself down around us. It had a faint chemical smell, only a whiff, nothing more than a faint gray cloud to my scent-sight, hardly there at all.

Biocrete lining the passage gave off a faint bluish-white glow, blurring and brighter near the water. The tunnel continued ahead several meters and then curved to the right.

After a few minutes of making my way along the tunnel, it widened, and there appeared a biocrete walkway on the right side. I stepped up onto it, pleased to find that I could stand upright. Drac still didn't let go. As long as we stayed beneath the scattering cloth, we needed to stay close.

This section of the passage was clearly

carved out of the rock, shaped, and then coated with biocrete. Even so, it looked rough, with odd outgrowths that swelled in circular rings on the ceiling.

Lights. Off, at the moment, but they must have hung grow lights down here to grow the biocrete when the tunnel was carved. The biocrete around the lights had grown faster than the rest. Now the biocrete was all dormant and fixed.

The stream flowed down a straight channel in the center of the tunnel. From up ahead came a faint hum. A faint vibration ran through the biocrete beneath my feet.

We were close to something. Hopefully an access point.

I took another step and heard metal sliding against rock. I stopped.

As far as my scent-sight told me, the passage was empty. The sound continued. A rasping, dragging metal against stone sound.

It grew louder, or closer. Maybe both.

"Can you see anything?" I whispered to Drac.

"No."

I concentrated on the scents in the passage. A damp breeze flowed through the passage, carrying with it an algae odor, and something else.

Focusing more, I took in deep breaths, pulling as much air as possible through the scatter cloth hanging over my face.

Faint blue sparks floated in the air, carried by the breeze. With them came traces of an electrical, ozone smell. A few darker metallic, oily specks drifted along closer to the floor. A cloud of biocrete dust mingled with the rest. It wasn't much, but it suggested something.

A non-organic, a synthetic. Somewhere ahead in the dark. It could be a simple machine, but I doubted it. This was the guardian of the passage. It gave off little scent, making it difficult for my scent-sight to see it.

I'd run into this before, aliens or other things that my brain couldn't imagine from the scant information their odors provided.

Like vision, the images that the scent-sight produced came as much from my mind's ability to interpret and extrapolate based on the scent as it did from the scents themselves. Scents were rich in information, adding a time component as molecules degraded, but at times a poor substitute for sight.

The rasping sound continued to come closer, sliding and grinding, a sinuous sound. Muriel and Dyami were lost while we pursued Kelwyn, a Moreau and mass murderer that had taken on a snake-like form, his lower body completely replaced by a serpent's tail.

This sounded like that, except metallic, and smelling like a non-organic. And too close for comfort.

"Slide off," I said to Drac.

"Leave the cloth and be exposed!"

"Run into a sentry, and we're exposed anyway. Slide off and stay put."

Drac let go and slipped off my back. I pulled out my Lottier 65 and flicked on the side light, sweeping up the scatter cloth and stepping out in the same motion.

CHAPTER 6

Terran Exploration Vessel: Australia

On the heels of the all-clear came a directed order. "Dr. Shaw, to command. Dr. Shaw to command."

Helen was already out of her chair, taking a look at Clay's arm. The tissue was bruising already, and the angle was all wrong. She looked up as the order came in.

"Command, Shaw here, I've got a wounded staffer. I need to go to medical."

"Negative, Dr. Shaw. Report to command. Medical is on the way to take care of your staffer."

Negative?

Clay managed a smile. "Go, Doc. Whatever it is, it must be important."

"Hang on," Shaw said. "Once I know what's happening, I'll fill you in."

Then she was moving, because Clay was right. If they were calling her to Command after what had happened, it must be important. What could have happened that they needed their head of xenology in Command?

Blue-shirted medical responders were coming down the corridor as she left. She pointed at the xenology department doors.

"Clay Yeager, in there with a broken arm," she said, still moving toward the elevators.

The one in front, a cute young guy with a black curl of hair on his forehead, nodded, all seriousness. "We've got it."

Good enough. Helen reached the elevator, stepping inside when the doors opened.

If *Australia* were on the planet, it would have most resembled an enormous skyscraper some 110 floors high. It was a flying city with everything needed to support the population of nearly two thousand men, women, and children. The Command levels were at the 'top' of the structure, all thirty of them.

Helen pressed her hand to the identification panel inside. "Hub."

The screen blinked green, accepting her command. Access to the Command hub was restricted. Only those with high enough clearance. Apparently, she had that clearance now, a change. Permanent or temporary?

The elevator took her up at express rates, stopping for no one. They must really want her in the hub.

After a minute the elevator slowed to a stop. The map on the panel blinked at the level, nearly at the top of *Australia*. The doors slid open.

A man wearing a brown security uniform stood outside in a corridor like any other on the ship. Same navy blue flooring and pale walls.

Not just any man, but Derek Constantine, the security director. A handsome man at sixty-two, with silver hair and a strong jaw. The uniform short sleeves showed off an arm thick enough to bend iron. He grinned broadly, showing perfect white teeth.

"Dr. Shaw! Thanks for coming so quick. If you'll come with me, I think you'll want to get to the hub right away."

Constantine was already moving. Helen ran after him. Caught up.

"What's going on? Why all the maneuvering? My staffer on duty broke his arm!"

Constantine glance at her, mouth

quirking into a quick smile. "Wasn't buck-led in, was he? We've got a bunch of bumps and bruises over this. Emergency drills, Dr. Shaw, practice them with your staff."

Helen's neck burned. "We can't stay strapped in twenty-four seven, Mr. Constantine."

"No, ma'am." Constantine gestured as a door opened in front of them. "Right through here."

They were already at the hub?

Helen went inside. It was dark inside and filled with a babble of voices. A woman's voice cut through it all, her tone loud and confident.

"People, coordinate with your team leaders. If it so much as blinks a light, I want to know."

Helen was walking between walls that were shorter and shorter with each step, stair-stepping down. Lights sparkled ahead, floating text and readouts.

She walked out into the hub, an amphitheater at the heart of Command. The center of the space was taken up by a large holographic display and surrounded by level upon level of workstations, stair-stepping up through the next couple levels above this one.

Right at the edge of the hologram, her back to Helen, stood Olivia Blackstone, *Australia's* Chief Director. The woman ultimately responsible for everything that happened on this flying city. She was tall and thin, with her trademark white hair hanging straight down her back to her waist. Simple bamboo sticks held her hair pinned back. She wore pale green workalls, the same sort of thing that most of the workers on board wore. Like many spacer-bred, her feet were bare.

The hologram itself tore Helen's attention away from Blackstone.

A black void hung in the center of the room like an absence of something, rather than anything solid. A spacecraft? Whatever it was, a holographic grid of green lines wrapped around the void, giving it shape and structure.

Two black egg-shaped ovoids shoved together, without any reflections or texture. The smooth lines and artificial material clearly indicated it was something manufactured rather than natural. Only it lacked any noticeable seams or openings of any kind.

Other holographic screens floated around the shape, offering additional information they'd collected so far. On one of the screens was a scale representation of the craft and *Australia*. The craft was a speck, smaller than their atmospheric shuttles. The readouts showed that *Australia* had matched velocities with the craft.

They had come to a stop relative to the craft.

An alien spacecraft? What else could it be? Helen scanned across the floating displays, drinking in the data.

What were the odds that *Australia* would discover an alien spacecraft out here? Or had —

Helen said, "Could it be one of theirs?"

Blackstone turned. "Dr. Shaw. Thank you for coming so quickly. Join me."

Security would have had to restrain her, to keep her back. Helen walked out into the amphitheater. Everyone was busy and on alert.

Up close Blackstone was tall and elegant, her features fine and beautiful. Ageless. Rumors suggested that her family went in for gene-sculpting.

"By 'their,' Dr. Shaw, do you refer to the Galactics?"

"Yes. Stories say that the Glittering Throng has ships that pass unseen."

Blackstone gestured at the hologram. "Yet we detected this one."

"How?"

Blackstone gestured, and the hologram rotated and expanded. Gases escaped through a scarred section of the ship. In that section, the black, featureless surface was ripped open like a tear in space itself.

"It's damaged," Helen said. She walked closer to the hologram, waving aside the data screens. They floated out of her way.

She didn't want to read the details right now. She wanted to see it for herself.

The tear ripped along the length of the craft, almost from one end to the other. The edges looked bubbled as if melted or cooked. The material inside looked more familiar, like metals, ceramics, and plastics. Blue lights crawled over the tear like bugs in a wound.

"What are those?" Helen didn't wait for permission. She reached out and gestured to expand the hologram even more, zooming in on the tear.

Insectile robots of some sort moved through the tear with glowing blue eyes. They were working quickly together to seal the tear. They spun out new material across the opening, which spread and solidified into more of that same featureless blackness.

Blackstone touched Helen's elbow. "Dr. Shaw, I would like your suggestions on how you think we should proceed."

"Contact them, if we can," Helen said. What else could Blackstone even be thinking about?

Blackstone's face might as well have been carved out of stone. Not someone to play poker with.

Behind Blackstone, Constantine's face was much easier to read, the deep creases in his frown showed how much he disliked that suggestion.

"We know nothing about them," Constantine said.

"And we won't learn anything by sticking our head in the sand." Helen tilted her head to look up at the hologram, then beckoned to the display showing the size comparison with *Australia*. "We're a little too big to try to tiptoe past and pretend we didn't see anything. I don't think that offering to help will be seen as threatening. And with that damage, they may need our help."

"Could either of you be more predictable?" Blackstone asked her right eyebrow-raising. "If I'd wanted the obvious answers I wouldn't have asked you to the hub."

"We still haven't detected whatever it was that damaged the ship," Constantine said. "We've sent out tri-eyes, but if there are more ships like this one, but undamaged, we might have a hard time identifying them."

Constantine had a good point. Helen looked back at the tear.

"Certainly Mr. Constantine is correct that we need to check, that's our safe bet. It's also possible that this happened because of an internal problem. The ship may be alone."

"Alone? This many light-years in interstellar space?" Constantine shook his head. "What sort of drive could a ship that size have?"

"That's the point," Helen said. "We don't know."

Blackstone pointed at the hologram. "Right. We don't know. Any other recommendations before I decide what we will do?"

"Non-interference," Constantine said. "Unless our aide is requested."

"And if they can't ask for help?" Helen asked. "We sit and watch that ship bleed out into space? If this is a Galactics ship, providing assistance might go a long way to opening a line of dialog with the Glittering Throng."

Blackstone folded her hands. "We don't even know if the Galactics exist, we've only dealt with two species that claimed to be intermediaries. We've had no direct contact. If they are as advanced as reported, what are the chances that we'd find the ship disabled out here?"

Helen opened her mouth. Blackstone had to understand what was at stake here, there were —

Blackstone held up both hands. "If I could have everyone's attention?"

The buzz in the amphitheater quieted. Data continued to build on the screens as the teams around the room analyzed what the detectors and tri-eyes were telling them.

Blackstone spoke. Her voice carried out through the hub.

"Facing the unknown always brings risks and opportunities in equal measure. I have to weigh the risks to the entire ship, with the possible rewards of helping fellow sentients in distress." She turned and looked steadily at Constantine and Helen.

"Mr. Constantine will provide security for Dr. Shaw's xenology team. Take a shuttle. Go over there and attempt to establish contact with whatever is inside. *Australia* will move off, so we aren't seen in a threatening posture. At the first sign of hostility, I want you out. Understood?"

"Yes, ma'am," Constantine said. "Dr. Shaw, how long do you need to assemble your team?"

"Give us thirty minutes," Helen said. "I'll have my team assembled in the bay."

Constantine nodded to her, to Blackstone, then turned on his heel and left.

Blackstone appeared at Helen's elbow, moving silently on bare feet. "I envy you this opportunity, Dr. Shaw. We will all look forward to your report."

"Thank you, Director. I'll go get my team ready."

Helen headed back down the passage she'd entered. Her mind raced ahead of her. First contact protocols. She touched her comm earbud as she walked and started placing calls.

CHAPTER 7

The Tretan Shuttle

A search of the cabin had failed to turn up a way to access the ship systems. Interface panels remained unresponsive. The only lights came from their comm screens, which didn't have any connection except with each other.

Muriel's reflection in the darkened wall screens was pale, barely illuminated by the meager light from the comm. Her eyes were dark shadows, the pale gray hidden by the dim light. Strands of her hair floated free around her head like a halo, faintly illuminated by the light from Dyami's comm as he drifted across the cabin.

The Eyotan caught the backs of two chairs and halted his forward motion behind her. In the reflection his face was a huge, wrinkled nightmare emerging from the shadows, eyes highlighted by the dramatic orange stripes around his eyes. Opening his mouth revealed massive fangs and crushing teeth.

"I have not found an access point," his translation band said.

At least she wasn't alone. That much was comforting. Muriel turned around with a light touch on the wall. As she came around facing Dyami, she brushed his arm to halt her spin. Tough bristles sprouting from his thick skin tickled her palm.

"Me either. I guess we wait until either Pilot gets systems back online, or a rescue team from Hansel arrives."

"They will send a rescue?"

"Yes, of course. Even if Pilot didn't get off a distress signal, sensors on the moon had to have detected the other ship firing on us."

"What of Brock Marsden? The other ship intercepted his escape pod."

"We'll track him down." No question. Except. "We'll have to stop Kelwyn first. We can't allow him to continue murdering people on Olinda."

Dyami thrummed. Vibrations traveled through his arm to her hand. The translator spoke. "Agreed. Will Brock understand this course of action?"

"Yes. He'd do the same thing in our place." Muriel's lips twisted. "Assuming we get out of this in one piece."

Dyami's breathing sounded like a bellows pumping.

"Are you okay?" Muriel patted his arm. "Your breathing sounds labored."

"Foul air," Dyami said.

Muriel had pushed aside the smoky air. She had modified her lungs in the Moreau Pod, adding capacity and efficiency adapted from water-dwelling species. She could hold her breath for up to a half-hour at a time and was equally at home in the depths as she was on high peaks.

It raised the question. How long would the air in the cabin last? If it wasn't being circulated and refreshed, and Dyami was probably equal to four people on his own given his size and bulk.

"I'm so sorry," Muriel said. "Try not to move. Rest, if you can. I don't have the same oxygen requirements. I can minimize my own use."

Beneath her hand, vibrations traveled

down Dyami's arm as he spoke below her hearing.

"Okay," the translation collar said, entirely too cheerfully for the way Dyami must be feeling.

Dyami remained where he was, his massive fingers just touching the seat backs to stay floating in place. At first, Muriel was going to leave him there, but if the artificial gravity kicked in, he might get hurt.

"Let's get you strapped back in," she said.

No response. Dyami's heavy eyelids were almost closed. Muriel bit her lip. Was he already unconscious? She had no idea what his atmospheric requirements were like. He might be extremely susceptible to a drop in air pressure.

She'd have to move him herself. Ordinarily, that'd be out of the question. Now? In a zero-gee environment? She might have a chance.

She got behind him. He had a lot more bristles along his backside, making a sort of ridge down his spine. The bristles matched the color of his stripes, black or orange.

Planting her feet against the seats, she

put her hands on his back. Tough skin, like thick leather, cool to the touch. She pushed.

Dyami drifted away from the seats back toward the padded bench near the front of the chamber. Muriel kicked off the chairs and floated past him. Halfway there she flipped over in mid-air and prepared to land on the front wall.

Her feet hit the wall, and she bent her knees to absorb her momentum. Dyami was coming across the room like some sort of Halloween blimp, and there wasn't much time before he overshot and hit the wall.

She couldn't let him continue to bounce around the cabin.

She grabbed the loose strap on the bench and used it to anchor herself, pulling in the excess until she had her feet firmly beneath her.

Dyami loomed before her. A massive, unconscious shape, but he was still breathing. Heavy breaths came in and out regularly, slowly.

At the last second, Muriel jumped up, reeling out the strap behind her. She flipped, hit the ceiling and pushed off again. This time her trajectory took her over Dyami, and down the other side.

He was still moving, pressing against the strap. Muriel reached out and caught the buckle on the other side. Dyami's motion continued pushing against the other side of the strap, and she rebounded, pulled up by the strap against Dyami's bristly side.

Through it all, she kept her grip on the ends of the strap. She pulled and ever so slowly, Dyami drifted back. She yanked the strap down using muscles designed to carry her deep into the ocean.

Snap. The buckle fastened in place with Dyami floating just above the bench.

Muriel twisted around and kicked off the bench on a trajectory to her chair.

Halfway across the space between a loud clang sounded through the cabin. It sounded like something had hit the side of the shuttle.

At her chair, Muriel pulled herself down into her chair and pulled the straps around to buckle in.

Another clang sounded through the walls.

"Hello?" Muriel called. "Hello? We're in here? Systems are down! Hello!"

More clangs and bangs through the walls.

Something was out there, but what? A rescue team or their attackers? Were they about to be saved or vented into space?

Chapter 8

Olinda

The Lottier's sidelight stabbed out into the darkness, sweeping across the damp biocrete tunnel ahead.

With a jolt, the world snapped into solidity as my eyes adapted to the light and filled in the gaps in my scent-sight.

A shape, something big, slipped across the tunnel. Water splashed. A large swell moved downstream.

No time to fire. I held the Lottier steady and eased on up the path along the stream. Behind me, in my scent-sight, Drac's luminous, rust and blood-smelling shape, stayed put beneath the scatter cloth shroud.

The only sounds now were those of dripping water and the stream rushing past. Plus the faint squelch with each step from my water-laden boots.

I stopped moving, sure something was watching me. Whatever sentry was down here, it hadn't just fled.

I took a step back.

Water exploded out of the stream. Screaming like a steam whistle, a sinuous metal shape rose up and up in front of me, curving as it approached the ceiling.

The sentry was at least a meter across and segmented. On each segment, two spots lit up with an ominous red light.

I thumbed the selector on the Lottier 65 and fired two shock darts at the sentry.

The sentry moved, curving aside, dodging the darts. I dove forward in a roll that took me closer. In my scent-sight, I saw pockets of biocrete behind me vaporize.

I fired again, a series of shots, anticipating it would dodge.

Two sharp pings and electrical snaps made it clear the darts had found their target — without effect.

The sentry twisted, tracking me. More spots vaporized in the biocrete. I was up, moving at a run down the walkway. It had to be firing some sort of laser from those spots on each segment.

Vaporized biocrete flared up right beside my foot. I dove to the side, rolling into the stream. The water might help shield me from the lasers, but it killed my sense of smell. My Euzebian neck slits sealed closed against the water. So did my nostrils. One of the perks to the modification, no more water up my nose.

With all of my modifications to reflexes, strength, speed, healing, and senses, I'd made myself a better detective. The C'lacktal hand, unsettling at first, wasn't my choice but it had proven useful. However, none of that helped me under water.

I immediately turned and swam downstream toward the sentry. The only light I had was on the Lottier. The beam didn't show much in the dark water.

Bubbles thrashed in front of me. The sentry? Shrill sounds, distorted by the water, echoed through the passage.

Drac. It was going after Drac.

I got my feet under me and managed to stand against the current, catching the side with my C'lacktal hand. I brought up the Lottier.

The light bounced off the reflective surface of the sentry. The scatter cloth shroud lay abandoned on the walkway.

A dark shape flew overhead.

The sentry turned, tracking Drac's flight. A gap opened between the top segments.

I fired the shock darts into the gap.

A loud snap and crack then a sharp jolt hit me. Pain burned through my nerves. The sentry crashed down, collapsing down into the stream. My muscles jerked and twitched.

My teeth ground together. I jerked. I fell. I couldn't stop myself. I had no control. I knew what was happening. I'd fired the shock darts into the sentry, and we were both in the stream.

Stupid. Stupid!

Helpless, paralyzed but aware, I fell back into the stream. Dark waters closed over my head. The current shoved me along.

A clawed foot grabbed my coat and pulled my face up out of the water.

"Esteemed One!"

I coughed. Feeling started to return but a billion pins and needles prickled across my body. The shock darts were designed to shut down non-organics. Good to know they'd work against organics too. My scent-sight returned, giving me a clearer picture of the tunnel.

Drac hissed and pulled, dragging me out of the stream up onto the edge. He stopped, panting heavily and held me there until I could move. In my scent-sight he glowed brighter than normal, pulsing with his rapid heartbeat. The rust smell was stronger, making my tongue taste metal.

"Thanks," I said when I could speak.

"We must go!"

He was right. We'd no doubt set off the alarms in the place. We had to move fast to get what we came for.

I crawled the rest of the way onto the walkway and managed to stand. I kept the Lottier out, using the light to illuminate the passage ahead.

Drac gathered up the shroud, stuffing it away as he moved on ahead.

Orlando Pike, collector and eccentric, made his living trading on galactic tech. He was famous in his day for going further in along the Rim toward the galactic core than any other human living. And he'd come back with new galactic tech to make him rich.

As I followed Drac, I knew that we were being watched. Pike's security had to be mobilizing to stop us. We had to get in and locate the tach field generator. It was the key to everything.

I was counting on his security being unprepared to deal with someone like me. A gamble that might pay off if we moved fast enough.

Less than a minute after we'd left the shut-down sentry behind, the passage ended. The stream rushed out of a pipe, under pressure.

Other than that there didn't seem to be any way to continue. It looked like a dead end.

Chapter 9

Xenology Contact Team

When they didn't receive an answer from the alien ship to any of their attempts to communicate, across a spectrum of frequencies, Helen agreed to Constantine's suggestion that they dock with the ship.

"Looks like most of their systems are down. Maybe they can't answer. Maybe they need medical assistance." His blue eyes had twinkled.

Helen clutched her chair arms while the shuttle grabbed onto the alien craft. The mood in the cabin was tense. Everyone waiting to see what, if any response the alien ship would give.

What if the engines fired? What if some sort of defensive shield fired? Could they even lock onto the alien ship?

Holographic screens floated in front of her, showing the entire approach.

Next to *Australia*, the alien ship had appeared small, a mere speck. Even so, it was nearly as large as their shuttle. And size didn't mean everything. If this alien craft belonged to one of the Galactics, it could be unimaginably more technologically advanced.

"We've got a hard lock," came the word from the pilots. "All systems report green."

"Attach the lamprey," Constantine ordered.

Helen couldn't believe her ears. "What are you doing, Mr. Constantine?"

"Moving ahead with the plan, isn't that what we're supposed to do?"

Everyone was listening, of course. In a space no larger than a bus, what else was anyone going to do? Their teams were evenly divided on each side of the aisle running the length of the crew compartment. Five each, from security and the xenology team, plus the flight crew of four sitting ahead and above them. All of them wearing space suits, helmets stored beneath the seats.

Everyone had holographic screens up, pouring over the data coming in from the shuttle sensors, except now all those eyes were on her. Including Constantine's blue eyes across the aisle.

"Doctor?"

"Deploying the lamprey only makes sense at this stage if you planned to force access into the ship."

"That's exactly what I plan to do. We've gotten no response. We're not going to get any answers hanging onto the side of this thing. We have a window of opportunity. This is the time."

"Or we could use the hard lock to try and communicate with anyone in the interior."

"And if they do need medical assistance and can't respond, we've delayed action. Dr. Shaw, I'm treating this as a rescue mission at this point, which means that I'm in charge. You and your team are along as advisors to whatever we discover inside. Understood?"

"I don't think that's what Blackstone meant when she sent us over here," Helen said.

Constantine grinned. "Maybe not, but decisions on the ground are sometimes different than those made when you're sitting back home looking at reports."

Constantine unbuckled his straps and rose out of his seat, all bulk and power. He bent and pulled his helmet out from beneath his seat, then straightened. He grinned at her.

"Well? Are you going to get your team ready? We go in as soon as we cut through that hull."

It was crazy. Helen gaped as Constantine walked forward to talk to the flight crew. He ordered the lamprey deployed again and this time the crew responded.

A whirring noise started in the belly of the ship. That was the lamprey moving out to the other ship. It'd lock on and drill through the hull of another ship, providing a quick method of entry in the event of an emergency when other access points were unavailable or inaccessible.

It was done. They were going in. Hopefully, Constantine's call wouldn't get them all killed in the process. Helen reached beneath her seat and pulled out her helmet.

"Come on, folks. Let's get ready. I want a full recording suite active. We get everything. Environmental, cultural, all of it. We don't know what we're going to find in there and we may need answers fast."

Faces turned to look at Helen. Her team, each of them hand-picked because of skills they brought to the table. Not all of her department heads, Clay wasn't with them thanks to his broken arm. If she could have, she would have brought along several teams of researchers and assistants as well. Instead, she had her most experienced people. If something bad happened, well, then those they left back on *Australia* would get promoted.

In the seat beside her, Ben Tol already had his helmet out. The xenolinguist was a small man and slender. Standing, he only came up to her shoulder and had the unfortunate habit of directing all of his remarks to her breasts. She might have suspected that he had a neck injury or something that prevented him from looking up, except he didn't have the problem with any of the men on the crew. If anything he almost stood on tiptoes to look up into their eyes. He'd complained when he came aboard that the regulations didn't allow him his high-heeled shoes. A necessary accommodation, he had called it. Blackstone shot that down.

Still, he was a fine xenolinguist that took

an evolutionary look at language develop-
ment in other species. His insights had transformed the way people thought of language.
Socialization issues aside, he was the best
person to take a look at any language artifacts
they might discover and give some insight.

Ben snapped his helmet in place and
stood up. "Ready to go, Dr. Shaw."

"Great, Ben. We'll wait until security
gives us clearance."

Mina Lange, the team's biologist, leaned
forward over the seat. Bright red hair, cut to
fall down to the middle of her ears, swung
forward. "Shouldn't we go first? I mean, it
hardly seems to make sense to have the ones
with guns greet the strangers."

Across the aisle one of the security team,
a man with dimples on both cheeks and dark
brown hair laughed. "Wouldn't you rather
the monsters go for us first?"

Mina glanced over and smirked. "What
makes you think anything would go for
you?"

Who wouldn't? Helen thought, not that
she'd say it. The man was obviously built,
almost as much as Constantine, and almost
unbearably handsome in a boyish way. Name

on the suit was Dustin. He was like a delicious morsel of candy just —

Dustin laughed and continued checking his equipment.

"Dr. Shaw?" The question came from behind Mina, from Lukas Zelenka.

"Lukas? What is it?" A medical doctor, with an emphasis on non-human medical practices, Lukas' helmet was on, but crooked.

"My helmet," he said. "I can't get it to lock into position."

"Mina, give Lukas a hand."

Helen headed down the aisle. Ben followed her. The last member of her team, Ross Gordon, was already suited up and waiting patiently in his seat. The xenopaleontologist hadn't wanted to come along on the mission. He was less interested in living aliens than in how life evolved. Plus he had this little thing called cowardice, what he liked to call prudent caution. He looked up as she reached his seat.

"Ready?" She asked.

"Yes, Dr. Shaw."

Ross followed orders. He preferred being off in his own world, but she had wanted another set of eyes on whatever they came across, and even if he preferred to study the evolution of life, he still knew more about more different types of species and aliens than anyone she knew. Between him, Mina and Lukas, they might have a chance at providing some sort of aid for the alien crew. And Ben to translate, if it came to that.

Leaving her, the head of the department to plug in the gaps. She loved aliens, and the more she learned, the more she wanted to learn.

Constantine met her back at the rear hatch with his team gathering around them. Dustin stood next to Constantine, a grin still playing on his lips.

"Alright, Constantine," Helen said. "How do you want this to work?"

"You want to go first?" Constantine asked, a cock-sure grin on his face.

"I don't want the crew of that ship shot. If you think you can manage not to do that, I'm fine with you going first."

Constantine laughed. "Why thank you, Doc!" He nudged Dustin. "I think we can manage not to shoot the natives."

Dustin laughed too, apparently some sort of private joke. Helen ignored them both. The rest of the security team had come down the aisle behind her and Ben. In the front was a woman, tall, with a long, regal face behind her helmet face shield. Pierre, according to the label on her suit. Beside her was a smaller man with a goatee. The name on his suit was Tam. Both looked serious. She couldn't see the face of the third, hidden behind the others. Her team crowed the aisle behind them.

All of the security team carried weapons, squat splat pistols. Named not only for what it did to the targets but also because it was designed not to penetrate hard surfaces like ship hulls.

"Let's not waste time shuffling around," Helen said. "Let's go in the order we're in now."

Constantine nodded. "If there's trouble, you two get down. Give my people a clear field."

"Sure."

"Everyone link up!" Constantine called out.

Helen lifted her helmet and pulled it down. She gave it the sharp twist to lock it in place, then slapped the safeties. Heads-up displays popped into place, floating at the sides of her view. One on the left flashed, the confirmation to link up with the rest of the team.

The display showed a three channel tree. Top level, just her and Constantine, the next the security team and the third her team. Constantine had both her and him in all the channels. A side channel linked them all back to *Australia*.

"*Australia* command, Constantine here, do you read?"

"We read you, Constantine. Status?"

"We've deployed the lamprey and are burrowing into the alien craft now. Preparing to move inside."

"Constantine." That was Blackstone. "Has there been any contact with the aliens?"

"Negative on contact. We're going in assuming they are unable to respond."

"Understood, Constantine. We're all watching."

On their private top-level channel, Constantine said, "I bet they are. Anything to add Doc?"

Helen eye-blinked to select the channel. "No, let's just get on with this."

"Understood." Then to all the channels, Constantine said. "Okay, everyone. Here's the drill. We go in careful. Identify hazards, whether environmental or in response to our presence. Non-lethal force unless I say otherwise. Understood?"

Affirmatives from the teams.

Helen's breath echoed in the helmet. Her palms felt slick, but she couldn't wipe them on anything while wearing the suit. It hadn't been that long since she had complained to Clay about being bored with studying reports from other teams, other expeditions. Good or bad, what happened here would get examined and cross-examined. Everyone would have an opinion.

At the thought, with a flick of her eyes, she called up the screen showing the lamprey's progress. The alien ship's hull was hard, unknown ceramic-type material, incredibly strong. Several different complex layers. More data than she could process at the moment.

Nothing there to stop a fusion torch from cutting through the ship. Anchors held the hull section secure. When they were done, the anchors would essentially turn the section into a door that they controlled. It was considered a minimally destructive method of gaining entry to another ship.

Meanwhile, the airlock at the end of the lamprey would maintain atmospheric integrity on both sides.

No one was saying anything. Everyone was waiting. Instruments on the lamprey indicated it would break through to an open area in thirty seconds.

Constantine and Dustin stood in front of her, facing the sealed hatch. They hadn't drawn their weapons, at least.

Helen tongued her teeth, picking up hints of banana and blueberry from her morning smoothie of kale, banana, and blueberries in almond milk.

Five seconds.

The last seconds seemed to pass all at once. The lamprey reported back access to the interior. Anchors holding strong, an interior atmosphere detected. The torch folded away.

That was something at least. Then the atmospheric sample came back. Earthlike with increased carbon dioxide levels, hazardous levels. Particulate traces showed signs of a fire and pressure levels were low.

"If you were over there without a suit, you'd be unconscious," Helen said, over the team-wide third channel.

"Maybe that's why they didn't answer our knock," Constantine said, on the same.

"They may have different requirements," Mina said. "We shouldn't assume they breathe the same mixture as us."

"Let's get in there and find out," Constantine said.

"Let's go," Helen said.

The readings bothered her. Mina could be right, of course. Still, the atmosphere looked awfully like what she'd expect on a Terran ship that had lost pressure and had a fire.

The first hatch into the lamprey's throat opened up. Constantine and Dustin moved inside, holding onto the tethers lit by slow pulses of blue light.

No artificial gravity in the lamprey, or apparently in the alien ship from the readings.

"Null-gee ahead, folks," she said over her team's channel. "Remember your training."

Helen followed the two space suits ahead of her into the throat.

Chapter 10

It looked like we'd reached a dead end. Drac hissed his annoyance, his head bobbing as he looked for another way out of this passage.

I'd paid for the plans to Pike's fortress, at considerable cost. When I'd studied this passage, it had looked like it continued straight on into the fortress, with other passages branching off to the lower levels.

I pulled the plans up on my tablet.

"Which way?" Drac asked.

"I'm checking!"

Did the plans just show the narrow pipe in front of us? No, they clearly showed the passage. That's when I noticed the faint line on the plans. I zoomed in on that section. At full magnification, I saw the reason.

The lines were superimposed over other

lines beneath them. The passage that continued on into the fortress was on a different level.

I studied the ceiling above and there it was. A hatch, hidden in a recess in the shadows. It was thick and armored. Not something that we could burn through the way we had gotten past the grate on the outside.

"Up there."

Drac crouched and jumped. His wings swept down, giving him a boost. He caught the edges of the recess and hung there, his head in the space. He chittered to himself.

"Can you open it?"

"Busy!"

We were running out of time. We had to expect that Pike's security forces were already moving in on us. If Drac couldn't get it open, we could lose our one chance at rescuing Muriel and Dyami.

"Drac?"

He hissed. Rusty waves poured off him, streaked with a sweet rot smell that set my stomach churning. With aliens I don't smell the right emotional cues, my human brain doesn't know what to do with the information received.

From down the tunnel behind us came a crash. A sharp sound of metal hitting biocrete. The sentry! The shock darts were wearing off.

My Lottier was in my hand, light slicing through the darkness. I didn't see the sentry yet. It might not come back online all at once.

A loud clunk noise above me drew my attention. A low hum sounded, of machinery activating. A bright bluish light, spilled down around Drac, illuminating him and turning his wing membranes a bright purple.

His head twisted around upside down. "Este—

His words were cut off. I smelled them, humans above. I spun and put my back against the wall even as Drac was yanked off the rocks, up through the hatch.

Bright light flooded the tunnel with him out of the way. Two men, one right after the other, dropped through the hatchway into the tunnel. I shot both with the Lottier's neuroparalyzer darts.

It didn't slow them down at all. They landed lightly on the biocrete, dressed in black uniforms, helmets and gloves. No bare skin. They leveled very lethal burrower guns at me. A very familiar weapon, usually armed with smart rounds programmed to seek out the target's vital organs or nervous system.

"Drop the weapon, Mr. Marsden," said the man nearest me.

Even with the uniforms, enough scent leaked out for me to get a whiff of what they were feeling. The one that had spoken was cautious and confident. His companion was also confident and uneasy at the same time. I think his unease had more to do with the tunnel than me.

Metal rasped against biocrete, followed by loud splashing noises, down in the tunnel. Down in the gloom, the metal sentry snaked closer, coming up the stream bed.

I lowered the Lottier.

"Drop it, kick it over."

The fact that they'd already identified me, as much as the guns and the sentry, convinced me to go along with them. I dropped the weapon and kicked it over.

The uneasy one picked it up and tucked it away behind his back.

In the tunnel the sentry stopped a couple

meters away and stood there, swaying slightly. It didn't fire.

"Okay. Up through the hatch."

Both moved back away from the brightest spot on the biocrete. I picked up smells drifting through the opening, a mix of different people, human except for Drac's odor. Tension, anticipation, and boredom floated in the mix with strands of yellow and orange.

For now, I'd go along.

The hatch was about three meters up. I crouched and jumped up, catching the lip and pulled myself up into a brightly lit corridor.

Not a dank dungeon corridor at all. Polished native stone floors, gleaming wood paneling, and artwork hung on the walls. It wasn't really a corridor at all, but a wide hall, an exhibition space.

No one was paying attention to the artwork right now. Two soldiers, covered head-to-toe like the ones in the tunnel, held Drac. He was awake and trying to bury his head beneath his wing, his dark face twisted up into a mask of agony. Bright chandeliers glowed above, hanging from a high arched ceiling painted with an impressive mural.

Bright light is torture for the Nosferans. They're nocturnal by nature, dark adapted and see more into the infrared spectrum than humans.

I don't like Nosferans. I don't have a choice about working with Drac. And right now I couldn't do anything to help him.

Not with a half-a-dozen guns pointed at my head. The rest of the soldiers were standing in a group facing me, burrower guns in their hands.

I've fought large groups before and come out more or less intact, but not a group armed with weapons like those. All they had to do was hit me somewhere, and that wicked ammo would burrow through my flesh to its intended target. Even my modified physiology wouldn't protect me from that sort of damage. Depending on how they had programmed their ammo, a single shot would either kill me or worse.

I kept my hands in view and stepped away from the hatch as the two below climbed back up.

I nodded at Drac. "His goggles? He can't take this sort of light."

The confident soldier from below shoved me. "Let's get going, Marsden."

I didn't move. If we were going to get out of this, I needed Drac able to function. "It'll only take a second. In his second pouch there, you can see the strap."

One of the soldiers holding Drac turned his head. I didn't hear any words, they were probably talking on a secure sub vocal channel.

Then he nodded. One of the soldiers from the lineup on me moved over to Drac and opened the pouch. He fished out the goggles.

Drac turned his head, eyes squinted shut, but making it easier for the soldier to slip on the large black goggles. His entire posture relaxed. Breath hissed out.

"Gratitude."

"We helped him," the soldier behind me said. "Now let's go before I put a bullet in him."

I agreed. "Okay, let's go."

The soldiers holding Drac spun him around and marched him down the hall. The others formed up around me, and we walked.

My scent-sight told me that all of the

soldiers were male. It's more than vision, I can sniff out all sorts of things about people. Less about aliens. But these guys, all human males, all of a fairly similar build. The last one closed the hatch behind us, the access point vanishing in the floor.

These men were professionals, and something more. They moved with precision around Drac and I, almost like a school of fish, or a flock of birds. Or Olindan diving bats swooping past flitters. Something was up with them. I didn't know what, but I didn't like our odds.

Chapter 11

Australia Expedition

The alien ship looked shockingly human inside. Comfortable looking chairs made two rows with three on each side, not that different than *Australia*'s shuttle. Fewer seats, but those seats looked more luxurious. Ahead of Helen, Dustin and Constantine's lights flashed across the space.

Both men stopped, hanging onto seat backs, lights fixed on a point at the front of the cabin.

"Doc?" Constantine said.

An alien floated just above a log-shaped bench at the front of the cabin. Big, like the size of a big bull. Not cow-like at all. Black with orange zebra-like stripes, the skin had a shiny, leathery quality, dotted with bristles. Massive, muscular arms floated loose and equally muscular but smaller legs. Not a biped, from the look of it.

The thick head was wrinkled, and the mouth hung open, revealing both pointed and flat teeth. An omnivore.

A strap anchored it to the bench. Belts on its body held bits or equipment, technological tools from the look.

"Doc?" Constantine repeated.

"I see it," Helen said. "Beautiful, isn't he?"

"He looks like he could take your head off in one bite," Dustin said.

"Is it alive?" Constantine asked.

As if it had heard Constantine, the alien inhaled a deep breath, huge chest expanding as it sucked air. Then it exhaled, blowing the air out.

"Unconscious, I think," Helen said.

Hanging back in the entry, she was blocking anyone else from coming inside. She lightly pressed off and floated up the aisle and caught herself on the men's shoulders. She twisted and pulled herself between them.

Constantine caught her arm. "What are you doing?"

"Getting closer. I can't help if I can't see

what's going on. I'm going to need Mina and Lukas in here too."

Constantine let go and pulled himself into the space between the seats. "Be careful."

Helen drifted forward, slowing her motion on the next seat back.

A head rose up over the front seat on her left. Helen jerked, yelped and lost her grip on the seat. She spun sidewise like the hands on a clock.

A hand caught her leg and steadied her.

"Move away!" Constantine shouted. "Move away, now!"

Move away? From what? Hands turned Helen, bringing her back around, and upright. A woman was helping her. A human woman, without a suit, so not one of theirs. Beautiful, with fine soft features and brilliant gray eyes, wide against the lights pointed at her.

She shielded her eyes from the lights with her hands.

"Wat? Yor the rescu tem?" The woman asked.

What? You're the rescue team? That's what she had said, with an accent that made it nearly unintelligible. Helen held onto the woman's hand.

"Yes," Helen said. "We're here to help? You understand?"

"Yest," the woman said.

Helen eye-blinked the comm to the team channel. "It's okay. She's human and part of the crew. There's no danger."

A flash on the private channel one. Constantine. "You don't know that Doc."

Helen responded on the same. "She's unarmed and isn't wearing a suit. We're lucky she isn't unconscious too. We need to get them back to our shuttle. This air can't be good."

"Can't do it," Constantine said. "Too risky."

"They might die if they stay in this atmosphere!"

"We'll share resources, pump, and filter through the lamprey. They stay here until we get some answers."

The woman was watching Helen speak. The sound wouldn't have carried outside the helmet. Helen turned back on her external speakers with another eye-flick.

"We're going to clean the air and

repressurize." Helen pointed at the alien. "Does he breathe a standard Terran atmosphere?"

It took a second for the woman to process the question and then she nodded. "Dyami? Yest. Too much cee o two, now."

"Okay. We'll fix that." Back on the team channel. "Okay, Constantine, let's do it. She says there's too much CO_2 right now."

Helen heard the orders passing at a low volume. The rest of the team was moving. She ignored them and focused on the woman. Helen pressed a hand to her chest.

"Helen Shaw. What's your name?"

"Muriel Reinhard."

Muriel. Definitely not alien. What the hell was going on here?

CHAPTER 12

The Tretan Shuttle

The air was much better. Over the past hour, the rescue team had replaced and repressurized the cabin. Small globe lights floated in the cabin, making it easier to see. Muriel floated beside Dyami's head so that he would see a familiar person when he woke. Her breath fogged the air. It was starting to get colder in the shuttle, and her outfit didn't provide much protection.

The young woman, Mina and the man with her, Lukas, had taken a look at Dyami. A biologist and a medic, from what their boss, Helen Shaw, had said. It looked like Helen was in charge of the scientists, while the man with the rock-jaw and steely eyes, Constantine, was in charge of the security team. None of them had identified their ship.

All of these people spoke with a strange accent. When Muriel had asked why it took so long to get a ship out to them from Hansel, Helen had pretended not to understand the question and then had changed the subject when Muriel tried asking again, pronouncing the words the way they did. It didn't make a difference.

It wasn't just that they didn't understand her. Something was going on. If she had to guess, she would have said that Helen and the others were surprised to see her.

Dyami moved against Muriel's hand. He snorted.

"Is he waking up?" Helen asked.

Helen had to be in her thirties, fit, a standard human as far as the eye could tell. She had been the first to remove her helmet after the atmosphere had improved, over the objections of Dr. Zelenka, the team's medical doctor. He had wanted them to follow strict quarantine procedures and had been overruled by Helen.

Behind her, Constantine, apparently in charge of security for the team, slapped the shoulder of one of his men and pointed at

Dyami. The security officers fanned out, using the empty chairs to brace themselves.

"That isn't necessary," Muriel said, focusing on matching their accents. "Dyami won't hurt anyone, we work together."

With the ten of them in the cabin, space was at a premium. The other two scientists from Helen's team were poking around the ship. Understandable, given its origins.

Dyami stirred more. He was breathing easier since they'd cleaned the air but hadn't woke yet. Muriel put her hands on each side of his face.

"Dyami? Can you hear me? It's Muriel."

The armband translator vibrated. She felt it through her hands. Helen was close enough that she must have noticed.

"What is that thing on his arm?"

That thing? How could someone in Shaw's position not recognize a common device like that? "Just his translator. He understands us well enough, but he can't speak our language."

"Ben?" Helen said.

The small man that had stared at Muriel's breasts when he first came into the shuttle drifted over from where he had been studying a wall panel.

"Yes?"

"Tell him about the armband," Helen said to Muriel. "He's our xenolinguist."

"What's going on here?" Muriel asked. "This doesn't seem like a rescue."

"We are going to help you," Helen said. "We just haven't seen anyone of his species before."

"The Eyotan don't tend to leave their world," Muriel said. Once again Helen was trying to shift attention elsewhere, why?

"What does the armband do?" Ben asked eyes focused again on Muriel's breasts.

"It translates languages. You have to have seen galactic translators before," Muriel said.

Ben looked up then, dark eyebrows like caterpillars rising above sunken eyes. "Galactic?"

Helen and Ben exchanged glances. Both of them looked at the armband and back at Muriel. They couldn't have looked more surprised if she had taken off her shirt.

Why? Why would a translator surprise them?

Dyami snorted and jerked his head.

Muriel braced her feet against the bench, curling her toes beneath.

One big eye cracked open, squinting against the light from the floating globes. Dyami's eye rolled and fixed on her.

His head rumbled beneath her hands.

"What's happening?" The armband translated.

Helen gasped.

"We're okay," Muriel said. "The environmental systems failed. I think there was a fire somewhere, and you lost consciousness. These people are here to help."

At least they weren't hostile, yet. But could she trust them? Helen's evasiveness, the presence of armed security, it could all turn out badly. What if they hadn't come to rescue them? What if they were from the ship that had taken Brock and fired on the shuttle?

With an audience, there wasn't a way right now to warn Dyami.

He reached down and grabbed the bench and used it to slide out from under the restraining strap, tucking his legs up between his arms, so it looked as though he was sitting on the bench. He blinked and then yawned, his huge head splitting open to reveal large teeth.

Through her feet, Muriel felt more vibrations from Dyami.

"What are those vibrations?" Helen asked.

Ben held up a tablet. "Infrasound —"

"I am pleased to meet you," Dyami's armband said. "I am Dyami, of Eyota, apprentice detective with the Shanley Walsh agency. Thank you for responding to our distress."

"Uh, you're welcome," Helen said. "I am Helen Shaw. These people are members of my research team, and security from our ship."

"What ship is that?" Muriel asked.

The security man, Constantine, coughed and beckoned when Helen looked over. "Doc, a minute please?"

"Excuse me," Helen said. She kicked off, drifting across the cabin to Constantine.

Ben stayed where he was, watching both Muriel and Dyami. His gaze frequently went to the armband.

"What is wrong with the ship?" Dyami asked.

Muriel didn't want to mention the Pilot. Not until she knew more about the intentions of these people. "I don't know. Systems are still down. They cut through the hull and used their environmental systems to restore breathable air to the cabin."

"Cold," Dyami said.

"Amazing," Ben said. "It actually sounded sad. It carries emotional cues as well."

Muriel moved to catch Ben's attention. "Maybe you can answer a question for me?"

He met her eyes, just for a second, before looking down. "Uh, okay?"

"Have you seen a galactic translator before?"

"Not..." Ben glanced at Helen and rubbed his gloved hands together. Sweat beaded on his brow despite the temperature. His suit should keep him comfortable, but he didn't look comfortable.

"Ben?"

"Not, um, exactly like that one. No."

"Why would an armband surprise you? They make them in pretty much any shape."

His head jerked up, lips parting in obvious surprise.

He had no idea what she was talking about. Yet Helen had introduced him as a xenolinguist, an odd title at that, but how could he not know about the galactic translators if languages were his profession? It didn't make sense.

"Who are you people?" Muriel said.

Dyami's lips drew back, revealing his teeth again. "We want answers. Now."

The translator did an excellent job of conveying a menacing tone.

Chapter 13

Olinda, Orlando Pike's Fortress

The room where they left us had two doors and no windows. Both doors were locked, I'd checked. The light was dim, from glowing strips that ran along the corners of the room up by the ceiling. Various ports and rings in the walls gave away the room's purpose.

A full-sensory immersion suite. No need to decorate when the sensie would take over all of the person's senses. Sensies didn't work on me any longer. Too many modifications to my DNA and physiology, too unique, and no one around to program a system that worked for me. Not that I minded.

Reality keeps me busy enough. I don't need unreality too.

Drac huddled in the corner. That was all

he had done since they shoved us in here and shut the doors behind us.

"Drac," I said, standing above him. "What do you think?"

"We've failed." He said. "We've fallen to rocks!"

A reasonable fear for a flying species. Not all that helpful right then.

"I'm not done yet. You came to me. You demanded that I help."

Drac's head turned. The goggles didn't give anything away and looked like pits to my scent-sight. Holes that gave off little odor at all.

"You wants the thieves! That is why you came." Drac hissed. "Esteemed One!"

Esteemed One. The ambassador. I turned away from the Nosferan. I didn't want to go back to that dark place, that time, all those years ago. They never forgot. I had thought that eventually, someday, it would all be forgotten. Not them. They remembered it all.

Not that they really had a choice. Their biology didn't make forgetting possible. Worse, they passed memories down through the Mother Sacks. How far back could Drac remember? Centuries, without a doubt.

They didn't forget and neither could I.

People, humans mostly, make assumptions about my age. They see Brock Marsden, Detective Moreau, as Captain Kynan Brice of the fine Olinda police force likes to call me. Not as strange as some Moreaus, mostly human, except the hand now. The Euzebian scent slits, like gills on each side of my neck, look like tattoos when closed. Unless someone gets really close, and right now that's only Muriel.

All the other changes are internal. Better eyesight pulled together from three different species. Faster reflexes thanks to the Veleckian nervous system, modified for the human anatomy.

It takes time, sometimes years, to simulate and test. Test and simulate. To research the possible side-effects of making a change with the Moreau Pod. Rushing through it too fast results in non-viable mutations, Dumpties, fortunate if they don't survive.

Even with safety features that I've developed, each time I climb into the Moreau Pod it is a gamble. That's why I haven't incorporated the Neridian neocortex modifications yet. Too many unknowns. Their DNA samples are the prize of my collection, the most expensive, and I may never unlock that puzzle.

One of the earliest modifications I made was incorporating regeneration traits into my genome. I wanted to promote faster healing. I combined traits from multiple species and didn't do sufficient research. I didn't realize it at the time, now I'm amazed that I didn't end up a Dumpty. Many first-timers that get a hold of a Moreau Pod do.

I was lucky.

The changes worked. It still takes time for me to heal. Just not as long as normal humans.

The changes had an unintended side-effect. I'm not aging at the same rate. I'm not immortal. I know that. I am a hundred and twenty-eight years old.

Like the Nosferans, I still remember. Drac didn't move from his spot. I leaned against the wall and rubbed my eyes with the hand that's still human. Over a hundred years ago, humans and Nosferans hadn't yet gone to war.

CHAPTER 14

The Tretan Shuttle

The air might be breathable now, but the atmosphere felt like the ocean right before a storm. Muriel floated beside Dyami, her left hand on his warm back, between the bristles. She used her toes to correct her motion and hold her position.

Dyami clutched the edge of his log-sized bench in thick hands, feet planted to drive him into action.

The scientists and the security personnel faced them from the scant protection of the shuttle seats. So far the security squad hadn't pulled weapons, but that was only a matter of time.

Straight in front, bracing themselves on the seat backs, were Helen and Constantine. They'd finished whatever they were discussing, and then Ben had moved off to the side. He caught the seat Muriel had used earlier and pulled himself down into it. His hand moved in slow stroking motions over the seat of the chair. The gesture looked somewhat obscene.

Muriel ignored him and focused on Constantine. The security man was the one to watch. Muriel didn't need to be a mind reader to know that, right now, Dyami made the man very nervous.

She used her hands and feet to swim through the air to a spot before Dyami. She kept her hands visible and grasped Dyami's restraining belt with her feet.

"Constantine. Is that your first name or last? Or something else? A title?"

"A Constantine," the one called Dustin quipped.

Constantine glanced at the man, and he fell silent.

"That's my name, ma'am."

"Great. I already mentioned it, but my name Muriel Reinhard. Have you checked that information? We're from Olinda. Our ship was fired upon by the same ship that captured an escape pod with one of our crew.

We have to stop the attacks on Olinda before it's too late. Do you understand?"

Constantine scratched his head. "Well, Ms. Reinhard, I grasp the words you're saying. I can't say that they all make sense."

Helen said, "Muriel, you are a surprise to us. We aren't here to harm you, or your companion."

"Why am I a surprise?"

Helen stepped forward, throwing herself into a slow spin. Constantine and Dustin caught her, rotated her back around. Her face was flushed.

"Not used to zero-gee," Helen said. "I'll hold still."

The other people were exchanging glances. Sub-vocal communications? Muriel caught the Mina and Lukas looking at some sort of tablet, and glancing her way. They knew something.

"What's the surprise?" Muriel demanded. Time to lay the cards on the table. "Are you working with Kelwyn? Is that it? Was he surprised I was helping Brock?"

Helen's forehead wrinkled. "No. I don't know those names. We didn't know anything about you before we came into your ship.

We didn't expect to find anyone human on board, we thought this was a first contact situation."

First contact? This wasn't the outer reaches, after all. "Why would you expect first contact around Hansel?"

"Hansel?" Constantine asked. "You mentioned that before. What is it?"

"A moon?" Were they serious? "One of the most populated areas in the system? Not even counting all of the habitats and ships coming and going."

Constantine shook his head. "There's no moon here."

"Or much of anything else." That was from the back, from one of the scientists. Ross, they'd said when they had introduced everyone.

Not much of anything else? "What is he talking about?"

Helen's lips pressed together, then she said. "We need to show you."

Muriel knew that tone. It was the way you said it when you had bad news to give someone, and you weren't sure how they'd take it.

One of Dyami's fingers curled around her wrist.

CHAPTER 15

102 years, 3 months and some days ago...

Standard Terran Time

Cold sleet fell from red clouds above. The light cast everything into red. Like blood. That's Seabrook, the bleeding planet.

Mix the light from the red giant with the organic smog in the atmosphere, and the thickened sleet hit with dull thuds, then oozed like blood while out-gassing a noxious sulfuric odor.

I tucked up my great coat, pulling the collar up around my neck. A few drops of melting sleet oozed and dripped off my broad-brimmed hat. As whiffs of sulfur reached my nose, I adjusted my nose filter.

Technically the atmosphere isn't toxic, but most of the inhabitants, the human ones at least, choose to wear nose filters. Some opt for more elaborate filters that also cover the mouth.

Only on Seabrook would filters become a fashion statement.

On that day long ago, I was impossibly young and fully human. Not yet a Moreau. Twenty-six STT years old, born on Seabrook and looking for a way off. I cupped my hands and waited beneath the awning of a closed up store along Mudport's boardwalk, watching what foot traffic there was mingling with bicycles, recumbents, and cars. Powerful searchlights stabbed up into the blood-stained sky from the Mudport's spaceport, around the bend in the bay. The haze turned the lights into dull bloody beams slashing at the sky, the shapes of the ships no more than dark shapes on the ground.

My desire to leave the wave-pounded shores of my home was regularly thwarted by any passing ship crew that stopped in at the port.

Seabrook sports one continent and a scat-tering of volcanic islands that are the tips of enormous volcanoes thrusting up out of teeming, world-spanning, ocean. Even the continent is nothing more than an upwelling over a cluster of super-volcanoes thought to be the result of a massive collision two billion years earlier that pushed the planet into a tighter orbit and left it with an expansive ring system.

A hazardous planet, at best, to approach without running into debris. Many ships didn't bother. Why trade with us, when they could go to more attractive and less hazardous ports?

Mostly, the highly-prized seafood. Although some species admire our planet and find beauty in a place that looks, and often smells, like an abattoir, for most, it isn't worth the bother. For those with a taste for exotic seafood, the oceans serve up a nightmare of aquatic life.

I didn't know that that would be the day my life changed. I'd wanted it for so long, waited for so many spacers, taken any job that Mudport flung at me. I'd muck out fish guts, shift cargo, drive loaders, anything that might help me secure a spot on one of the visiting ships.

I had my eye on a berth with a Torlian crew, a ship I called the Gourd-O-Pod, based on the way the fat ship resembled a green flying gourd. It had landed at Mudport two days earlier, to pick up a load of deep-sea crustaceans from the depths of the ocean. Terrorlobs, nothing like Terran lobsters, despite the name. Green-brown, and each half the size of a man, squat and ugly, with claws powerful enough to cut armored fish in half. Difficult to dredge up, as they fought like mad and shredded traps, and yet the Torlians kept coming back for them.

As aliens went, Torlians didn't seem that bad. They resembled Earth's restored Apatosaurus, a biped with a tail and a crest rising up from a duck-billed face. The most common coloration was some shade of yellow with a paler underbelly. A few ran to dark colors, even stripes. Not a species with a fondness for clothes. They usually went everywhere without clothing. Usually, the only thing they carried was some sort of wearable tech for communication.

Not a violent people, sometimes abrupt. On their last few visits, I had done my best to act the helpful human. Guide, arranging services, even putting them into contact with harvesters that wouldn't rip them off.

They knew me, and I thought I knew them. They were my best option for getting off the planet.

They liked the waterfront. Knowing that they'd come in last night, that's where I went and why I was hanging out along the boardwalk, eyeing those passing by, waiting for those distinctive crests and booming voices.

The boardwalk stretches ten-kilometers along Mudport's waterfront, the result of over-enthusiasm for the city's potential. The businesses running along the boardwalk are eateries, clothing stores, and odds-and-ends places. Most of the seafood merchants take care of business outside of Mudport, right on the docks where ships unload their hauls.

Tired of standing beneath the awning, sleeting rain dripping through the tattered fabric, I went looking for someplace drier to wait.

I stomped through the rain, keeping an eye out for the Torlians. How hard could it be to find a group of yellow dinosaurs milling around our boardwalk?

There were places I wanted to check out anyway. The most thriving businesses along the boardwalk catered mostly to the crews of the fishing vessels. Bars and brothels, what-ever your kink or drink.

I hadn't known the Torlians to frequent the brothels, so that cut it down a bit to the bars where much of the business of Mudport happened.

And I could rule out the joints that catered exclusively to humans. Technically illegal, but tolerated by Mudport's exclusion-ists leaders. They'd serve aliens, all the while doing their underhanded best to encourage one of their regulars to rough up the aliens in exchange for a free drink.

Ruling them out worked for me. I never spent time in those places anyway. Wasn't the sort of place to find spacers, human or not, that could give me a job.

I went with the rest of the crowd, another human in a great coat with sleet like blood dripping off my broad brim hat, hands tucked in deep pockets.

On the side of the boardwalk, a cart ven-dor called out to the passing crowd.

"Fresh caught! Fresh caught! Crisp and hot!"

I knew that voice. His name was Wednes-day. He worked the boardwalk, him and dozens of others, pushing or riding their carts from place to place.

His cart had a bicycle front on it, with the cart in the back, covered in a steep synth-canvas awning. Lines of scaly, armored fish hung beneath the awning. Fat and glistening in the reddish light, with massive jaws.

Wednesday himself huddled up close to his cart, his coat wrapped around a massive frame, fabric straining against the buttons. A curly white beard spread down across his broad chest in an impressive cloud.

I dodged some cyclists, stepped around other pedestrians, and made it through the crowd to Wednesday's cart.

"How's business, Wednesday?"

"Same as any other day!" Wednesday laughed at his own stale joke. "Broke Brock, you down here hustling the boardwalk again? Still, think that someone is going to haul your ass off this bloody rock?"

"A man has got to have his dreams."

Wednesday snorted at that. "Dreams! Dreams'll get you sucked into the deep. A man doesn't need dreams. He needs his belly full and a dry place to sleep if he's fortunate. And if he's really lucky, a woman to polish his rod now and then. That's it, the great secret of life, and it isn't going to change no matter how far we go!"

"You're not going to blame me for wanting more than that, are you?"

"No." Wednesday shook his head. "What's the point? You're young, you already know it all anyway."

"I think the galaxy offers a bit more than this." I gestured at the stream of humanity passing Wednesday's cart. I couldn't accept that what he said might be true. If I had, I think I might have thrown myself from the boardwalk.

"Sure Brock, and standing around isn't helping me pull in customers. How about you buy something? Crispy hot fried fish? That'll lift your spirits." Wednesday pulled back the lid on his side of the cart.

Even from this side, I felt the heat. Steam flew up around Wednesday, carrying the smell of spices, fat, and fish.

My stomach growled at the thought, but Wednesday wasn't wrong when he called me broke. Scrounging jobs where I could, I never had much money. I'd turned down offers of regular pay, afraid to get chained down in the rut that Wednesday described.

"Not hungry," I said. "I'm looking for some Torlians, ship came in, I've done some work for them before. Any chance you've seen them go past?"

"Torlians? Sure, they went by a while ago. Heading down to lands' end. Maybe they think they'll go swimming, a vacation on the beach!" Wednesday laughed again. Swimming unprotected in these waters? Not likely.

"Thanks, Wednesday, stay dry." I turned to leave.

"Hey, Brock."

I stopped, looked back. Wednesday held out a roll, stuffed with shredded fish and sautéed greens, half wrapped in waxy paper.

My mouth watered. I wanted the sandwich. I hadn't eaten since the night before. Wednesday shook his head before I said anything.

"Take it. It's been sitting too long. I'd have to throw it out anyway soon, and I know you're not going to buy it." His eyes narrowed. "Ain't giving it away. People see you eating it, you're going to tell them where you got it. Gonna advertise for me. Deal?"

I knew the score. I'd do it too. I'd send him as many customers as I could. I took the sandwich, warm in my hand.

"Sure thing, Wednesday. You got it. Thanks for the job, and the sandwich."

"Umpf. Let's see how many people you send my way. Get enough, and I might have some more work for you." He laughed. "You might need it when those dinosaurs don't take you off in their spaceship!"

I raised the sandwich. Thick round roll, crust golden and toasted, soaking the fat from the fish. Stuffed with oily strands and greens. I took a bite, savoring the buttery taste, the crunch of the crust and the way the fish melted in my mouth, rich in spices. Heat flowed from my mouth down through my body, warming me against the bloody sleet falling. Almost like a sun-break in my mouth.

A thin guy, face pale beneath his dripping hat, nearly ran into me. His eyes went to my face as he mumbled something, a curse or an apology, then went to the sandwich. He hesitated, and I saw his nostrils flare.

"No problem," I said. I nodded at Wednesday's cart. "I got it from Wednesday, right there. Best sandwiches on the walk. Can't beat the price."

I walked away, slipping around a slow-moving cyclist, eating as I went. That first bite had stirred my hunger, fanning the flames. I glanced back once and saw the pale man duck beneath Wednesday's awning.

True to my word, and with gratitude for what Wednesday had done, I did tell other people about his cart as I looked for the Torlians.

I'd nearly reached land's end, where Mudport gave way to the tumbled rock of the jetty reaching out across the bay. The boardwalk ended beside shops battered by wind and wave. These places took the brunt of the weather. None more than a couple floors high, exteriors peeled and warped by conditions. Low rent, high crime neighborhood. Not where I expected to find the Torlians. If I'd been guiding them, I would have turned back before getting this far.

I didn't see them and was about to turn back when I heard a loud trumpeting sound and distressed hoots. A crack like rocks striking, or a shot being fired, split the air even over the wind.

I ran toward the noise. It came from an alley between two of the dilapidated buildings. Women lounged in the windows of one, hardly dressed, looking tired and bored. As I ran, they started rising, leaning against the glass, trying to see.

The noises continued. I skidded to a stop at the mouth of the alley. It was dark in the narrow space, but not so dark that I couldn't see two long yellowish backs, streaked red with sleet, bending over another yellowish body lying on the ground. It was the ones standing making all the noise.

I took a breath and walked down the alley. I didn't know what had happened. Whatever it was, I wanted to help. I liked the Torlians if one was hurt I wanted to help.

And part of me, that dark voice we all have, was telling me that this was my chance. My opportunity to get off this bloody rock once and for all.

CHAPTER 16

Australia's Shuttle

Muriel fought the sick feeling in her gut. It didn't have anything to do with moving from a null-gee environment to a standard gravity.

The shuttle looked old.

Nothing specific that she could put her finger on, like seeing someone dressed in an old style. Antiquated. Come to think of it, even the space suits that the scientists and the security wore looked old. Not old as in worn out and patched, in fact, the suits positively gleamed, as if they hadn't seen much use at all.

It was the fashion, the design of the suits that had a retro look to them.

Add to that the linguist's surprise with

Dyami's translator and their clear surprise when she asked about Hansel.

Helen and Constantine had led the way through the umbilical airlock that connected the ships. Now Helen turned, watching Muriel as she stepped down into the shuttle.

Just like stepping onto land after spending a long time in the water. Muriel moved forward, making room for Ben Tol to step down.

On the surface, the shuttle didn't look much different than the Tretan's ship. Seats arranged in front-facing rows. Like the team's spacesuits, it had a pristine, freshly-constructed look to it. At the same time, who picked such dull colors? All muted grays and whites. Shiny, shiny, a style that brought to mind old recordings.

"Is everything alright?" Helen asked. "Are you feeling okay? It can be disorientating returning to a gravity field."

"I'm fine," Muriel said.

Helen and Constantine moved forward, and Helen followed, turning sideways to let Ben slip past her. The scientist hurried after Helen.

Muriel stopped and turned back, waiting

for Dyami. His big hands appeared first, grasping the hatch frame. He pulled himself forward, swung his legs up between his arms and dropped with a loud thud onto the aisle. He barely fit, and he filled the passageway with his bulk.

"Small spaces," he complained.

"At least there's air to breathe," Muriel said.

"Muriel?" Helen called.

Muriel turned. The other three were toward the front of the cabin. Constantine was ahead, speaking to more people, a flight crew at the front of the shuttle. Helen had activated a large holographic screen on the left cabin bulkhead.

Muriel glanced at Dyami. "Come on, let's find out what's going on."

She went up the aisle, and he followed her. Whatever else happened, she was glad to have him at her back. Distant voices, the sound of the hatch opening and closing, told her that the other members of the team were following.

Muriel reached the end of the shuttle and Ben moved, taking one of the seats, making room. Helen pointed to the holographic screen. It showed deep space, nothing but darkness and unfamiliar stars.

"What am I looking at?" Muriel asked.

Dyami leaned over her shoulder to see, his bulk taking up the aisle.

"This is where we are," Helen said.

"Nowhere," Constantine added. "Right smack dab in the middle of nowhere."

"Interstellar space," Helen added. "Feel free to pan the view around, it all looks much the same."

The pressure grew in Muriel's gut and in her head, like pushing a dive into the deep, deep dark. How far was too far to go?

She stepped up to the display and reached out, reaching into the holographic interface and dragged her hand across that emptiness. The stars moved in response. Muriel swiped several times more, and the view didn't change. She couldn't even tell if she had gone all the way around or not, none of the stars looked familiar. She flicked up, and the display rotated the other way.

Nothing. Nothing. Nothing.

The space around Hansel bustled with activity. The moon was a bustling hive of activity, serving as a major spaceport for the hundreds of habitats and colonies scattered throughout the Olindan system. The space above Hansel looked like a cloud of fireflies, a dance of lights moving in an intricate ballet around the mining-scarred surface.

Nothing like that here. Only deep blackness and stars. In many ways similar to the deep dark of the Olindan ocean. Tiny organisms down there glowed, but they also moved, swam, fought and died. These stars were static.

"Where is Hansel? Olinda?" Dyami asked.

"Where are we, might be a better question," Muriel said.

A bright splinter in space caught her attention. Whatever else was here, that wasn't a star. She grabbed the display on that spot and spread her hands, expanding and zooming in on the object.

Not an object. A ship. One from the history books. Even at this distance, surrounded by nothing, it looked big. A long structure stretched out and speckled with lights. Muriel pointed at the ship.

"That's your ship," she said, watching Helen and Constantine's faces. "Why don't you tell us about that? Answers would be good."

Constantine reached out to Helen, pulling her back. Muriel's gut tightened. They were in the deep, deep dark here. She clenched her fists and waited for an answer.

CHAPTER 17

Australia's shuttle

Helen was searching for a place to start when Blackstone's image replaced the star field and *Australia* on the holographic display.

The director smiled at both Muriel and Dyami. "Excuse me for eavesdropping, and allow me to welcome you. I am Olivia Blackstone, director of the Terran Expedition vessel *Australia*."

"*Australia*," Muriel said. "How is that possible?"

Possible? What was the woman talking about? Helen looked at Blackstone, waiting for the director to answer. All eyes were focused on the screen. The rest of the team hung back, unwilling to get too close to the large alien, but she saw many of the seat back displays mirroring the front cabin display.

"You wanted the answer," Blackstone said. "My turn to ask a question. You spoke of a place, Olinda? Hansel? Where exactly are they?"

"Not here, obviously," Muriel said. "Olinda is a planet around a G-type star about four hundred and thirty light years from Sol. Hansel is one of the moons. The world, and its system has attracted colonists and trade from countless species."

Listening to Muriel, an almost electric shock ran through Helen. What the hell? She hugged herself to stop the trembles. Four hundred and thirty light years? Humanity didn't have people out that far. It was so far beyond the scope of explored space, it was almost unimaginable. And yet, if Muriel could be believed, and she sounded sincere, the place was real.

Blackstone broke the silence. "You have to forgive us, we're a bit taken aback at your answer. Our expedition is en route to CY-HC-2347, a habitable moon around a gas giant. We had thought maybe you came from there. Even now, still a light year out, it's the nearest world."

"No Director," Muriel said. She pressed her hands together. "I'm sure I already know the answer, but I have to hear it. What year is it?"

Year? She was asking about the year? A cold realization swept over Helen like someone had opened a door and let in a winter breeze. It couldn't fucking be...

"2876," Blackstone said gravely. "Are you implying what I think many of us suspect, Ms. Reinhard?"

"Implying? I don't know that I'm implying anything." Muriel looked up at the alien.

Helen couldn't decide what the look they exchanged meant. The alien's lips curled back, making him look even more like something from a nightmare. The contrast between him and the lovely young woman standing in front of him was unreal. This whole conversation had taken on a feeling of unreality.

"Director?" Muriel said. "You say it is 2876, confirming what I thought, what I know."

The floor shook, and the armband

translator on the alien spoke. "It isn't possible! The universe does not allow this."

Muriel kept talking as if he hadn't said anything, but she patted his arm. "We're from a time just over a hundred years in your future. And Director Blackstone? The proof? I know about your secret orders."

The woman's word's made no sense, and yet it was like the shuttle's atmosphere had just been evacuated into space. No one said anything, not even Ben. Blackstone's face on the screen revealed nothing, as calm and composed as if Muriel had said it was sunny outside. It was Blackstone herself that broke the silence.

"I see, Ms. Reinhard. I feel it would be better if we continued this conversation in person. Please accompany our team back to *Australia*, as our guests."

"And if we refuse?"

Blackstone's eyes narrowed slightly. "It is my understanding that your ship's environmental systems are inoperative. I think there are few options remaining to you."

The big alien growled. Helen stepped back and hit the bulkhead. Blackstone glanced at her and then back at their visitors.

"Dyami, is it?"

The alien stopped growling.

"I am not threatening you or Ms. Rein-hard," Blackstone said. "I want to help get to the bottom of this, and we also have a mission to get on with. Your ship is disabled. We can bring it aboard. Maybe help with the repairs. I would very much like to meet you in person."

Muriel bit her lip, her eyes went to the alien, to Dyami, and she reached up to touch his face.

The two had a bond. A friendship, which said something about wherever they came from. Helen pushed away from the wall. Deal with the facts in front of them and to hell with the consequences.

"I'd like a chance to get to know you better too," Helen said. "Where you're from, it sounds fascinating."

Muriel looked back to Helen, and her eyes glistened. Her lips parted as if she was about to say something. Helen's breath caught in her throat, waiting.

Instead, Muriel gave one nod. Just the one. Her shoulders sagged.

"Thank you," Blackstone said. "I will see you when you arrive."

Helen could breathe again. Whatever Muriel wanted to say, it'd probably come out at some point. Until then, she just had to do what she could to help their guests and make sure that they didn't fall under Security's purview.

"Let's get you settled," Helen suggested. "We'll need to figure out something for Dyami."

Constantine moved forward talking to his team and the flight crew, arranging for their trip home.

Home. Helen went with Muriel as she found a seat in the front room, dislodging Ben Tol. He moved back, easing carefully around Dyami. The big alien crawled up front and lay down on the floor in front of the bulkhead at their feet. He folded his arms and rested his head on them. His big eyes closed.

"Is he okay?" Helen asked.

Muriel nodded. "I think just over-whelmed. And worried. We've left someone very important to us back home. I don't know if we'll see him again."

Helen fought the urge to ask questions and instead said, "Let's just get back. We'll deal with the rest then."

Once again Muriel opened her mouth as if to stay something and stopped. She looked away.

Helen studied the young woman. Was she from the future? Was it even possible? Science said no, but the rumors about the Galactics, whatever you called older alien species, had a lot of scientists running scared, afraid that they didn't know nearly as much as they thought they did. So far they hadn't even been able to answer how the artificial gravity worked, and that was with generators in hand.

If it was true that Muriel was from the future, how much did she know about *Australia*'s expedition? Did her presence, and the alien's, mean that things had changed? Was it possible to change the past?

Had it already changed?

CHAPTER 18

Orlando Pike's Fortress, Olinda

I was back in the empty sensie room, Drac still huddled in the corner muttering to himself. The light hadn't changed, but two other things had changed.

I was hungry. *Ravenous.* I needed to pee, the pressure like a knife in my gut.

A human man stood beside the door. Thin and hard, wearing a tight white shirt without sleeves. The thin material revealed a body sculpted and heavily muscled. His skin was dark brown and marked by patterns of scars along his bulging muscles. His hair was long and gray, matted into tendrils, and within each glinted glistening strands. He wore black shorts that, like the shirt, clung to thick hard thighs and ended just above the knee. His lower legs and feet were bare.

I knew the man. Orlando Pike. Infamous collector, pirate and benefactor of enough politicians to make sure he didn't have to worry about any legal issues on Olinda. A safe, neutral refuge for a man wanted on dozens of worlds for crimes.

Convenient.

He watched me sitting there, his square jaw clenching.

"Brock Marsden. You're an interesting case. What happened next?"

He smelled of apples, sour and tart. He wanted something from me, and he was sure he was going to get it.

Was already getting it, and had been since I was put in this room.

He was scanning my memories. *Why?*

Pike squatted, the motion smooth and easy. "Because I'm a collector. I acquired this technology from someone you knew. Groct, I believe he was called?"

Groct. Alien, non-humanoid, lemon-scented. He tried to kill my friend Calanthe, and he killed some others. Cut off their heads and downloaded their memories. It drove him crazy.

"I refined the techniques after I acquired

the technology. Really ingenious, except the scanning methods were primitive. I have a nanowire web that is not only more accurate, it also leaves the subject alive. And I want you alive."

"You're reading my mind."

"Yes. I want to know why you came here."

"Then why start with things that happened so long ago?"

"Because I want to understand you, completely. My people don't keep anything back from me."

"I'm not your people," I said.

Pike smiled, a flash of white against his dark lips. His laughter was easy, warm and filled the cell. Through it all Drac remained huddled in the corner.

"Oh, nothing's wrong with him," Pike said. "The technology doesn't work well with Nosferans. All those inherited memories. The calibration isn't set up for that. We'll get it eventually."

"For what? What are you doing with our memories?"

"Memories are information. When we're done, I'll understand everything there is to know about you. Information to be used, to be sold, whatever I wish."

I wanted to leap up, attack him. Despite his impressive musculature, he smelled fully human. I wasn't. I also didn't move, not so much as a twitch.

Pike laughed again and smoothly stood. "Don't worry. I'll give you some time to take care of necessities, eat, and then we'll get back to it."

CHAPTER 19

Seabrook, long ago...

I didn't want to startle the two aliens, not when they resembled dinosaurs and each massed at least twice my mass.

I called out as I entered the alley. "Hello? Do you need help?"

One of the Torlians spun around, surprisingly nimble for such a big sentient. The thick skin around his eyes wrinkled and flushed a bright orange color that radiated up along the crest extending up from his head. His beak-like mouth opened and blasted out a noise like a fog horn.

I got it. I stopped and held up my empty hands. "I'm Brock Marsden, I've helped your crew before, on other trips."

I pointed one finger at the fallen Torlian. "What's happened? Maybe I can help?"

The other Torlian turned now. I recognized her by the way her crest widened at the top. Jun'lack was the captain, if that was the word, on the Gourd-O-Pod.

"Jun'lack, it's me, Brock Marsden."

Jun'lack's tail smacked against the ground next to her fallen crew member. She spoke, her voice intelligible, if a bit high-pitched. "You don't think this is a good time."

I don't know if it's in their wiring, but the Torlians sometimes have a hard time with pronouns when speaking our language. They tended to switch them around or avoid them. Jun'lack meant that she didn't think this was a good time.

I took a couple more steps forward, watching the flushed male while focusing on Jun'lack. "Maybe I can help? Tell me what happened. Do you need medical help for your crew member?"

Jun'lack's waved her crest in the negative. "Dead. That one is dead. Killed!"

Murdered? "What happened? A robbery?"

The orange flush was draining now out of the male's crest. His tail drooped, and he turned slowly back to the body.

"It isn't known," Jun'lack said. "That one

came out alone, to this place for reasons not shared. We followed too late, that one was already shot dead."

Crime wasn't unknown on Seabrook, especially not in places like Mudport. With the off-world traffic, it brought all types. The constables, at least the honest ones, tried to keep it in check but received little support.

"Let me help," I said. "I know Mudport, and I know people here. I can find out who murdered your crew member and turn whoever it is over to the constables."

"No!" Jun'lack clacked her beak. "You want the killer beneath your feet."

Her feet, she meant. She didn't want the killer turned over to the constables but to her.

"If I do this, will you give me a spot on your crew? I want a berth off this planet."

"I will have a position with the crew, if I bring this killer to you," Jun'lack said. "This you swear!"

Once I turned that around in my head, it made sense. She swore that I'd have the position if I brought her the killer. It was a way off the planet. And if it meant living with whatever happened to a killer? That was okay.

I had to get closer to really see the body. If I'd had better eyes, I would have stayed back, but as it was, I had to get close to the Torlians. They smelled of fish and plant decay and seemed not to notice the sleet splatting and oozing off their backs.

The dead Torlian was male. With a long, thin crest that widened only slightly at the end. Females had broader crests at the top that fanned out. The body still wore a sash, the one piece of clothing it did wear, that doubled as a carrying strap for various pieces of tech. Compared to the other two, he had been carrying quite a lot of devices. Electronic screens flickered and danced, unaware that their owner had died.

The living male crouched in the alley, tail curled around his feet, knees up against his chest and face buried beneath him. His crest rose straight up into the air and a low thrumming noise pulsed from the crest. Some sort of song for the dead? Crying? I didn't know.

Jun'lack loomed over my shoulder while I walked around the body and studied the ground.

"I'm looking for any evidence the killer might have left behind," I said.

"That is the only evidence I need," Jun'lack said, pointing at the bloody hole in the dead Torlian's broad chest.

The wound was big, tissue peeled outward. It was the exit wound. I leaned over enough to see that, yes, there was a smaller — still big enough for three of my fingers — hole in the Torlian's back. Someone had shot him with a large weapon.

I took out my phone and snapped pictures of the body and the area around him. The Torlians made no move to stop me. Jun'lack watched, while her nameless companion continued to sit in the mud, rocking and humming through his crest.

The wound surprised me. Why do something so violent? What could the Torlian possibly have that was worth all of this?

"Did he have anything valuable?"

"No. We came to trade for fish. Blauek was still in training, a branch of your family. He would have done well if he had continued the training. Perhaps in time, even to have run a ship of his own."

"Why kill him like this? This was a violent weapon. Messy. Who does something like that?"

"There is no reason!" Jun'lack blasted an angry horn at the red skies.

I shivered. The day, such as it was, wasn't nearly long enough. Soon it would get dark, and with it, the chance of any of us finding out the truth would decrease.

What if Blauek hadn't been the target? I rephrased the question for Jun'lack. "Could someone had thought that they were taking you out?"

"It's possible, why?"

"Contract disputes? Any conflict you can think of, they might be leads to explain what happened here."

"Who would hire someone so incompetent that they couldn't identify their target?"

I took more pictures of the body and studied that wound more. It was big, but also the edges of the entry wound were cut in four places like whatever cut through Blauek had a cross shape.

Like a harpoon, one of the armor-piercing varieties that were used to hunt down the sorts of fish that the Torlian enjoyed.

I pictured him standing in the alley. The killer shot him from behind. So they hadn't been arguing or anything like that, at least when it happened. The bolt would have ripped through him and ended up — there!

The harpoon stuck in the wall of the structure on my right, the tip sunken into the wood. I took pictures of it, then pulled on gloves. Jun'lack followed me to the harpoon.

Her crest thrummed over the patter of the sleet. "That is what killed Blauek?"

"Yes. As I see it, Blauek was in the alley, facing this way, when he was shot from behind. The bolt ripped through and embedded itself here, in the side of the building."

The male behind us hooted loudly, a call of alarm that I recognized.

A group of constables piled out of a flitter at the end of the alley. A dark shadow passed overhead, another flitter, rotating and coming down on our other side, to block off the alley.

The male stood again, uncoiling and eyebrows coming together as he focused most of his attention on the constables straight ahead.

"Don't do anything!" I called. "Don't say anything. You've asked me to help, I'll handle this."

And if I couldn't? Then I'd get left behind

here on this rock. I walked around the male, and the fallen body, and stood in front of the corpse as the line of four constables made their way closer. Three trailed behind the leader.

I knew them all. Never in too much trouble with them myself, I had even helped out on a few cases. Trouble was, Kenneth Holburn didn't care for people stepping on his turf.

He marched ahead of the following constables. A tall man, thin, nearly sixty years old. His broad hat hid his hair, but his blue eyes shone brightly beneath the brim. His white beard was trimmed short. He wore a great coat, just part of the standard issue on Mudport, but the constables' coats were all rusty red. The sleet just seemed to vanish when it hit them. Their badges glinted golden in the dim light.

I walked out to meet them.

"Mr. Marsden," Holburn said. He stopped, hands lose at his sides. "What's going on here?"

I obviously couldn't hide the crime. "A Torlian crew member has been killed. Murdered."

"Murdered? Maybe you ought to let me determine that."

"He was shot through the back with an armor-piercing harpoon. It's stuck in the wall back there. And his captain, she's the one with the broad crest, the name is Jun'lack, believes it was murder."

Holburn's eyes narrowed. He didn't say anything for a couple of long seconds. I'd seen it before. Holburn knew how to let people wait. So I waited. I resisted the urge to fidget or cross my arms. It wasn't quite a staring contest, but after the first couple heartbeats, it started to get into that territory.

Holburn broke the silence. "What's your interest in this, Mr. Marsden? How did you happen to be here?"

"I'm working for the Torlians right now."

"So what did you see? Any ideas on how this happened?"

"I wasn't with them at the time," I said. "I heard them hooting and came running. When I arrived, it was too late. I didn't see anyone else in the area."

Holburn nodded. He looked past me, at the waiting Torlians, then back. "Do they speak our language? You can communicate with them, right?"

"They speak pretty well. Sometimes they mix up pronouns."

"Thank you." Holburn stepped close, and his hand fell heavily on my shoulder. He squeezed a bit harder than necessary. "Why don't you run on now? This is a constabulary matter now."

I turned my head, looking him in the eyes. He didn't have anything on me in height. "I told you, I'm working for them. I take my orders from Jun'lack right now."

The squeeze tightened and then released. It left my shoulder throbbing. Holburn stepped on past. "Don't get in my way."

I turned around and followed. The other three constables trailed behind us, while the two at the far end of the alley stayed put.

When we got close Holburn turned and pointed at one of the constables behind us, a woman with bright red hair and pale, freckled skin. "Alicia, call in a wagon, then let's get some pictures of this."

He spoke loudly, clearly waiting until that moment so that the Torlians would hear him giving directions. I moved away from him to stand near Jun'lack. If necessary, I could run interference between them.

"Captain, Jun'lack, is it? I'm constable Holburn, I'm in charge here."

The living male, whose name still escaped me, had sunk down on his heels again, making that humming noise through his crest. Jun'lack's brow darkened toward orange.

"You want answers. You want the person responsible," Jun'lack said.

"That's right," Holburn said. "And we'll get those answers. We'll catch the person responsible."

He didn't get it, that she meant that she wanted the answers, and the person responsible. Although when it came down to it, I didn't see that it matter. I stayed silent.

"Take us through it," Holburn said. "What happened?"

"It is not known what happened," Jun'lack said. "That one was alone, we found him too late."

"Does he have a name?"

"Blauek."

Holburn pointed at the grieving Torlian. "And what's that one's name?"

"He is called Gorge."

"Gorge? or Jorge?"

"Gorge," Jun'lack said, clapping her bill for emphasis. "Gorge and Blauek shared sex."

Holburn blinked as he absorbed that bit of information. I'd been around Torlians enough to know that their relationships and reproduction were entirely different things.

"But Gorge and Blauek weren't together. Gorge was with you?"

"Yes. You were conducting trading business for terrorlobs. Blauek was junior-most on the ship, and went out to explore the city."

"I see," Holburn snapped his fingers at me and gestured.

We walked over by the wall of the building. Alicia moved around the body, taking pictures.

Holburn got in my face. "What the hell am I supposed to do with this, Marsden? Alien wanders off on his own, gets himself killed in the process. You realize what a mess this is?"

"I do." Holburn wanted to talk. That was a first. "I think we can help each other out here."

"How's that?"

"Keep your constables out of it. Give

me time to do some digging around on my own. I might turn up something that you won't find."

"Because you're so charming?"

"People know me," I said.

"If they know you, they know you keep your nose clean. They know you want to get out of here. Hardly reasons to confide in you."

I shrugged. "If that's true, then I don't get anywhere. Either way, no problem for you."

"There's a problem for me if you get yourself killed in the process. Some alien gets himself killed, that's one thing. You get yourself killed, that's a lot more paperwork."

"I can keep the Torlians off your back," I said. "Like I said before, I've worked for them. If they think I'm handling this, then they won't be pestering you."

"Finally, a reason I can get behind." Holburn rubbed his jaw. "Fine. Here's what we do. I'm going to stick this as an alien matter, under alien jurisdiction. You do what you want to help them, or not. We'll do a crime scene survey for you, hand over the details and then we're done."

Nice to see how much he cared about

the visitors to Seabrook. Unfortunately, his attitude wasn't uncommon.

"Works for me," I said. "That's what the Torlians want anyway. I think Jun'lack has her own justice in mind."

"Hey, as long as they take care of it on their ship, not a problem for me!"

Holburn slapped my arm, hard, and walked back over to where Jun'lack stood. Holburn pointed at me as I came back.

"I'm appointing Brock Marsden as our special liaison on this, and we're putting the matter under your jurisdiction. He'll find out what happened here."

"One day," Jun'lack boomed. "We depart at sunset tomorrow. You want to bring us the one responsible by then!"

"I'm sure he'll do his best," Holburn said. He winked at me, then went over to talk to his people.

I turned around and found Jun'lack's face in mine. The skin around her eyes was still flushed orange, but fading. Her hourglass pupils searched my face.

"I will find the one responsible?"

She meant me. "I will."

"One day," she said.

"I got that. I bring you the one behind this, and you give me a position on your crew." I stuck out my hand.

Jun'lack tipped her head to the side, then took my hand. Her skin felt slightly oily, warm against my palm. Three long fingers curling around my hand. A strong grip there, not too much.

She let go and warbled. Gorge stirred, rose and stomped around Blauek's body. The two of them walked off without another word.

Alicia paused in her photography and came up beside me. "Huh, what are we supposed to do with the body when we're done?"

"Send it to the spaceport." I gave her the berth number. "That's our ship."

Our ship. It gave me a shiver to say the words, but I was convinced. I'd find the person responsible and deliver him to Jun'lack, and secure my place on the ship and off Seabrook.

Did I feel guilty about that? No way. The killer deserved justice. If he'd killed a human, I wouldn't have hesitated before turning him over to the constables. No reason to

hesitate before turning him over to the Torlians either.

No reason at all.

CHAPTER 20

Terran Expedition Australia

The room was something from the history books. All sleek lines and gleaming surfaces. The table at the center of the room looked like glass but was undoubtedly some sort of smart polymer, popular in this time.

Time travel. The idea was as chilling as breathing deep space and just about as possible. Muriel paced the room, circling the table with its padded chairs. Since coming aboard she and Dyami had been moved quickly, through cleared corridors, to this conference room somewhere in the depths of the massive Terran ship. Between the elevator and the blank corridors, the place felt like a maze.

For his part, Dyami sat at the head of the room, on the floor, his short rear legs between his thick arms. His wrinkled face watched her pacing.

"This is the time that was?" Dyami asked. "The past? Such things defy possibility."

Muriel stopped, leaning on one of the anchored chairs. "That's what we thought. We're here. What do you know about *Australia*?"

"Nothing," Dyami said.

"Let me handle the talking. I'm sure they're listening to us now, that's okay. I know the history. I studied it as part of my education."

Let Blackstone, and whoever else was listening, chew on that. Right now Blackstone had to be coming up with all sorts of other explanations for their presence, for the Tretan's shuttle, and what Muriel claimed to know. Explanations that didn't involve time travel.

So far the *Australia* crew hadn't given any indication that they were aware of Pilot. Was the Tretan creation even still online? Since their brief contact, there hadn't been any more indication that the Pilot was functional. If it was, then there was a chance that it might have some idea how this had happened. Until she knew more about their situation and status on this ship, however, she wasn't planning to say anything about the cyber mnemonic clone.

The door opened and people filed in, led by Olivia Blackstone, *Australia*'s director.

Tall and thin, white hair hanging down her back. Bamboo sticks held her hair back. She wore plain green workalls, not any different than the rest of the crew and it didn't matter. All eyes focused on the director. She moved as if she was both unaware of the attention and expecting it. Her feet were bare, and her eyes, when they met Muriel's, were hazel with specks of green and gold.

She wasn't old, the white hair wasn't an indication of age. Her skin was flawless, perfect, and unlined. She looked as if age might never touch her, just like the historical images.

Beautiful, like Subha or Calanthe back home on Olinda. Women that she admired and had emulated before striking off on her own. Strong women, accustomed to getting what they wanted. Except for Brock. He had rejected them both, and chosen her. Unbelievable, and yet it had happened.

Those women were Moreaus, like her, their genes sculpted to their own chosen version of perfection. Subha, for her aquatic life in Olinda's oceans, and Calanthe focused on enhancing her sexual powers, a sensie actress in growing demand.

Blackstone wasn't a Moreau. The Moreau Pods hadn't been available in this time. Her family had used gene-sculpting, human technology to modify and improve genetics generation after generation. Artificial engineering done before birth, on the base DNA. One change at a time, different modifications tried with different offspring. Nonviable offspring were terminated. Those that lived continued the tradition, with the most successful and reliable traits being combined with the latest modifications. It was similar to what could be accomplished with a Moreau Pod, only over generations, and without studying alien DNA. The big difference? Moreau's made the choice for themselves. The gene-sculptors decided it for the unborn.

Blackstone walked to the head of the table. With her were Helen Shaw and Derek Constantine. The security chief showed his age. The three of them took seats at the head of the table, as far from Dyami as they could get in the room.

Concern? These were people that supposedly were going out to explore and seek contact with aliens. Dyami was intimidating when he wanted to be, but right now he stayed sitting, watching the Terrans come into the room.

Muriel stayed standing, mid-way along the table.

Blackstone folded her hands on the transparent tabletop. "Ms. Reinhard, will you have a seat? Do you need any refreshment?"

"No, thanks, I'll stand."

With a small nod, Blackstone looked down the table at Dyami and smiled. "And you, Dyami? Is there anything that you need?"

Vibrations flowed through the chair beneath Muriel's fingers. The armband translated Dyami's response. "No, thank you."

"Well," Blackstone said. "If either of you needs anything, or want to take a break, let me know. You're our guests. I want you to be comfortable on our ship. Quarters are being prepared. If there is anything we can do to make you more comfortable, let us know."

"Thank you," Muriel said. "I think we should see to our ship's repairs and be on our way as soon as possible."

"I can understand your desire to do so," Blackstone said. "We've resumed our course for CY-HC-2347. Along the way, we'll see what we can do about your ship. I think we stand to learn a great deal from each other."

Sometimes, when diving in the ocean, Muriel swam out over the deep dark chasms. Places where the ocean floor was far, far below and the temptation to dive deeper and deeper welled up inside. A giddy, dangerous feeling, the same that swam in her gut now.

Tell them the truth? Tell them anything about the future? Or keep that to herself? Had they already changed history just by being here? Was that even possible?

"Muriel," Helen said. "You looked troubled. We only want to help."

"Put yourself in my place," Muriel said. "If you found yourself back in time at a key moment in history, what would you do? Does your presence change things? What if you make the wrong choice?"

Constantine leaned forward, his hands flat on the table. "I'm sorry, I'm finding it hard to accept that you are from the future. I'm not a scientist, but everything I've learned makes it clear that time travel is impossible."

"Not entirely," Blackstone said. "The drive that powers this ship could be considered a form of time travel. We move while staying in the same time reference as the rest of the universe. We're essentially standing still while moving, only the information about our position changes."

"I've never understood that," Constantine said. "We only have to look outside to see that we've moved."

"Yes," Helen said. "That's right. We've moved. Each STC shift adjusts our position, without any real motion. The only time we really move is when we have to use the conventional engines to adjust our local velocity, as we did when we matched trajectories with Ms. Reinhard's ship."

Dyami rose up, and the Terrans all went still. He walked slowly around the table, a massive orange and black nightmare. He stopped when he reached Muriel. He sat down again close to her.

Muriel rubbed his shoulder until his eyes closed part way.

"This is as hard for us as it is for you," Muriel said. "I know exactly the problems you're having with this, I've got them myself. Nothing the Galactics have revealed has ever indicated that time travel was possible."

"You didn't intend this, then?" Blackstone asked.

Sharp. The director had caught that right away. No point in denying it.

"No, of course not," Muriel said.

"And the Galactics," Helen said. "They really exist? The Glittering Throng isn't a myth?"

Muriel shook her head. "You're using a ship powered by Galactic technology."

"We know it's advanced alien technology, and that we still don't understand it," Helen said. "But many people, even myself sometimes, have issues accepting the idea of a civilization of super-intelligent aliens living around the center of the galaxy."

"The Glittering Throng exists," Muriel said. "They just aren't that interested in lesser species out on the Rim."

"Then why share anything?" Helen asked.

"Some groups among them want to help the Rim species advance, others that just want to see what happens if we're exposed to this or that. They don't always give their reasons, and contact is rare."

"Meddling aliens," Constantine said. "We should be finding our own way."

"If we did that we'd still be stuck in the solar system," Helen said.

Blackstone pressed her hands together. "I think we're getting off track. Our guests claim to come from the future, and I'm inclined to accept Ms. Reinhard's word about that."

The other two settled back in their seats. Muriel felt a yawn build. She covered it.

"You're tired," Blackstone said. "You've been through a lot. I want to wrap this up and let you rest in your quarters. Before we do, we need to talk about what you mentioned on the shuttle."

"Which was?" Muriel asked. As soon as she asked, she knew what Blackstone was getting at. Her orders. "You want to talk about your secret orders."

Helen was watching Blackstone. Constantine looked at his hands. Blackstone's elegant features didn't reveal anything.

"Yes. You've put me in a difficult position.

There will be talk among the team members that heard our conversation."

"Sorry if I made things awkward."

"That is done. I need to ask you not to discuss the matter with members of the crew while you stay with us."

"I can do that."

Blackstone looked at Dyami. "And you, Dyami? Will you keep what we discuss here between us? In time I will inform the crew, but for now, I want to keep it to those in this room."

"I will keep the matter private," Dyami said. "A detective is good at secrets."

"Indeed," Blackstone said. Her attention came back to Muriel. "What, exactly do you know about my orders?"

The abyss was beneath her feet. It wasn't just the orders, but everything else that followed from the orders.

Muriel swallowed. For now, she wouldn't reveal the details. Not unless she had to, anything else threatened to change the future, if that was possible.

"I know that you're not just going to study a habitable planet. A scout ship, an Open Universe ship, was already lost in the system, reporting being attacked by aliens. It would have been too difficult to change *Australia*'s mission, but you've been ordered to locate the aliens and find out all you can about them, and not to reveal the alien presence to your crew until you reach the system. It was thought that revealing the truth too early would jeopardize the mission."

After she spoke the silence in the room grew and spread. Blackstone's lips pressed together.

Chapter 21

One day to track down whatever xenophobic low-life killed the dinosaurian alien, and in doing so secure passage off Seabrook.

I'd never investigated a murder before. Holburn's people finished up their documentation of the crime, stamped the reports as an off-world matter and sent them over to me. In a private message Alicia also included her contact details.

Nice, and not anything I had time to pursue if I was going to catch a murder and get off-world.

I took my tablet and went around to the brothel at the front of the alley. Those girls were always out in that front window. They had to have seen something.

Three women occupied the display front when I left the alley. A blond, artificially tanned to a golden brown, lay back along the red velvety couch while two pale, dark-haired girls caressed and kissed their way along each side of her flawless skin. None of them wore anything except for iridescent scale jewelry, a popular item made from native fish. The one nearest the glass, on hands and knees, as she tongued the blonde's taut breasts, wore a string of scale jewelry that looped around her waist and dangled down between her firm ass cheeks.

The display certainly caught my attention. It took me a few seconds to tear my gaze away. I had to focus. The crime was the key right now, no matter how tempting distractions might look.

I walked past the display window and went inside.

Where the outside of the building had the worn-down look of many buildings at land's end, the interior was much better maintained. Wall panels glowed with a warm amber light, like sunlight through honey. The dark veins of the panel shifted and moved, causing the light to dance and flicker.

The air smelled far better than the muck and sleet outside, a dry, flowery smell, faint, not overpowering.

I was greeted by a tall, statuesque woman wearing nothing except a gauzy white robe that hung over her right shoulder, leaving the left bare. Or mostly bare. A gold chain hung down from a scale jewelry necklace and clipped to her nipple with a scale clap. She had no hair whatsoever that I could see, perfectly smooth scalp, no eyebrows, and her bare arms were hairless as well. Her skin glowed a rich gold color in the light.

"Good morning," she said, her voice a deep warm purr. "Whatever we can do to make you comfortable, please let us know. Male, female, mixed gender or anything more exotic, whatever your desire, here you will find it fulfilled."

"Thank you," I said. "That's great news. I'm investigating the murder of a Torlian visitor, he was just killed around the corner. I wanted to speak to the girls that were in the window earlier this morning, to ask what they saw."

Her lips parted, and the tip of a pink tongue appeared, just a second, then she smiled. "Let me show you to a room where you can wait."

"Okay, thank you."

She led the way, walking with an enticing sway. Another woman, her double in every way except the robe went over her left shoulder, passed us on her way to the door. Twins? Other, more surgical, modifications? I didn't know and didn't ask.

The entryway opened up into a wide lobby and bar. Beautiful women and men moved around the room, each different, and each fantastic. The clients were easily identifiable in that crowd, with their dark coats still wet from the sleet outside.

I was taken around the room, through a beaded curtain into a hallway lined with doors. My guide opened the second room on the left, a green door, and gestured for me to enter.

The room was small, most of the space taken up by a large bed with shimmery black blankets. An open doorway on one side obviously led to a bathroom, where I caught a glimpse of a large black tub.

"Make yourself comfortable," my guide said. "I'll send along the girls presently."

"Thank you."

The guide stepped close, her fingers gliding up my wet coat. "Would you like me to take this for you?"

"Uh, okay. Sure. Thank you."

Skilled hands slid around the coat, and her long fingers nimbly undid the buttons. With it open she reached inside and placed her hands flat on my chest. Heat radiated from her hands, even through the thick weave of the shirt. She slid her hands up across my chest, over my shoulders, and the coat slid off. She caught it before it pooled on the floor.

I reached up and took off the hat. I kept Blauek's image in my mind, and Gorge crouched, mourning beside his body. Anything to avoid an embarrassing reaction to my guide's touch.

She collected the coat and hat without comment. "The girls will see you soon."

She left, giving me time alone to recover before the next assault on my senses.

I didn't have long to wait. I paced, as much as I could, in front of the big bed. The door opened, and two women entered the room. Not the same group that was in the window just now as I entered, but I recognized one. She had amazing blue hair that cascaded down her back like waves. She had been one of those in the window when I reached the alley. She wore a shimmery, plastic dress with what looked like water drops, except they didn't roll down the material.

The other was a brunette, hair cut short, mid-way down her ears, and straight. She had large, almond-shaped orange eyes split with an oval pupil. The tips of her ears had tiny tufts of golden hair. She wore a silky green tunic, very short, and open in the front with generous mounds of white flesh nearly spilling out.

"Thanks for talking to me," I said quickly.

The woman with the blue hair reached for me, the light catching scale's glued over her fingernails. "We do whatever you want, honey. We get paid either way."

Paid? I couldn't buy a sandwich, I certainly couldn't afford the rates these women charged.

I took a step back, which brought me closer to the orange-eyed woman.

"Maybe it wasn't explained to you. I'm

investigating the murder that happened ear-lier, the Torlian that was killed outside?"

The orange-eyed woman blinked. "Tor-lian? What's that?"

"That dinosaur-looking alien, the yellow one," the other said.

I nodded. "That's right. The alien. He went into the alley between this building and the next. Someone went in after him and killed him with a harpoon. I need to find the person responsible."

The blue-haired woman shook her head. "I'm not getting mixed up in anything like that."

"Right," her companion said. "Besides, we're not even getting paid. And we don't know who you are. You don't look like a constable."

"I'm not, I work for the aliens. Constable Holburn has declared the murder theirs to deal with. You must have seen someone go into that alley."

The woman in the blue dress reached for the door. "We were a bit busy with each other and Talina, at the time. We've got to put on a show out there. And it's our chance to take a break from clients."

"Talina? Who is that?"

The orange-eyed woman shook her head. "She was there too, but she's off work. Probably at home already. And I don't think she'd want to talk to you anyway."

"An innocent person, even if he was an alien, got killed right outside. You can't just ignore that."

"We're done here," the woman in blue said.

She opened the door and walked out. I reached out for the orange-eyed woman, but she avoided my hand. "Don't touch me. You didn't pay to touch me, you didn't pay to talk, you paid for nothing. You need to leave, or you will get more trouble than you imagine."

I held up my hand. "You're really going to let a killer get away with this?"

She hesitated in the doorway. "I'm not involved. And I'm certainly not going to risk pissing off some harpoon-wielding crack diver."

With that last, she left the room, slamming the door behind her. I grabbed the door, and it wouldn't open. I jiggled the knob and nothing. Somehow they'd locked it, and locked me inside.

A crack diver, she'd told me that much at least. Crack divers went into the deep geothermal vents off the coast, fishing for giants. Massive deep water creatures that feasted off the bottom feeders. A whole ecology of nightmarish, armored fish. Crack divers used harpoons in their fishing, and they didn't usually stay on land long. Even without the Torlian's deadline, I'd have to find the killer right away, or he'd be out of reach, beneath the waves where I'd never find him.

CHAPTER 22

Olinda, present day

I came back out of my memories not knowing how much time had passed.

Not much from the look of the room. Orlando Pike remained squatting only a few feet away, his eyes on my face. Drac was still gibbering to himself in the corner, wings over his head.

I tried lifting my hand. It didn't move. The way Drac twitched and muttered, it looked like he was still unaffected by the nanoweb device Pike was using on my brain.

"You really wanted off Seabrook, didn't you?" Pike asked.

My mouth unlocked. With it, my senses cleared up. To my scent-sight Pike was a glowing, crackling cloud of bluish ozone, pouring off his head in pulses. It was tinged with yellow contentment, and strands of red contentment. At least that's how my brain handled the signals. I concentrated on the older smells, and ghostly images of Pike formed in place around him. I pushed it back until one of the ghost images rose and walked backward to the door.

I can't judge time well with my scent-sight, but it still gave me a sense that not much time had passed. Only moments, maybe since he returned me to the room after the last session.

"You've seen the place," I said, responding to his question before he lost patience. "Wouldn't you want out of there?"

"The women were very beautiful. It looked like a wild, invigorating world. A cauldron to forge strength and resilience. Two qualities I believe you possess in great quantities."

"Yeah, it's great. Why don't you move your operations there? I'm sure you would fit right in."

Pike laughed.

The laughter faded, replaced by a friendly grin as if we were just a couple friends hanging out and reminiscing.

"I'm curious to see how this develops," Pike said. "You were under pressure to get the case solved before the Torlian's deadline, and so far you weren't getting much help."

"It's all about the legwork," I said, copying my partner and friend at the agency, Shanley Walsh. "If you're going to sit through all of my memories, it's going to take a long time."

"Not as long as you'd think. We're sharing an accelerated playback, time compressed. And most of the uninteresting bits are indexed and archived by my system. I'm just choosing the parts I find interesting."

Pike stood, rising smoothly from his squat. "But I will give you another break. I can't sit and watch your memories all day. Take advantage of it, I'll be back later to see what happened."

I couldn't move until the heavy door closed behind him. Then my muscles unlocked. I rolled over onto my hands and knees, then got up. I felt tingly all over, my nerves jittering from the way they'd been treated.

I swung my arms. If I didn't have long, then I needed to find a way to escape, and undo what Pike had done to me.

Chapter 23

Australia, 2876

A scout ship lost to aliens? Time travelers from a hundred years in the future? Confirmation that the Galactics really were some sort of uber-smart aliens near the center of the galaxy? A conspiracy to send the *Australia* to a system, without telling them what had happened to the scout ship?

Helen stopped in the corridor outside her lab. Just stopped. Leaned back against the wall, her palms flat against the cool surface, and breathed. In and out.

Whatever she had ever said about deep space missions being boring, she took it back. This wasn't boring. This was the crazy opposite of boring.

Studying the *Cristobel* data didn't sound so bad now. And they did have those interesting symbiotic relationships that cropped up over and over in the Cristobel ecology. Symbiosis gone crazy, one of the researchers had dubbed it, with up to seven or more species living collaboratively. Mirrored humans and their domesticated plants and animals, in a way, except without the inequality in the relationships. Or the intelligence.

That sounded a lot more interesting right now.

Especially since she couldn't tell her team the facts of what was going on. But they were there, aboard the ship from the future. Did that make it a time machine?

A couple women in pale green workalls walked past, heads together talking. Helen caught a few words.

"...don't know, a ship..."

A ship. With a human woman and a Halloween alien. With the knowledge that could change everything about this mission.

The door to her department slid open. Clay Yeager stepped out, red hair still flying out in all directions. His left arm wrapped in bright yellow, with a sling holding it close to his chest. He looked the other way, at the women walking away, then turned his head and saw her.

"Doc! Everyone is inside, waiting for you, just like you asked."

Helen pushed away from the wall. "I'm coming, thanks, Clay."

"Great! When can I meet him?"

"Him?"

"You know, the alien?" Clay followed her inside. The door slid shut behind them. "They've been telling me about him, sounds amazing. Ben said that he has some sort of universal translator."

It was good to be back in her own space. She could handle her department. Past the workstations, through the conference room's transparent walls, she could see the others had already gathered, standing and looking at holographic screens which floated around the room, displaying the information that had been gathered. Raised voices drifted out the open door.

"Let's get this over with," Helen said.

"Get what over with?"

Helen ignored Clay and went on into the conference room. The talk stopped. Everyone turned and faced her. Clay quickly sat down in one of the high-backed chairs, kicking to spin it around to face her.

"Go ahead and sit down."

They all moved to take seats. Ben took the chair at the far end of the table. Mina and Lukas took the chairs on her left, Mina across from Clay, her red-haired bookends. Which left Ross sitting beside Clay.

Mina leaned forward on her elbows. "When is Blackstone going to release the information about our guests? I'm getting a ton of pings from our people wanting to know what we found!"

"We need to get both of them into medical," Lukas said. "I want full work-ups. No telling what we can learn from them. And I still think that we need to take precautions, if not full quarantine measures for the contact team and anyone that has come into contact with them since they came aboard."

"If I could get time to study the alien's translator device, it would be very useful," Ben said. "Clay could assist me with the technical aspects."

"Yeah!" Clay pumped his good arm.

Helen leaned on the table. "I appreciate the ideas, and the pressure you're under from the rest of our people, and from the crew at large. Right now we are under orders not to discuss the mission with anyone."

Mina laughed. "You can't be serious!"

"The director realizes the difficulty that this puts on us —"

Ross interrupted. "The director runs the ship. She doesn't set scientific policy. Her position isn't dictator or captain for a reason, it's director."

"In this case, she has orders granting her additional authority."

"How can she have orders unless they knew that we'd find this ship?" Clay asked. He rocked back in his seat, mouth dropping open. "Oh hell, they knew?"

Mina shook her head. "She can't really expect to keep it quiet, the whole ship knew that we matched velocities with Muriel's ship. Think of all of the crews prepping our shuttle, and what about everyone that saw us bring in the alien ship?"

Blackstone's orders were hard. Impossible, even. The crew would talk, but that's all they could do right now. Gradually, as needed, others would be brought in to help, but right now they had to keep the full situation to a small group.

"I get it," Helen said. "I really do, Mina. And you're right. They'll talk. Let them talk. Right now that's all they can do. There are aspects to this situation that can't be made public yet."

"What are you talking about?" Mina shook her head. "I didn't sign on board to be kept out of a significant discovery. They've just demonstrated that time travel is possible!"

Suddenly everyone was trying to talk at once. Clay was hammering questions across the table, Ben and Ross were arguing about something, and Lukas was trying to get in a word between Mina and Clay.

"Please," Helen said. They all ignored her. "Please!"

The conversations trailed off.

Helen raised her hands. Mina opened her mouth, and Helen raised a finger. Mina threw herself back in her seat.

"This is the deal," Helen said. "We investigate. We can use our resources, with isolation protocols in effect. No one else gets the full picture. The director wants more answers before we go public with any of this. Agree now, and we'll finish the briefing."

"If it gets me access, I'm in," Ben said.

Ross nodded. "Me too."

"Hell, yeah!" Clay said. "No way I want to get left out of this."

"I would also like to be included," Lukas said.

Mina ruffled her hair. "Fine! I don't want to get shut out. I don't like this. What are we going to do about a physicist?"

"I have a physics degree," Clay said. "On top of engineering and computing technology. And I've worked on projects with alien tech that I can't even talk about, they're so classified."

"Which is why Clay was brought in on this," Helen said. "We need him, broken arm or not."

"Hey, thanks for including me, boss. When do we get started?"

"If only it were that simple." Helen went to one of the holographic displays in front of the wall. At her touch the screen turned blank, asking for security authorization.

Time for all cards on the table.

Helen tapped in her authorization code.

The screen filled with panels. The centermost panel showed a massive Saturnesque planet banded with orange and red clouds. Massive storms churned across the face, making pockmarks of the cloudscape. A ring system spread out on either side, gleaming in the light from the star. It was a brighter world than Saturn, closer to the star, and bathed in its light.

A tap and the view zoomed in, not on the planet itself, but on a nearby speck that soon resolved itself into a whole world, a moon with a complex atmosphere full off-white clouds. Blue areas, oceans, showed through the clouds. With the gas giant in the background, the world looked small when it was actually a little larger than the Earth.

The world was familiar, the high-resolution images were not. The team had only seen the initial pass by a long-range dark interstellar probe, designed to stay out of the inner regions of the solar systems it passed.

"CY-HC-2347," Helen said.

"Where did you get these images?" Clay asked.

"I'm getting to that." The image grew in size until the gas giant was lost to the background, the clouds lit only by reflected light while half of the moon remained sunlight. The image continued to fly closer, focusing more and more on the nighttime side of the moon.

It wasn't the moon that had focus now. Dim light reflected off objects above the planet. The image stopped moving.

Helen reached out, circled the area with her hand, and expanded it. The objects were massive solar wings spreading out from dark, non-reflective cores. Three of them hanging above the moon, in this section.

The mood in the room froze. Her team, caught up moments again by their guests, were all riveted by the image.

"Those look like solar power stations," Clay said.

Helen nodded. "That's the thinking."

"Wait," Mina said. "You're saying that Cyeechie is inhabited?"

"And they knew about it," Clay said. "You knew this?"

Helen shook her head. "I only found about it at the briefing with the director. This is what Muriel meant when she talked about the director's secret orders."

Inhabited. The world that had been full of possibilities, full of the unknown, had become even more complex.

"That's what they were keeping secret," Clay said. "Aliens?"

Ben leaned forward and interlaced his hands. "Obviously, a technically advanced sentient species is good news for me. I am wondering, however, why we weren't informed about the previous mission?"

Just like ripping off a bandage. They'd already had to swallow several impossible things, what was one more?

"A scout ship, twenty-three crew, independent, not part of the company, visited Cyeechie first. Contact was lost, not before reporting being attacked by the natives."

Mina stood up, stepping back from the table. Lukas twisted around and reached for her, but she shook him off.

"That's, that's..."

"I know," Helen said. "I know all of your questions, hell, I've been asking them myself. Mina, sit down."

"How could they not tell us?"

"Sit down. We're in this now, and right

now we're still months out from Cyeechie. The thing is, Muriel, knows about us."

Mina's hand went to her mouth.

Clay snapped the fingers of his right hand. "She knows? If we accept that she's from something like a hundred years in the future, why would she know about our mission? With how fast we're spreading out, how much is going on, why know anything about us?"

Helen's feet hurt. Her back hurt from standing. And she couldn't have put their situation any clearer than Clay had already done. She spun her chair around and sat down.

She gestured at Mina's chair. "Sit down. Let's order some food up and start coming up with a plan."

Mina came back to the table. The rest of the group started pulling up tabletop screens. Unbelievably, it was time to get to work.

Chapter 24

Seabrook, 2874

With less than a day to solve the murder and escape from this planet, I had to track down a crack diver without a description, and without any idea if he had already disappeared beneath the waves. For all I knew, he could be deep in the geothermal vent regions already.

I left the brothels under the glares of the tall, hairless women that I saw as I entered. I got the feeling that they didn't want to see me back.

I couldn't simply go to the port and start accusing every deep water diving operator I saw with murder. It wouldn't be healthy, for one thing, and I doubted that it would elicit any sudden confession from someone capable of shooting a harpoon through an alien.

I'd have to do what I told Holburn and

Jun'lack that I could do, go into some of the places along the boardwalk and see what scurried out when I started turning over shells. People wouldn't want to talk. Holburn had that right. At least they wouldn't want to talk at first. They might have something different to say if I was paying the bar bills.

Only problem with that, I didn't have any credit with anyone.

It was Jun'lack's crew member that had died. If she wanted the killer, she was going to have to cough up expenses. I should have asked about it before she left.

And I couldn't show up at the ship without information.

The sleet fell harder, and colder, almost ice balls pelting my coat like frozen chunks of gore.

As tough as things sounded, I wasn't about to give up now. Not only because I wanted the berth on the Gourd-o-Pod, but because of Blauek. Young, unaware of just how dangerous and xenophobic some humans could be, and he'd gotten himself killed. That shouldn't happen. I couldn't bring him back, maybe I could turn the scum responsible over to Jun'lack for justice.

Or revenge. That was her call. Mine was catching the guy.

A few fronts down the boardwalk from the alley was a bar. Buckets, the sign read, weathered by salt spray and time. Salt crystals clustered like ice on the corners of the narrow windows along the front of the place. Around me, the crowd was thinning as people sought refuge from the icy sleet pelting the boardwalk. It sounded like thousands of hammers pounding against the wood.

Δ

I'd done work there a few times, bartending for Sammy MacDonald. If you could call it bartending when the drinks are served in buckets.

I blended with the rest of the crowd and followed a couple crusty-looking men on into the bar. Hot air blasted out of the place as we shuffled in, carrying with it a rich soup of odors. Fried fish mixed with the dizzying cocktail of alcohol fumes and sleet-washed humanity. You could almost get drunk just breathing the air in the place.

The dark stone-wood floors were scuffed

and slick from all the melting sleet that people had tracked into the place. Dehumidifier fans hummed in the ceiling, and one of them had developed a clunky noise with each revolution. Clunk. Clunk. Clunk, it beat behind the vents.

The two men that had gone in first stomped off to an unoccupied corner booth with the familiarity of regular customers. Besides them, however, the place was fairly empty. A couple men at the bar, bookends to the empty stool between them. A group of four others sat around a table in a booth in front of the windows. A small forest of empty glasses grew from the stone-wood table. Their conversation was the only life in the place, as voices and glasses were raised in some private celebration.

Sammy was behind the bar, as she so often was. Her black hair was tied back in a red handkerchief. Age hadn't diminished her good looks, even if her skin was more weathered, and her face more lined. They were good lines, happy lines, mostly.

When her green eyes fell on me, there wasn't anything happy about her face. Her eyes narrowed, lines formed between her brows and her lips tightened.

"What are you doing in here?" She demanded when I reached the bar.

"That's not exactly the welcome I was looking for, Sammy."

"The last time you worked for me you gave away a free round of drinks and then closed the place early."

Oh. Right. She was right. I'd forgotten about that, I knew she was sore at the time, but I hadn't imagined that she would still be angry over it.

"I'm sorry, I had a call from —"

"I know! You told me, Brock. One of your precious aliens called, and you went running off to help them. Sure told me where your loyalties are, not to anyone who thought they were your friend!"

I leaned into the bar. "Sammy, I'm truly sorry. It was wrong of me to do that, I know. I can't make it up to you, I know that —"

"And can't pay me back for what I lost, either."

"I'm sorry Sammy, money's been tight —"

"I'm not talking about money!" Sammy turned around and went on into the back, slamming through the doors like a squall coming in off the water.

The two men at the bar were looking at me. They could have been twins separated by a few decades. Both whiskered and worn by the ocean outside. Fishermen, of one kind or another, but that's the clientele Sammy brought in. It was that kind of place. She tried to make them comfortable.

I nodded at them and went around the bar, and followed her through the doors into the kitchen. The smell of fried fish was even stronger back here, and the air hotter. The lights were also much brighter, the ceiling panels glowing a bright Earth-sky blue. The color was jarring, nice, but alien. I'd never seen a sky like that on Seabrook.

Sammy stood a couple feet away, her back to me, arms wrapped around herself. Past her was Thomas Pierson, her regular cook, and Charlene Anderson, one of the waitresses that worked for her. Both of them looked at me, questions written plainly on their faces.

"Charlene, can you look after the guys out front?" I asked.

Sammy whirled around. "Brock, just get out of here! You don't come back here, you don't work for me, and you don't tell anyone here what to do!"

Charlene froze for a second, then moved. "I'm just going to check and see if anyone wants anything."

Thomas lifted a basket out of the fryer and clipped it in. He wiped his hands with a towel. "I'll give you a hand."

The two of them hurried out of the kitchen without another glance. Sammy wasn't looking at me. She ducked her head away.

"I had no idea," I said.

She still wouldn't look at me. "I didn't even know if you were still on Seabrook. You called, you told me what had happened, apologized, and that was it. I figured you'd really gone off with the aliens."

The Pluffs looked a bit like sea lions or walruses, semi-aquatic species that spent most of their time in artificial realities. Fascinating species, the ship that had come to Seabrook had been interested in a guide to show them around, and arrange underwater tours. They were part of an entertainment company making some sort of artificial reality adventure set in Seabrook's oceans. Given the wildlife, it sounded like a pretty terrifying adventure. I'd jumped at the chance to work with them, but when the time came to see if they'd take me with them, they had looked at me with huge soulful, uncomprehending watery eyes. And then they had left.

"That didn't happen," I said. "They weren't interested in a human tagging along."

Sammy shook her head and finally looked at me. Her green eyes were hard and dry. "Too bad, Brock. Stuck here with the rest of us. When did you start hating your home so much?"

"How about when my father went under the waves and never came back? Or when my mother was raped and killed by a roughneck? Or seeing people hate other species simply because they're different? I went off to help the Pluffs that day because everyone else they tried to talk to laughed at them, made fun of them. The universe is big, and some of it has to be better than this!"

Sammy bit her lip. Then she took a breath and said. "Okay. Look, Brock, I was hurt, okay? And pissed. I thought you'd just left."

"No, I knew you were pissed. I figured I

should give you some space. I didn't know that you thought I had left with them."

"Yeah, well, when you do go you'd better not do it without telling me!"

"I wouldn't. Look, I'm here on a job."

"What job?"

"Earlier, a few places down from here, in the alley beside the brothel, a Torlian was killed. Shot with an armor-piercing harpoon. I'm working for the Torlians to try and find his killer. Holburn is calling this an alien matter, leaving it up to them to deal with."

She laughed. "Again with the aliens?"

"Yes, looks that way."

"So what is it that you want from me?"

"I need to know if you've heard anything? Did anyone come in here looking like they might have just killed someone? Maybe lugging around a harpoon gun?"

"No. Nothing like that." Her head tilted to the side. "Is that it? That's really why you came in here again? To ask about my clientele?"

As if I could feel any worse than I did already. I hadn't realized it before, how Sammy felt. I liked her, I really did, but me and attachments, it didn't work out.

"Sorry, Sammy. Really, for letting you down, for all of it."

She shook her head. "I don't need your apology."

"You've got it anyway. Will you call me, if you hear anything? I wouldn't ask, but we're talking about a killer."

"Yeah. Sure. I'll call. Not for you, but for the alien."

"Thank you."

Sammy pointed at the door. "If you don't mind? I've got a business to run."

"You'll talk to Charlene and Thomas too? In case they hear anything?"

"Yes!"

I mumbled a final thank you and hurried out of the kitchen feeling like I was one of the gutted fish waiting to get tossed in the fryer. Thomas passed me as I went out, we nodded at one another, and then I was out by the bar, and he was through the door.

Charlene came around the bar. "Brock? What's going on?"

"Ask Sammy," I said. I managed a smile. "I screwed up, didn't I?"

She nodded. "Yep. Pretty bad too, from the sound of it."

"Thanks, that's what I thought. I'll see you, Charlene." I headed for the door.

"You might want to wait! It's really coming down out there!"

I didn't need her to tell me that, I could hear the hail pounding on the metal roof as I got closer to the door. It was as if some angry god had decided to dump a load of gravel right on Mudport.

I should have stayed inside. That would have been smart. The storm outside was getting worse, and no one was going to be out in it.

I shoved the door open, and the first hail balls struck my arm like being hit by a thrown rock. It wasn't only hail either, now. Snow was mixed into it all, a swirling, blinding mass of reddish snow splatting to the ground around the hard knots of ice.

Chapter 25

2876, Terran Exploration Vessel, Australia

As prisons went, this one wasn't all that bad. Muriel's room was plain for the most part, although there was a large holographic wall screen which could display any scene she wanted.

And which refused any attempt to access the ship's systems. Anything beyond pleasant scenery and entertainment was locked out. A few tablets lay on the tables, equally locked from anything beyond the most basic entertainment and controls.

She was pacing when the double doors connecting her suite to the next swung open, and Dyami barreled through, a large black and orange knot of anger. His bristles nearly vibrated with it, and his lips had drawn back to show a mouthful of teeth.

Muriel raised her hands, beckoning for him to stop. "Dyami! What's wrong?"

Dyami slapped his own left arm, two hard smacks. His armband translator was missing.

"What happened to your translator?"

Dyami responded with a low rumbling growl, giving her a look that was as clear as any words.

"Right. Sorry, I know you can't answer. Where was it?"

Dyami beckoned and turned back toward his rooms. He glanced back as she followed, then walked stiffly through the open doors into the adjoining suite.

It was the mirror image of her room if a tornado had somehow formed inside the suite. Couch cushions had been tossed around. The furniture was anchored down, at least. Dyami stormed through the mess, batting aside the scattered cushions, moving relentlessly toward the bedroom.

Like the suite's main area, the bedroom was in disarray. The bed had been stripped of blankets, which lay on the floor.

Dyami stabbed a thick finger at the nightstand beside the bed. Other than a floating holographic clock, there was nothing there.

Dyami patted his arm and pointed again to the nightstand. Then he touched his chest and pointed to the bed, closing his eyes.

"You took off the armband, and put it on the nightstand, then went to sleep."

Dyami bobbed his head.

"And when you woke up, it was gone?"

Another head bob. Dyami rocked back, sitting up, and dragged a finger across his chest from left shoulder to waist, then again from his right shoulder to waist. His belts? He ordinarily wore belts with pouches to carry tools, his tablet, and other items. Muriel looked around the room and didn't see any sign of his gear.

"Your belts and other stuff are gone too."

Another head bob of agreement. Then Dyami's lips curled back, revealing teeth. He punched a fist against the wall, a loud bang against the panel. The wall flexed and didn't dent.

The message was clear. Dyami blamed the *Australia* crew. Muriel didn't have any other explanation. His gear didn't walk off on its own. Apparently, they waited for him to go to sleep, which suggested that they were continually monitored, and had come in to steal his things.

Ben Tol had to be behind it. The linguist had been dying to get his hands on the translator since he had seen it work on the shuttle.

She looked up at the glowing ceiling panels. "I know you're watching. I want to talk to Olivia Blackstone now! You can't simply come in here and take our belongings. We agreed to be isolated from the crew, for everyone's safety, but we didn't agree to be treated as prisoners. We have rights. Now get Olivia Blackstone!"

"Muriel? Dyami?"

The voice came from behind them, from the living area. It sounded like Blackstone.

Muriel led the way back into the other room.

Blackstone stood in front of the holographic wall screen. Except she didn't look quite right, realistic, but lit up from within. She was a hologram, like when she had talked to them on the shuttle only this was a full version of her.

"We need you to return what you took," Muriel said. "Some of that is Galactic technology, and all of it is from the future."

"Which is precisely why I asked that it be removed," Blackstone said. "It'll be kept safe, and studied under strict protocols."

"You have no right to do that."

Dyami hit the floor.

Blackstone pressed her hands together in front of her chest. "You must see this from our side. How can we pass up the opportunity? Especially when you are reluctant to share what you know?"

"We're the least of your concerns," Muriel said. "Treating us like prisoners, ignoring our rights, none of that is going to encourage our cooperation."

"I understand your reluctance. It is smart. Wise, even, from your perspective. We didn't believe that time travel was possible, but then we wouldn't have believed that the Space-Time Coordinate drive was possible either, and as has been pointed out it allows faster than light travel."

"Except it doesn't," Muriel said. "It alters your space-time coordinates, making a quantum jump. It isn't motion through space-time."

"Yes, and yet I can watch a ship with an STC drive move. We can't perceive those quantum jumps. And we still don't have a solid theory on how it works."

"If it is any consolation, we still don't in my time."

Blackstone shook her head, lips tightening. "No, that is no consolation at all. And a perfect example of why you are right about not sharing information. I have colleagues spending their careers studying this technology, and with a slip of the tongue you've doomed their work and made it pointless."

Muriel's gut tightened. She shook her head. "Not pointless, I didn't say that we haven't learned from the effort."

"True." Blackstone lowered her hands. "Yet this gets me back to my point. Your reluctance is smart, from your perspective. It protects your time from changes if that's even possible. We don't know. From where I stand, however, your knowledge could help so many. Take those colleagues I mentioned. What you know could help them avoid blind alleys, help us narrow in on —"

"No." Muriel walked several steps closer to the hologram. Dyami stayed with her. "No. You can't force us to do that. There's too much at stake, and you can't know the consequences. It could make things worse."

Olivia nodded slowly. "Worse? I see. As in, things were bad enough already? By coming here, you're afraid that you'll make things even worse."

Olivia smiled a sad, small smile and turned as if to leave.

Muriel's heart slowed like it did when she dived deep. "That's not what I said. And all of this is beside the point when we should be talking about Dyami's ability to communicate."

Olivia had started to fade, but now she solidified again. She looked directly at Dyami. "This must be frustrating for you. You clearly understand us, and yet can't speak. I will assign someone to come to teach you sign language, teach both of you."

"That's not the same thing," Muriel said. "You can't..."

It was no good. Olivia had faded away between one step and the next.

Dyami walked around in front of Muriel and sat down, which still left him taller than her. He stroked her arm with one big finger, very gentle despite his size.

"It isn't fair, or right, what they're doing," Muriel said. "I'm sorry. If there's a way to get out of this, I'm not seeing it right now."

They were prisoners on a doomed ship, stranded over a hundred years in the past. Almost no time had passed since they escaped from Hansel, planning to meet up with Brock and stop the mad Moreau, Kelwyn from murdering people with his Moreau Pod-based weapon.

And now this! She had no idea what had happened to Brock. Hopefully, someone else would get a chance to stop Kelwyn. Although it might not matter if Olivia Blackstone was determined to change history.

CHAPTER 26

2876, Terran Exploration Vessel Australia

Helen called the team together for a daily meeting and update on their progress with the project. Three weeks since they intercepted the alien ship from the future, and she didn't know what to call the project. Clay had suggested the Yankee Project, but she thought that revealed a bit too much about what was going on.

"Aw, come on, Doc! How many people would have even read a Connecticut Yankee in King Arthur's Court?"

"That's not the point. We can't let it get out that our guests are from the future. The quarantine story is holding so far."

At least it seemed like the story was holding. Most of the crew was focused on reaching Cyeechie, now only a few weeks away.

There was curiosity about their guests. Helen still called them guests and tried really, really hard to believe it. Curiosity from the crew, tempered against the heavy workload as they approached their destination.

More and more, however, she had the feeling that there were things that Blackstone was keeping back from them all.

Maybe it was all in her head. Hell, maybe it wasn't even what it seemed. At least things weren't dull anymore.

Ben Tol was the last to come into the conference room, his head down, focused on a tablet he carried in his hand. Clay had taken the seat at the end of the table. Ben reached the chair, nearly sitting down before he noticed that Clay was in his usual spot.

"Wow, man," Clay said. "I don't need a lap dance that badly." Clay grinned and winked at Mina. "Unless our resident biologist wants to give it a go."

"I'd sooner give our guest a lap dance."

Clay laughed.

The whole time Ben stood silently beside the chair, hands folded together around the tablet.

"Fine," Clay said. He got up, and bowed, gesturing to the chair. "Your chair, sir."

Clay went around the table and dropped into the chair opposite Mina, a grin still plastered on his face.

"Okay," Helen said. "Let's have everyone's reports, then we can get back to work. We've got a lot to do with the project and Cyeechie approach coming up."

Clay leaned forward on the table. He flicked up a hologram above the table. An image of the alien ship that had brought Muriel and Dyami back in time appeared floating above the transparent table top. It showed the ship in the hangar, the hangar walls and floor indicated by faint lines. The ship itself was a pool of emptiness, reflecting nothing. The only spot that had any volume or texture was the airlock attached where they had cut into the side of the ship with the lamprey.

Standing, Clay reached out to the hologram, turning it and stretching it out, zooming in on the damaged section on the opposite side. When they'd first seen the ship that section had been scored, as if from an impact. Spidery robots had been repairing the damage.

Now that side of the craft was unmarked, nothing to indicate any damage.

"Following the director's orders, we didn't do anything to stop the little buggers from working. Yesterday they finished the last of the repairs and vanished inside. We haven't seen any activity since."

"What are you doing now?" Helen asked.

Clay swiped the hologram away and dropped back into his chair. "Nothing with that. Not until the director lets us go inside. She's ordered the entire hangar sealed, remote observation only. It's dangerous, Doc. What if the systems on that thing power up? We have no idea what it could do to the *Australia*."

"The director feels that the ship is too much to handle right now, with everything else going on. She wants it taken back intact and undisturbed."

Clay shrugged. "Could be our funeral, that's all. It's obviously not dead. If those little buggers can patch it up, they might take out our airlock too."

Lukas said, "The lamprey had no problem

cutting through before, we could again if we needed to."

Clay laughed. "Right. We did that when the ship was crippled. If they've fixed their systems, we have no idea what defenses it has. We might not get another chance."

"Okay," Helen said. "Point taken. I'll bring them up again with the director. What are you working on now?"

"Helping Benny with the translator, you should ask him. I don't know what he wants me to do."

Helen looked across the table at Ben, apparently involved in whatever was on his tablet. "Ben?"

He raised his head. Seeing everyone looking at him, he placed the tablet on the table. "Yes?"

"Report?"

"Yes." Ben coughed into his hand. "I've, um, been working on the translator as Clay said. We have been trying, without success, to establish an interface with the device. It appears coded to the specific user. As yet, we haven't established any non-destructive way of accessing it."

"You've got to let me take it apart," Clay

said. "I'm telling you, man, that's the only way we're going to get anything out of it."

"And I've told you," Ben said, irritation clear in his voice. "That it is a piece of Galactic tech and a monkey would have a better chance of understanding a fusion reactor. We cut into it, we might easily destroy it."

Helen shook her head. "And the director has forbidden any destructive actions with any of the devices. What about the interpreter's work, what's her name?"

"Fiona Davidson," Ben said. "A talented linguist and translator. I believe she's making good progress in communicating with the alien. It helps that he already understands our language."

"Good." Helen turned her chair. Ross had sat silently through the meeting, and in fact looked as if he might nod off.

"Ross?"

The xenopaleontologist blinked and sat up. "Yes?"

"Your report?"

"Well, I've had little to do with all of this. I've spent my time more productively working on the data, what there is, about CY-HC-2347."

Lukas spoke up. "We've found something interesting."

All eyes focused on the doctor. Lukas got up from the table and opened a holographic window on the wall. Muriel's portrait appeared, fully rendered and animated, so it looked as if she was watching them.

Creepy, if realistic. Helen focused on Lukas instead. His cheeks were flushed, and he looked at Mina. She gave him a bright smile. *Interesting.* The two of them had been working a lot together, and their fields overlapped. Maybe it had led to other overlapping.

A chuckle nearly escaped from Helen's lips. She coughed, waving to Lukas. "Go on."

Lukas pulled up additional screens from the portrait. DNA renderings rotated beside the portrait, and detailed genetic charts appeared, with certain sections pulsing with bright glows.

"Here, here, here, and in many more places." Lukas touched each of the glowing spots, opening a cascading storm of data screens. "You see? Right? She isn't human."

"Not human?" Ross asked. "I don't believe that another species evolved that looks so much like one of us. She's so pretty."

"Wow," Clay said. "Ross has got himself a crush!"

"I don't," Ross said. He settled back in his seat. "It is an objective fact of pleasing symmetry."

Lukas pulled out several new screens. Too much for Helen to process. She ignored the screens and focused on Lukas.

"I don't think she evolved that way, it looks like her DNA has been modified. She was human, once."

"So she's gene-sculpted," Helen said. "That doesn't make her inhuman. Lots of people are gene-sculpted."

"Lots of people, like Blackstone," Clay said.

Mina leaned forward on the table. "It's more than that, this isn't gene-sculpting."

"Mina is right," Lukas said, his words coming faster. "Not gene-sculpting at all. That process leaves trace markers that we can track. Some of those are present in her DNA, inherited markers from generations ago, not anything that was done in vitro. The modifications we see in her come from multiple species are incredibly precise and integrated as if whoever did this procedure knew exactly where to modify her DNA and did it everywhere, in all of her cell matter."

Okay. That sounded impossible. Helen asked, "How would someone do that?"

Lukas shrugged, laughing. "I don't know. We followed protocols, all samples were divided and analyzed independently, and all point to the same result. She is not human any longer. Her DNA includes material from whales, among other things, and polar bears."

Clay whistled. "Yikes. Shades of Dr. Moreau!"

"Pretty much, she's a chimera," Mina said.

"Chimera?" Helen pressed her fingers against the smooth surface. When she slid her hand, it didn't leave any fingerprints on the surface. "A chimera. Why? What do these modifications do?"

"Adapt her for a semi-aquatic existence," Lukas said. "She has increased lung mass, her eyes and hearing show aquatic adaptations, and she has more efficient storage for fat cells."

Clay cupped imaginary breasts.

Helen shot him a scowl. He dropped his hands beneath the table.

"Okay," she said. "How could these changes be made?"

"I have no idea," Lukas said. "I can't think of anything that could make all of these changes to the human body, and yet I see the same thing throughout the samples."

Mina jumped in again. "It's really incredible. Every cell in her body displays the same meticulous changes as if they've all been rewritten. It's beautiful, really. I have no idea how that could possibly happen, no delivery mechanism I can think of could do the job and get to all the cells. You'd have to take the body entirely apart, make the changes and put it back together again. Impossible, except here she is."

Another mystery. One of the many piling up around their guests. And the biggest mystery of all, what lay ahead of them at CY-HC-2347? Muriel knew, and for the past several weeks had refused to divulge any details. Constantine was pushing Blackstone for a change in Muriel's status, and permission to get the answers out of Muriel, or failing that, out of Dyami.

Was he wrong? Helen looked at her team, talking among themselves about the discover

Mina and Lukas had made. *Not human.* Statements like that might give Constantine the leverage he wanted.

Chapter 27

2874 Seabrook

I screwed up with Sammy, and the thought of that chased me out into the hail and snow. These sudden storms often happened in Mudport. It was like the planet herself had decided to stone me for how I had treated Sammy. Reddish snow swirled around me, obscuring the abandoned boardwalk while the hail drummed down.

Hunched in my coat, I trudged up the increasingly treacherous boardwalk. The storm would pass soon, then the snow and hail would melt away. Right then I had no choice except to take the beating while I looked for the next likely place for the murderer to seek shelter.

Ahead, through the battering hail and swirling snow, another figure trudged along the boardwalk. He was only a shape, a dark silhouette in the storm, hunched over in his long coat beneath a broad-brimmed hat. He could have been me, a few seconds in my own future, staggering down the boardwalk.

Except that he also had something over his shoulder, worn across his back, and sticking up above his shoulder. Indistinct in the storm, but the shape certainly suggested a harpoon gun.

The odds were against it. Except who else would come out in the storm? The regular denizens knew these storms and used them as an excuse to hoist another drink. For him to be out here, he had to have a good reason.

Perversely the fury of the storm increased. I slipped and skidded on the boards. My left knee slammed into the wood hidden beneath the slushy coating of snow and hail.

Pain shot up my thigh.

The shape ahead blurred, hidden by snow.

I gritted my teeth and stood up. A sharp hail ball smacked into my jaw. The pain was immediate and cold.

I ducked my head. I put more weight on my leg. The knee protested, and I ignored it. It hurt, but not enough to stop me.

I shuffled forward, hurrying as much as I dared. The figure ahead swam in and out of visibility like a ship appearing and disappearing on a storm-tossed ocean.

That was his plan. I knew it. Get out during the storm, while everyone was occupied with drink and other diversions. Get to his sub and dive. Disappear beneath the waves. Wait out the storm and any interest from the constables in the murder of one more alien.

He'd sit down there in the dark, gloating over his cleverness, until he was forced to finally surface. Then he'd come up, his holds full of his catch, as innocent as a newborn.

I had to catch up to him before that happened. If I caught him, I could show that the harpoon gun he carried shot the harpoon that killed Blauek.

Or I could catch him and discover I was entirely wrong.

At first, it didn't look like I was going to catch him at all. He danced in and out of visibility. My knee slowed me down. I pushed harder, ignoring the pain. I shrugged off the pounding from the hail, though I'd have a bruise that stretched across my shoulders and neck.

He had to be going to the docks, at the other end of the boardwalk. It was only a matter if he could get there fast enough to get away.

We were almost to the docks, he was still leading me, half-hidden by the storm, when he took off running. I didn't see him look back, but he must have seen me and realized I was following.

He ran, and I chased him.

Each step my knee flared with pain. The hail and the snow made the footing uneven and slippery. Hailstones turned beneath my feet, threatening another fall. I must have looked ridiculous, running through the storm, arms wind-milling to keep my balance. I didn't fall again.

He beat me to the docks. He ran down the ramp and along the floating docks between the bouncing fishing vessels and subs.

The storm kicked up waves. Salty, sulfurous spray stung my eyes.

I was closing the distance, running down the bouncing dock ramp. Then he fell. At least, it looked like that, at first, as he dropped to his knees. Except he had turned and unslung the harpoon gun on his back.

I threw myself to the side. A loud cough and crack cut through the storm before I hit the slick boards.

I landed hard and slid in the slush right over the edge of the dock.

There wasn't time to react. One split second I was on the ramp, the next in free fall over the waves below. The waves reached up, as if eager to grab me.

Another heartbeat and I plunged into the icy waters. Thick briny slush engulfed me. I sank down, my thick coat pulling me into the water until I hit the rocky bottom.

A cold icy chill sank its teeth into my limbs. My chest screamed for air. I got my feet beneath me and pushed off the rocks, stroking hard for the surface. The cold and weight of my clothes threatened to drag me back. My head broke the surface, and immediately a wave smashed me down again.

I broke the surface once more, coughing and gagging. Another wave threatened to swamp me, but I took a breath and ducked beneath, and through the wave, coming up on the other side in more control.

The cold was like thousands of tiny cold needles piercing me everywhere. My strength melted like ice on a hot stove.

I found the docks through the storm and struck off, swimming with everything I had.

With each stroke, the weight grew heavier and heavier. The cold sank deeper into my limbs. I ducked beneath waves that threatened to swamp me, each time it felt like a vise closing on my head.

I banged my numbing fingers into the slick wood. I managed to get a grip on a tiedown and hung on. I sucked air and pulled, heaving myself out of the water, landing gasping on the deck.

I was alive. Nothing had attacked me in the water, with the banging of the boats and the fury of the storm my own struggles had passed unnoticed. I got up onto my hands and knees, the left protesting through the cold.

The diver was gone. A harpoon was stuck in the dock ramp, just visible through the snow and hail, right where I'd been standing. But the man himself was gone.

I couldn't have lost him. The thought drove me to my feet even as I shivered and my teeth chattered from the cold. Moving was the best thing I could do. I couldn't just lay there on the dock, I'd freeze.

He must have gone for his sub. I fought my way through the storm, shielding my eyes with my arm as the wind blew snow into my face. The hail was disappearing, at least, but the snow itself was icy and stung where it hit my cheeks.

The dock branched out, a fern shape fanning out into the harbor. If it weren't for the light poles mounted on the dock, I might have lost all sight of the wood and tumbled back into the ocean. I cursed the limited visibility. I couldn't see far at all, most of the ships and subs were merely dark shapes rising above me.

I was out on one of the branches of the dock when lights flared on the next row up.

It was a sub powering up.

I turned and ran down the dock. The snow and spray slicked wood bucked beneath me, threatening to spill me into the water.

Then I did fall, my feet slipping out beneath me. I hit the boards and slid forward, fortunately, rather than falling into the water again.

I scrambled up and kept running.

I made it onto the dock, using the light pole to swing around onto that branch, and pelted down toward the end where the sub was powering up engines. A few more moments and it would slip beneath the storm-tossed waves and out of my grasp.

As I got closer, the stub-nosed shape of the sub took shape. The sub had the look of a wingless insect, with the front sphere lit up and several round windows in a band across the front of the sphere. Behind the front were two more sections, increasing in size. Water churned around it from the water jets dotting the sides.

The sub had already cast off the lines from the dock and was struggling to turn against the pounding waves. Each wave shoved it back, threatening to smash it against the docks. The jets whined, kicking up more spray into the air.

Two loose cables lay piled on the dock, secured to the tie-downs.

I grabbed the first line I reached and jumped off the pitching dock onto the side of the sub. My feet slipped on the wet surface.

I pitched forward, hitting the hard shell,

and scrambled for purchase while hanging onto the rope. I slid, and then I caught the tie-down on the sub.

I pulled myself up and quickly wrapped the line I held around the tie-down over and over. The line snapped taunt just after I jerked my fingers back. The sub pitched and tossed, throwing me from its side. I caught the line to the dock and held on as my feet dragged through the frigid waters.

The sub struggled to escape. I swung my legs up and got back onto the dock. I didn't know if the line could hold the sub or not. I grabbed up the second line as the sub's head swung back around, lights stabbing through the blowing snow and spray into my eyes.

The glare from the lights blinded me. The sub's windows were nothing but dark blurs through the snow and lights. The waves heaved and tossed it. The engines screamed against the forces of the storm and the rope that tethered it in place.

The dock heaved beneath me. The boards groaned. The waves tossed the sub. Then it dropped, and the dock rose up, riding a swell, and I jumped.

Again I landed on the treacherous surface

of the sub, carrying the second line. I looped the line quickly around the tie down on the sub as it jerked against the lines holding it. The scream of the engines rose higher, but the two lines held the small sub securely. I stumbled and caught rungs rising up to a hatch at the back of the sub's head.

Hand-over-hand, I pulled myself up to the hatch. The engines died suddenly, and the sub rocked back toward the dock.

I hung on. It bounced in the waves. The hatch opened, and a head popped out. I grabbed the front of the man's coat. He had a grizzled face, with a scar across his chin. I yanked him forward, and his head cracked into the edge of the sub.

He dropped bonelessly back down into the hatch. I was nearly done, but I managed to pull myself up to the hatch and climbed down after the groggy diver.

CHAPTER 28

Olinda, 2978

I jerked out of the memory, back into reality. The plain, familiar gray walls of the sensie room in Pike's fortress, replaced the storm-tossed seas on Seabrook. I shivered, still feeling the memory of the cold and snow.

"That was something," Pike said.

The pirate stood leaning against the door frame, arms crossed, a white sleeveless shirt hung loosely over baggy white pants.

Drac wasn't in the room any longer.

"Where is he?"

Pike kept staring at me. "Was he the guy?"

I tried to move. My legs and arms lay as limp as a corpse's. The chill from the memory was fading.

"Don't you know? Hasn't your system scanned that much of my memory?"

"The system has scanned nearly thirty percent of your memories and is working even now. I want to hear it from you."

Thirty percent. If it was going sequentially through my memories, then it would only have a few more years from Seabrook.

I wanted to keep him talking. The more he said, the more answers I got. "Yes. He was the guy. After shooting Blauek, he went to his favorite pub to restore his courage. When the storm hit, he took his chances to get back to his sub, just like I thought."

"You didn't know. You guessed," Pike said.

"A hunch. If he'd stayed put in the pub things might have gone differently."

"So that's how you got off Seabrook. You solved the case, turned the diver over to the aliens, and they took you with them."

I laughed. "If only it were that easy. No, Jun'lack wasn't happy when I turned him over to the constables."

Pike dropped his arms and stepped away from the wall. "You didn't give him to the aliens. Why? Why pass up the chance to get off that planet?" A broad smile split Pike's face. "Ah, the woman, wasn't it? Sweet Sammy, you stayed for her, didn't you?"

"No. Not for Sammy. I waited out the storm in the sub. Mac Bloch, that was the diver's name. He came around before the storm ended. I had him tied up by then. He came to, and he was just as vile and xenophobic as I would have expected. He took great pleasure in telling me how many ways he was going to kill me and feed me to the fishes. No body, no crime. That'd been his plan for Blauek if he hadn't been interrupted. Listening to him, I realized that his crimes went a lot deeper than killing one alien."

"So that's why? So that you could get justice for his other victims?"

"Partly. More, it was the xenophobic attitude. Bloch was more extreme in his xenophobia than some, but it was an attitude I saw a lot on Seabrook. They resented those ships even as they depended on them for trade. If I turned him over to Jun'lack, other people on Seabrook would resent the aliens that much more. Forget his crimes, if he were executed at the hands of an alien, it would have touched off a firestorm."

Pike paced in front of me. "I see. Very interesting. Noble of you. You had your chance. Turn over a man that deserved punishment to the aliens that would likely do just that, and get a ticket off the planet. And you didn't do that. Remarkable. Most remarkable."

I shrugged or would have if the paralysis let me.

Pike stopped in front of me and crossed his arms. "If the Torlians didn't take you off the planet, how'd you get off?"

"What did you do with Drac?"

Pike squatted in front of me. He rocked forward on the balls of his bare feet, expertly balancing. The metal strands woven into his hair glittered in the light.

"Why does he call you the Esteemed One? What is your connection to the Nosferans?"

I didn't answer. I matched Pike's stare and waited. I wanted my answer first.

Pike smiled again. "Okay. You want to trade. It is very funny. Eventually the scanner will have all of your memories, and I will review them at my leisure. But I will give you your answer. I've taken him out of here, to more appropriate quarters. We've removed the nanoweb since the technology proved incompatible. Instead, we've found another way to motivate him to cooperate."

Pike reached behind his shirt and pulled out a supple, dark leather sack. The material bulged and moved from something inside. A new chill ran down my spine that had nothing to do with the storm on Seabrook.

The color and texture of the leather. It was a match for Drac's wings. The bag wasn't large, a pouch of wing material, but the Nosferans didn't regenerate. If Pike had cut it out of Drac's wing, it wouldn't regrow.

Pike cupped the pouch. It moved as the thing inside squirmed.

I knew what he held, I knew what was in the bag. Smiling still, Pike pulled the mouth of the bag open and reached inside.

"Don't," I said. "The light —"

Pike lifted his hand out, clutching something white and shiny, a fleshy grub around twelve centimeters long, like a giant maggot. Except this maggot had a wrinkled Nosferan face, with an upturned nose and dark eyes sunk into pits. Those eyes twisted closed, the whole thing thrashing in Pike's grip.

A Mother Sack, the Nosferan female, that lived in the male's reproductive pouch. The Mother Sack's puckered mouth shrieked, an ear-piercing wail of agony and fear. The cry rose higher and higher.

Pike chuckled and stuffed the Mother Sack back in the pouch. It stopped screaming. He closed the drawstrings and tucked the pouch back beneath his shirt.

"It can't survive without the host male," I said. "You'll starve it to death."

"So long as the Nosferan does what I want, I will give them time together."

Pike stood back up, towering over me. I burned for a chance at him and still couldn't move.

"Let's explore your ties to the Nosferans. Even now, with the fate of his tribe in my possession, he continues to defy me for your sake. I wouldn't have imagined such loyalty. Are you a traitor to humanity, Marsden?"

Laughing, Pike didn't wait for an answer. He walked out. *A traitor?* If anyone in that room was a traitor, it was a pirate like Pike.

I had my chance to betray humanity with Bloch when I could have taken him out of the sub and turned him over to the Torlians. If I'd done that if I'd gone with them, who knew? They make great coffee, but knowing what I know now, I think I was lucky not to go with Jun'lack's crew.

I wasn't a traitor. Although Pike wouldn't be the first person to call me one.

Chapter 29

2875, Pohl Station, Mars

It never rained on Mars, but I kept the great coat and wide-brimmed hat that I had brought from Seabrook. The hat at least served a purpose, it helped block radiation. At least in my mind. The Martian domes supposedly provided some protection, but most of the native inhabitants were gene-sculpted colonists who had watched their grandparents and great-grandparents struggle with cancers and other illnesses born from colonizing the red planet.

I couldn't get away from the color red. I sat at a table in the Pohl Station food court, my chair angled so that I could look right out through the dome wall at the rocky red surface outside.

Years of wind and dust storms had erased

the tracks and signs of construction outside and would have coated the entire dome in a layer of corrosive red dust except for the scutters that worked outside the dome, working to keep it clear.

Banana trees grew out of a container just past my table. Similar planters radiated out into the food court from the dome walls like spokes on a wheel, turning the interior into a riot of green. Far above bright full-spectrum lights supplemented the light from the distant sun.

Looking ahead, along the dome wall, Pohl Station was a crescent shape of domes, like bubbles scattered across the landscape, curving around to give all of the domes optimal exposure to the sunlight. Each of the domes burst with green and life. Each a fragile foothold on an inhospitable world.

I hadn't planned to come to Mars. My chance to leave Seabrook came from a passing antimatter hauler needing crew members to replace several lost in a radiation leak. Dangerous work, skimming antimatter from the accretion disk of a black hole. Fortunately for me, they were on their way back to the Terran system with nearly full containment vessels. High risk, but good pay and free transportation away from Seabrook.

And yet, despite the distance I'd traveled, I found myself right back on another red planet. I longed for a planet with a blue sky, blue oceans, someplace warm. Not Earth, too overpopulated and developed. Something further inward along the Rim. It was a dream at least.

For now, I was stuck inside the station, looking out at the stark landscape outside. In the distance a row of hills rose up, rounded by time and weather, colors muted by dust and distance. That was the distant wall of the crater housing Pohl Station.

A plume of dust moved across the horizon. A dust devil? One of the colony vehicles? It was too far to see. I needed better eyes, or binoculars.

Turning my attention back to the food court, I watched the colonists. Sharply, uniformly dressed in black, small in stature and lithe. Cute. They made me think of stories of elves, busy working to change the whole planet. They wore little in the way of adornment, except for their technological aides, and plenty of those.

On Seabrook, tablets were the norm, in a variety of sizes from small to large. I'd seen holographic displays, robots, and even the Pluffs' direct-to-brain artificial reality. The Martians existed somewhere in between. They all wore glasses equipped with retinal displays, a sort of augmented reality system. They'd demonstrated the system to me when I arrived. I had found myself surrounded by floating displays, small until I focused on them. It was distracting, seeing the windows always buzzing around, like being surrounded by a swarm of bees all the time. I quickly opted out of using the system.

The Martians moving through the food court didn't look like zombies lost in their own reality. They were friendly, engaged with one another, quickly greeting friends as they arrived together at the tables. It was odd synchronicity repeated over and over. Except it wasn't that odd, not really. They were always immersed in the social ebb and flow of their society. They arrived together because they were in constant communication with each other.

While I sat outside, by the barren red rocks of Mars, watching them. I might as well have been actually outside the dome looking in.

I hadn't come to the food court to socialize, or even for the food, although I had a bowl of chips and salsa in front of me, and a plate of steaming spring rolls.

I was waiting to catch an adulterous spouse.

I sipped my water, genuine Martian water, preserved in the permafrost that surrounded Pohl Station. Guaranteed free of any industrial contamination, as pure as when the solar system was formed.

For all of its potential, life never rose on Mars. At least not that anyone had discovered in centuries of exploration. With life discovered throughout the solar system, the Martian gap was odd and unexplained. And a bigger mystery than I could solve.

I'd been granted provisional status with the colony because they had a use for private detectives. The colonists did keep a small police force, but they didn't have the resources to look into all of the sorts of things that a private detective could investigate.

Like Arthur Stinson. I picked up my tablet, thumbing through the information I'd already reviewed a half dozen times. Forty-one, native Terran, at six feet tall he was just under the upper height limit for the Martian colony, most of whom were significantly shorter. Blond, chiseled features, muscular, particularly compared to the lithe Martians. An easy man to spot in this crowd.

I'd been hired by Regina Stinson, his spouse, who had immigrated to Mars along with her husband. Supposedly the move had been prompted by her husband's desire to seek out new adventures, to explore a new world. She had believed it until she was contacted by Lizzy Hamilton, back on Terra, his former mistress who thought she should know what Arthur had done. He had left Lizzy back on Earth in an apartment he no longer was paying for and pregnant with his child.

That was bad enough, but it was Arthur's behavior since arriving on Mars that had prompted Regina to hire me. I suppose if she really thought that he had come to Mars to start over with her, she might have been able to put Lizzy's sad story out of her mind. Except that Arthur wasn't paying any more attention to Regina on Mars than he had on

Earth. He was coming home late, claiming that he was working, when Regina knew otherwise.

Pohl Station wasn't a big place. With a little work, Regina would probably have been able to find out the details herself. Except she didn't want to do it herself. She wanted to catch him in the act, and she couldn't stand to be the person that did that.

So it fell to me. I even had a license, courtesy the Martian government, to work as a private detective. That was the only thing I could do unless I applied for a career change. It wasn't chasing a xenophobic murderer through a storm, and that was okay by me.

A quiet inquiry to Arthur's work, at the Pohl Station water extraction facilities, revealed when he left work for lunch. I learned he had gone offline, odd among the Martians, but behavior excused because of his off-world origins.

This food court was closest to Arthur's work. The planters gave each section a little privacy, and meeting in a public place gave Arthur the excuse that he was simply there for a lunch meeting.

Unless my hunch was wrong. I put down

the tablet and picked up another spring roll. The crisp crust was still hot, flaking and melting in my mouth. Not too greasy, filled with a mixture of rice, vegetables, and mushrooms. No meat. Pohl Station's agriculture didn't produce enough excess to feed livestock. The population lived on a plant-based diet. It was hot, a little spicy, and reminded me of the sandwiches that Wednesday made back on Seabrook.

I finished the spring roll in a couple more bites. I wasn't going to turn nostalgic for Seabrook. I had a job to do. I didn't plan on staying on Mars forever, but for now, this was home.

Arthur Stinson stood out as he entered the food court from the west entrance. Even though he wore a black work suit like any of the Martians, his coloration and size were all wrong. He towered above the elfin Martians. His head turned, eyes scanning those at the tables, searching for someone.

I raised my tablet and started recording while pretending to adjust my positions and read with my back to the outside. While I watched, I munched on the chips and salsa.

A hand shot up from the section past

mine. Even through the banana trees, I had a good shot of the table. A petite Martian woman, her dark hair spilling around her delicate face in waves and curls. She waved her hand again. That wasn't typical Martian behavior, not when their augmented reality systems told them exactly where to meet their friends.

She was as offline as Arthur. The difference was there in the way they moved, watching the people around them. Colonists did look up as Arthur passed. His size and bulk guaranteed that much attention. His attention was all on the woman.

They came together at the table. She crushed her ample, for her petite size, chest against him, her head against his chest. The separated slightly, and he bent to kiss her. The kiss lingered for a second before they broke. The woman looked around as if checking for anyone watching. I didn't change my position. As far as they could tell, I was reading my tablet, not watching them.

The couple sat at the table. I saw giveaway gestures as they connected long enough to place orders, individually, before disconnecting again. Other than that moment, they only had eyes for each other.

It was enough for a start. I devoured the last spring roll and rose. I left without another look back at the couple.

There's no public transportation in Pohl Station, and no real need of it. End-to-end, the entire station was only two kilometers long, though made of multiple levels. The surface levels beneath the domes were only part of the story. Most of the station was sheltered beneath the Martian surface, dug down into the permafrost layers. Although the domes provided some radiation protection, the rock and permafrost beneath the surface provided much more.

My quarters were in a residential dome, Opportunity, near the center of the crescent-shaped Pohl Station. The central section was a cluster of domes piled together like soap bubbles, one merging into the next. It was the oldest section of the station, the domes' surfaces fogged slightly despite the best efforts of the scutters.

The main surface level of the Opportunity dome had gradually been converted into both a park and an agricultural space.

The path leading into the dome turned and spiraled around down into the depths of the dome past tier after tier of rice plantings. Other sections grew fruit and nut trees. The whole thing also worked to purify water used by the residential sections beneath, pumping it up to spiral around through the plantings and back down to the residences for reuse.

In an emergency Opportunity, like the other domes, could seal itself off from the rest of the station and function independently. In the early days of Pohl Station, such safety features were considered essential and had become part of the culture.

In that sense, very different than life on Seabrook.

All around me, people continued going about their business. Few Martians sat still while working. They roamed. They walked, and with their augmented reality, remained productive and healthy. I saw the advantages, I just wasn't ready to immerse myself that deeply in the culture.

I took the elevators down into the residential levels, down to the eleventh level, and returned to my small apartment.

Living space was at a premium when Pohl

Station was built. My apartment consisted of a single room, divided by panels into three connected sections. The first that I entered was a living area, Spartan ceramic furnishings, worn with long use. The next section held the bed and clothing storage, and the last a private bathroom.

Plain reddish walls and reddish furniture, made from ceramics mined from the Martian surface. The walls were polished bedrock, sealed with glass-fiber panels. No decorations anywhere. Unnecessary for Martians, as their augmented reality system provided any decoration and themes desired. Public art, public messages, and communication systems.

I'd linked my tablet into the system on arrival. If I used the tablet's cameras, I could tap in and view the world the way the Martians saw it. There wasn't much reason to do so.

I sat on the firm couch and pulled up the footage on the tablet. My next step was to identify the woman with Arthur, discover her story, and then present Regina with a complete package. What she did with it then was her decision. All I cared about was getting the final payment.

Chapter 30

2876, Terran Expedition, Australia

Dyami sat in the doorway between their suites. His hands moved in signs he had learned from Fiona. *Ready?*

Yes. Muriel signed back.

Helen Shaw had insisted that they were guests. That they were being isolated from the crew simply because they had traveled through time. But Muriel that wasn't the whole story. If they didn't get out now, it'd be too late.

Each time Constantine questioned her he became more forceful. The polite fiction of being guests was evaporating. Soon *Australia* would reach its destination, and they couldn't be on board when that happened.

Their only chance, the only way out she saw, was getting back down to the Tretan's ship. Hopefully, the Pilot had the ship operational. Constantine wouldn't have let anything slip about the Pilot if it had been discovered, but she didn't think that the other members of the investigation team would have kept that detail secret. She and Dyami had, carefully, agreed not to mention the Pilot. From what she had gathered in talking to the investigators, based on the questions they asked, they hadn't reentered the Tretan's shuttle, which suggested that the Pilot remained hidden.

If she and Dyami could get to the hangar where the shuttle was kept, they might actually manage to escape. Returning to their own time? That was a bigger problem, but one that they could worry about when they got away.

If they could get away. They were being monitored, which made planning an escape difficult. Careful signing gave them a way to communicate. Muriel had tried to guess where the cameras were located. Up in the ceiling panels made sense. A bunch of fiber-optic lines, running back to a collector, would probably give the *Australia*'s watchers a good view of the apartment. She couldn't be sure.

The trick was keeping the conversation about the escape embedded within other conversation. Ambiguous, not spelling out exactly what they had planned.

Fiona had given them their best option yet to escape. The young woman was sweet and excited to have this chance to talk to Dyami. She was under the impression that this was a big step forward in her career, to be selected to communicate with the alien. That also meant that she was more susceptible to being manipulated.

It was almost time for the translator to arrive. Muriel signed. *Move now.*

Dyami moved into her apartment and dropped down on the bare floor in front of the door. He rolled onto his side, letting his head roll back, big purplish tongue dangling out of his mouth. His limbs lay limp and unmoving on the floor. His chest heaved once. Twice. Then, shuddering, he stopped breathing.

What he'd done back on the shuttle, she had discovered, he could do at will. It took concentration, but he could shut down most obvious signs that he was alive. He'd stay that way until she gave him the sign.

Right on time, she heard someone at the access panel outside.

"Dyami!" Muriel screamed his name and brought her hands up to her mouth.

The door whisked open, and Fiona stepped inside. She wore the standard green workalls that everyone seemed to wear, but on her it actually looked good, hugging her hips and chest. Her auburn hair was pulled back from her face and trailed down her back.

Fiona rushed in, stopping in front of Dyami. Her eyes went wide. Her head snapped up, and her eyes locked on Muriel.

"What happened to him?"

Muriel bit back a sob. She shook her head. "I don't know. I thought he was waiting for you and he just collapsed. Is he even breathing?"

"Oh no," Fiona said. "Dyami? Dyami! "

The translator crouched beside him and leaned in close to his head.

She listened.

Fiona looked up, her face even paler than usual. "I can't tell if he's breathing."

"It's his condition," Muriel said. "Oh, no. We don't have much time."

"I'll get help." Fiona got up. "Dr. Zelenka, we'll call him!"

Muriel grabbed Fiona's arm. "There isn't time. There's a treatment on the shuttle. We get there, get it, and he'll be okay. But we have to go now!"

Fiona pulled away. Her eyes narrowed. She looked down at Dyami and back at Muriel. "Really?" Her voice hardened. "You think I'm going to believe that?"

She backed away toward the door. "I'm going to have to report this, you know? It's —"

Dyami surged up onto his feet in front of her, roaring.

"Dyami!" Muriel moved, but Dyami moved faster.

He grabbed Fiona around the waist with one hand and lifted her up into the air. Fiona screamed. Dyami swung her up and released her up into the air. Fiona screamed again as she flew up toward the ceiling and then dropped.

Dyami caught her with one arm as she fell

down, then set her down on her feet. Fiona staggered and shook, sobbing.

Dyami rocked back and signed. *Take us there.*

"I can't," Fiona said, crying. "They won't —"

Dyami leaned closer. Fiona shrank back.

Muriel moved close to the young woman. "He's upset how we've been treated. Your people stole his translation device and locked us up, ignoring our rights. I wouldn't anger him."

"They'll stop us if I take you out of here," Fiona said. "Maybe—"

Muriel shook her head. "No. We leave now. Open the door. Lead the way to our shuttle. If they try to stop us, say you've been asked to take us to the shuttle. The teams studying it have questions, and you're going to translate. Do you understand?"

"Yes, but it won't work."

Muriel took Fiona's arm. "You'll make it work. If you are convincing, they'll believe it. And there isn't another option for you. They might stop us. This is a big ship, lots of people, but to do it they'll have to sacrifice you. Understand?"

Fiona nodded quickly. Muriel resisted the urge to feel sympathy for Fiona. The young woman had gone along with their imprisonment. She had participated. The threat wasn't idle. She'd take care of it herself. Despite Dyami's aggressive posturing, it was all bluff with him. He couldn't hurt the young woman. He wouldn't.

Shoving Fiona at the door, Muriel stuck beside her. Dyami followed behind them. Fiona wiped her tears and then sent the access code for the door. It slid open.

They walked out side-by-side. The corridor was empty at the moment, a plain corridor that stretched off into the ship. Just stepping out of the suite of rooms was progress.

"This way," Fiona said. "We'll have to go to the elevators."

Muriel remembered the route that they'd taken from the shuttle to the suites, but that had included going to a medical facility on the ship for initial scans. They had discovered that she wasn't entirely human thanks to samples taken during the exam. So far she had put them off as far as any explanation. The last thing she wanted to do was make them aware of even more details about the future. Moreaus, Moreau Pods and the rest, that was information they didn't need. And it wouldn't help them with what was about to happen.

Since their route had included that detour, she knew that it couldn't be the most direct route. She leaned close to Fiona.

"Don't waste time. Take us the quickest way. Don't try to avoid anyone. The more confident we look, the less likely people are to stop us."

Fiona nodded and didn't say anything.

Down the corridor, then it turned, and two security guards stood at a station in the hallway.

Muriel did her best not to look alarmed. She recognized the guard on the right side of the corridor, Dustin. He had been on the shuttle when they were rescued. The other was a young man, close-cut sandy hair, with a cleft chin.

Both security guards put their hands on their weapons. Dustin looked at Muriel, Dyami and then focused on Fiona.

"What's going on here, Ms. Davidson?"

"They need our guests down in the hangar

bay," Fiona said brightly. "I guess they have questions and want me to translate."

"I don't have any orders to move our guests," Dustin said.

It wasn't going to work. These men were professionals. They'd never agree to the story without confirmation. The ruse was already up, and they hadn't gone far at all. The men hadn't drawn their very lethal splat guns yet. Muriel knew about those guns. Brock had taken her to a range on Olinda to familiarize her with weapons when she joined the agency. His Lottiers were a much more humane weapon.

All of that went through her head in a second. There wasn't time to warn Dyami. She moved, shoving Fiona hard at the younger security guard while moving to attack Dustin.

Her first kick was nothing but a distraction, one that he easily blocked. Even that showed his training. Muriel moved faster, striking and moving inside his guard.

A loud roar behind her told her Dyami had joined the fight. She left him to handle the other guard. Fiona screamed.

Dustin knew how to fight. He was a

better fighter. Her Moreau modifications, designed to help her with deep dives, made her much stronger than she looked. That strength made the difference.

She delivered a sharp uppercut that got through, knocking Dustin back, stunned. His guard dropped. Her next kick took him in the gut, knocking out his wind. A final blow sent him to the floor.

The other guard hit the floor hard and didn't get up. Muriel bent and took Dustin's splat gun. The squat pistol fit comfortably in her hand. Obvious safety, she clicked it off. Then she retrieved the other from the second guard. Blood ran from his nose, but he was breathing.

Dyami stood over a cowering, weeping Fiona. Muriel leveled the gun at the translator.

"Get up," Muriel said. "Our cover is blown. We have to move fast now. Let's get going."

Glancing at Dyami, she said. "Pick up Dustin, and bring him. We're going to need hostages."

It was bad and getting worse. At least Blackstone wouldn't get any more information out of them if they were killed in the attempt to escape.

Dyami scooped Dustin up and tucked the man beneath his arm. Muriel pulled Fiona up, pointing the splat gun at Fiona's gut.

"This will rip you in half. I'm not interested in hurting anyone, but we are leaving. Show us the way to the hanger."

Sobbing, Fiona stumbled ahead down the corridor. Muriel followed, and Dyami brought up the rear, moving pretty easily on three limbs instead of four.

The corridors lacked the shiny and polish of the shuttle. The ship was more lived in than the shuttle. They passed more doors, some areas with transparent walls. People working, turned, watching them pass. This all looked like research labs. People doing who knows what, studying data about the planet ahead. Or about them.

Muriel stayed alert for interference. Alarms had probably been raised already. Opposition had to be coming. She prodded Fiona in the back with the splat gun.

"Where are they studying the things that were taken from us? Nearby?"

"I don't know, please," Fiona's voice broke. "I don't know."

It didn't matter. All that mattered was getting off this ship before it was too late.

"Never mind," Muriel said. "How much farther to the elevators?"

"Just up ahead. If I show you, will you let me go then?"

Muriel shoved Fiona. "No. Keep moving. Your director did this, she's the one responsible. And if we get what we want, then we'll leave you alone."

Fiona told the truth. They reached the elevator a minute later without encountering anyone in the corridor.

"Call it," Muriel ordered.

Fiona used her access to call the elevator. A display panel showed the elevator rising along a simple graphic of the ship. It moved quickly, without stopping. An express elevator?

It arrived on their level, and the doors slid open. Muriel was behind Fiona, her hand on the woman's shoulder, splat gun in the small of Fiona's back.

Dustin groaned in Dyami's grip.

The elevator was empty. Muriel shoved

Fiona inside and followed. She went to the back so that she could stand behind Fiona and the two of them moved back toward the rear right corner, making room for Dyami.

With the hulking alien in the elevator, there wasn't much space left. Dyami put Dustin on his feet. The guard was waking and managed to stand, rubbing his head.

"Take us to the hanger," Muriel ordered.

Using her access code, Fiona sent the elevator moving. Muriel wasn't surprised when, a couple levels down, a holographic screen formed beside the door.

Olivia Blackstone's severe face formed and took in the scene in the elevator. "Ms. Reinhard, that's not behavior I can tolerate. I would have thought you were beyond such things in the future."

"We're not in the future," Muriel said. "And we haven't changed that much. We're going to our shuttle. You know the price if we're stopped."

Blackstone nodded. "Yes. I do know. I'm sorry. I can't allow this."

The elevator stopped moving.

"No." Fiona pulled away from Muriel. "Please, they're going to kill me!"

Blackstone looked right at Muriel, meeting her eyes. "No, she isn't, Fiona. Try not to worry."

It was the moment. Blackstone was calling her bluff. *Was it a bluff?* Muriel didn't pull the trigger. Apparently, she was bluffing.

"We only want to leave," she said, trying to salvage something. "Let us go, and we'll leave you alone."

"You know I can't let you leave."

"You can't lock us up and violate our rights, either, but you didn't have any problem with that one."

"The safety of my ship and crew is paramount."

Dyami signed. *Let us go.*

"He says to let them go," Fiona said. "Please, director. We have to let them go. This isn't right."

"I have to believe you came back here for a reason," Blackstone said. "You've hinted at what waits for us in our mission. If you start cooperating, you'll find me much more agreeable. I might even restore Dyami's translation device."

Violence wasn't going to get them out of this. Muriel took her finger off the trigger of the splat gun. She thumbed the safety on and lowered her arm.

They weren't going to get out, not this way.

CHAPTER 31

Olinda, Orlando Pike's fortress, 2978

B right light stung my eyes as I stepped out of the corridor into the sunny courtyard.

Two guards, covered head-to-toe in black uniforms complete with helmets, had walked with me from the sensie room where I'd spent the past few days. The passages leading out were mostly biocrete but covered in rich tapestries and other works of art. Sculptures stood in alcoves and in the centers of the halls. The whole place seemed to be a never-ending collection of expensive works of art.

More statues dotted the courtyard, many suggesting inhuman hands. Native Olindan plants mingled with plants from many worlds to create a rich, layered garden. Left alone the plants would have quickly swamped the place, which spoke of the time it must take to maintain. Even as the guards guided me out into the sunlight, there were gardeners at work among the plants.

Thin-limbed, nimble, with shiny green skin, the Waltangian gardeners were reputed for their skill with plants. From the look of the place, it was a reputation well-deserved. What about the big-eyed aliens made them such good gardeners? The familiar Moreau itch scratched at my mind. Granted, growing plants wasn't a trait that I really needed right now, but their genetic record might have all sorts of surprises.

Except this wasn't the time to worry about my collection. I assumed that I was being taken out for another chat with Pike. After the trip down my Martian memories, I had expected him to show up sooner.

I was learning. Pike had wanted to learn about my connection to the Nosferans, and instead, he was a guest at a routine case during my time on Mars. The brain scanner wasn't quite as capable as he had appeared to believe.

I'm sure he had questions about that. Since he had taken the Mother Sack from

Drac, I had to assume he already knew why we'd come to his fortress. I still couldn't believe that Drac had concealed the fact that he was carrying the Mother Sack. If I'd known I wouldn't have brought him. He could have gotten another member of his tribe to come with me.

I couldn't even be sure that he was still alive, although Pike was a collector. I didn't think he'd throw away anything if he didn't have to.

The Waltangian gardeners continued their work without paying the guards or me any attention. When we passed by one, I breathed deeply, opening my scent-sight slits in my neck.

The Waltangian was picking through the leaves of the plant, looking intently at each. In my scent-sight, rich orange and yellow colors flowed from the Waltangian and sur-rounded the plant. Thin green streamers rose from the plant to the Waltangian. The gardener stroked the leaves, leaving behind those same orange and yellow scents. Some sort of botanical stimulant? It was fascinat-ing. All around me in the garden was a trail where the Waltangian had been. The plants looked lively, vibrant and healthy.

Ahead I picked up another scent trail. This one human. I concentrated and a ghostly image formed before me. It was Orlando Pike, walking through the garden. He had a sour, agitated smell about him.

Following the guards, we walked along after Pike's shade. The scents grew stronger the farther we went into the courtyard, weaving around in the labyrinthine garden. We crossed a flat stone bridge, crossing a long finger of a pool. Looking east, where the pool widened out into a small pond, I saw Pike waiting on a bench around on the other side. He sat with his back to us.

Then we crossed the bridge and continued following Pike's shade. The sour agitation smell faded as he walked, even as his scent grew stronger. As my scent-sight locked onto him even more, it was almost as if he was really there, walking just ahead of us. The plants around the path all glowed with the Waltangian touch. It was a calming odor. Maybe he was in a better mood by now.

When we finally reached the other side of the pond, Pike looked up at me and smiled. I stopped paying attention to his shade, and it evaporated, replaced by Pike's current scent. The agitation was still there, but faint.

"I like it out here," Pike said. "It helps calm me, gets me into the right frame of mind to consider what I need to do."

This might be my only chance. I wasn't paralyzed, the guards at my back wouldn't be able to move fast enough to stop me. I could reach Pike, and sting him with my C'lacktal hand. The poison wouldn't kill him unless he reacted badly. It would induce a coma.

All I had to do was jump forward and grab him. Simple. Nothing to it.

I didn't move.

I wasn't paralyzed. My C'lacktal tentacles writhed with frustration, I glanced to either side, checking out the guard's positions.

And still, I didn't attack.

Pike smiled. "I know what you're thinking, Brock. It'd be so easy, right? Except that you don't want to hurt me."

True. I didn't want to hurt Pike. I'd do it if I didn't have any other choice, mostly I wanted to get what I came for, get Drac, and get out.

"People are funny things. Even someone

capable of extreme violence might be incapable of harming something or someone they hold dear. Why? What is it in the mental landscape that creates those inhibitions?" Pike rose easily to his feet. He moved closer until he was within reach.

All I had to do was reach out and sting him. It'd take a split second. No more than that.

"I demand loyalty from my people. Absolute, unconditional loyalty. They'll lay their lives down for me. I have no doubts about that, none, because I implanted that loyalty."

"Artificial loyalty isn't the same thing," I said.

"Isn't it?" Pike shifted to the side, looking at the guard on my left. "What do you think?"

"I serve you, sir. Absolutely."

Pike shifted his attention back to me. "See? However it comes about, it's still the same. You of all people should understand that. You take genetic traits from other people and use the Moreau Pod to incorporate those changes into yourself. Don't you see the similarity?"

I did. With his nanoweb devices, Pike

could essentially reprogram a person, make them do or think whatever he wanted. *Puppets*. Meat puppets with brains.

Pike waved a hand. "Never mind about that. We will have a long time to discuss the possibilities, but before we can do that, I have a job for you."

"A job?"

"Yes. The Nosferan was quite forthcoming about your purpose for coming here. He told me that you planned to steal the Galactic tach field generator, that it was a key piece in creating a device capable of traveling back in time."

So Drac had talked. I didn't blame him. "What does that have to do with a job?"

Pike shrugged. "I sold the generator. I want you to go and get it back."

"What's going to stop me from getting the generator and keep it for myself?"

Pike stepped closer. Our faces were only inches apart. He reached up, and his hand ran down my face in a light caress. "You work for me now. You'll go get the generator. Maybe you'll tell yourself that you'll run off with it, but when it comes down to it, you'll bring it back to me."

"I doubt that," I said.

"Doubt it all you like, it doesn't make it less true." Pike leaned in close, and his lips brushed mine.

I didn't move. In my mind, I recoiled. In reality, I reached up with my human hand and found Pike's waist. I pulled him close and kissed him back hard. Our tongues fought and just as my chest burned, Pike stepped back out of reach. He smiled at me.

"Go on now, they'll take you to the ship. All the details are on board."

I fought against the turmoil in my brain. "What about Drac?"

"The Nosferan is free to accompany you if you like. My technology doesn't work on him, but I think his loyalty ultimately lies with you."

I'd take his ship. And I'd find a way to get rid of the hold Pike had over me in the process. Even if that meant killing him.

CHAPTER 32

2876, *Terran Expedition, Australia*

After the escape attempt, Constantine was questioning all of Helen's people. Including her. She walked out of the lift onto the security floor and was met immediately by two guards.

Helen didn't know them. It was a big ship, after all. They took her palm print, registering her biometrics. The screen clearly displayed her heart rate and blood pressure. Elevated, although not much.

That was good. She didn't want to appear too nervous.

The guard handed her a visitor badge which she clipped to the front of her workall. While she was doing that another guard walked up.

"Chief Constantine is expecting you." It

was Pierre, the woman from the mission to the shuttle. Made sense, keep information to those already exposed.

"Thank you," Helen said.

Pierre made no comment as they walked down the short corridor and turned to enter a door on the left. It was a small interrogation room, with a single table in the center of the room. Two chairs sat opposite one another on each side of the table, standard issue ergonomic chairs except that the one on the far side sported a number of leads and monitoring devices.

Helen folded her hands and looked at Pierre. "I thought Constantine was expecting me?"

"The chief will be in once I have you prepped." Pierre gestured to the chair with the monitoring equipment. "Please be seated and strap yourself in. For your own safety."

"Regulations to a tee, is it?" Resisting the polite request would only force Pierre into an awkward situation.

Helen walked around the table and sat down in the chair. The straps were ordinary safety straps, required on any seat and often ignored. She snapped the chest piece beneath her breasts and locked in the base. The straps automatically tightened snuggly around her.

Pierre lifted a light pair of glasses from a pocket on the side of the chair. "If you'll put these on?"

It looked like a standard augmented reality set. Helen slipped them on. Her view of the room didn't change. Most likely the glasses monitored her pupillary responses to questions. Pierre slipped a wireless biometric monitor on Helen's right index finger. Then she lifted a lead attached to the chair, trailing a thin wire and stuck it to Helen's right temple. The procedure was repeated on the left.

"Does all of this tell you that I have to pee?"

Pierre didn't laugh. The woman went over and stood beside the door, hands folded in front of her. Her eyes remained fixed on Helen.

It was all procedure. Helen rubbed her palms together, slick with sweat. Great. She hadn't done anything wrong. None of her people had, not even Fiona. The recordings showed how Dyami and Muriel had attacked and threatened the young woman.

And yet, the questions had to be asked.

Did any of them help their guests plan the escape attempt? It was ridiculous, especially with the upcoming entry into the Cyeechie system. The mystery of their guests was about to take a back seat to a whole new system.

The door opened. Constantine walked in with the same quick confidence he always showed. He came straight to the chair opposite her and sat down.

"Hello, Dr. Shaw," he said politely, as he strapped himself in.

Regulations, all the way.

"I have a question, if I may?" Helen asked.

"That is?"

"Are the security staff being vetted as well as the research staff? We weren't alone on the alien ship."

Constantine nodded. "Yes. Everyone with contact with our guests, or their technology has been vetted. You're the last."

"That's good to know."

"This is necessary," Constantine said. "We must know if anyone assisted them in the attempt. Shall we begin?"

"Yes," Helen said. "Although I can assure you, I didn't have any knowledge of the attempt."

Even if she did sympathize with their motivation, she wasn't about to condone their actions.

The interrogation didn't take long. Constantine was thorough, reviewing her actions and activities in the weeks leading up to the attempt. Any contact she personally had with their guests, as limited as that had been.

Finally, Constantine unstrapped and stood up. "Thank you for your cooperation, Dr. Shaw."

"You're welcome." Helen waved the biometric monitor at him. "Can I take these off now?"

"In a moment. Director Blackstone wants a word before we do."

That was a surprise. Helen accepted it with a nod. Constantine left the room, with Pierre following on his heels, leaving her alone in the room. She was expecting a holographic projection when the door opened, and Blackstone walked in, barefoot and in the flesh, wearing her usual workalls like any other crew member.

Except she wasn't just another member of the crew, she was the director.

Helen smiled. "Excuse me, they've got me a bit tied up here."

Blackstone didn't sit. She stood in front of the table, beside the chair, with her fingertips resting on the surface.

"Your department has been doing good work finding out as much as possible about our guests. This escape attempt makes things more difficult. We're about to enter the CY-HC-2347 system. We need to know what they are hiding. It could be crucial to the survival of this ship and crew."

"You're going to change their status?"

Blackstone's expression didn't waver. "They created the situation themselves. Everyone that has had contact with them has been cleared. They acted alone and threatened our people. I'm beginning to doubt their story."

That was new. "You mean about being from the future?"

"Yes. The information they have given us indicates that they are well-informed, but nothing specific that would prove their claim to be from the future. It may be that they wanted to divert us, convince us to turn back. Or to lead us into a trap, scout out our capabilities. That ship is very advanced stealth tech. If it hadn't been damaged, we wouldn't have detected it at all. What if they set up the whole thing? Maybe escape wasn't even on their plan, but sabotage."

"In the recordings, Muriel insisted they only wanted to get away."

Blackstone shrugged. "In any case, we need answers. I want to know if we're going to have a problem with this decision. How are your people going to react?"

"What exactly are you considering here? Even if they have lied to us, they still have rights."

Blackstone raised a finger. "Do they? Your own research, the work of your team, has shown that neither of them is human."

The room suddenly felt very cold. This was what Helen had feared the moment that she heard Mina and Lukas report on Muriel. Blackstone couldn't use the science as an excuse to cross lines that shouldn't be crossed.

"Dyami's an alien, but Muriel is no less human than anyone that has gene-sculpting in her background." Helen paused, letting that point sink in. Blackstone had been gene-sculpted herself, the latest in generations of improvements. "And alien or not, we're talking about sentient beings. They have rights!"

"Sentience can't be the ultimate criteria for rights, the courts have already determined that with the A.I. trials. Sentient or not, an artificial construct is legally defined as property and a tool."

Helen couldn't believe her ears. It was the whole *souls* argument again. Intrinsic worth and all that nonsense. She was also walking a dangerous point here with Blackstone. The way Blackstone's eyes tightened, the firm press of her lips, Blackstone was a few words away from pulling the whole thing.

"Let's go along with that definition for now." Even though it made her sick thinking about it. "Constantine isn't the best choice to get information out of them. My team is."

Blackstone straightened and crossed her arms. "Your team? You've had weeks with them, and we have few answers. Time is critical here. We need to get this done before we arrive at CY-HC-2347."

"We haven't pushed, given their status as guests. If you're changing their status, we can try other methods, while respecting their rights."

"All I care about are results," Blackstone said. "Get them for me, or I'll be forced to get someone else to do it. I need to know what they know, particularly if they're telling the truth about being from the future and what they know about our mission."

Helen's throat was dry. She swallowed to little effect. "Understood."

Blackstone turned and walked to the door. She stopped before it opened. "I'll have someone come and get you out of that, Helen. Thank you."

Helen managed a nod, but by that point, Blackstone was already gone.

It hardly counted as a win. Helen put her hands flat on the table, doing her best to look unconcerned. She breathed easily in and out. They'd look at her scans during the conversation, looking for duplicity.

She'd told the truth. Her team would do a better job than security, and it'd be better for Muriel and Dyami. Maybe Blackstone was right, maybe they had other purposes for being here. If that was the case, she wanted to know too. If not, then she'd find that out,

hopefully without having to cross the line
that Blackstone was too quick to cross.

Chapter 33

2875 Pohl Station

Life on Mars was different than Seabrook. Alien, in many ways. At first, I didn't realize how alien Pohl Station was, not until I had my first big case.

Seabrook never felt like the frontier. Only twenty light-years from Earth, one of the first inhabitable worlds colonized. Despite the somewhat harsh conditions and predatory aquatic species, it was in many ways a nearly perfect match for humanity. Right temperature, compatible biochemistry, gravity within a few percentage points of Earth's, and free of much of the radiation and pollution that came with Earth's long history. Ideal, until you had to grow up there.

Strange, then, to discover a true frontier

in the Sol system, so close to Earth that you could see it in the sky.

Yet Mars was a frontier. Nothing matched Earth. Not the gravity, the atmosphere, the temperature range or the radiation exposure. No compatible biochemistry, because unlike so many bodies in the solar system, life hadn't developed on Mars. With fossils and extremophiles found on Venus, the rich sub-surface biospheres of the Jovian moons, and the wide-spread existence of life in other systems, Mars remained an anomaly.

The gap.

Was it an impact event right at a critical stage in the formation of life? A stellar eruption that baked the planet? Research to hunt down the reason was ongoing, but it wasn't the drive behind the colonists.

Many of those living in Pohl Station, I found, didn't want to know what had happened. Or, more accurately, they were afraid that life might turn up in some remote sub-surface pocket and spoil their plans.

The Martians planned to engineer their world and themselves. They didn't call it terraforming, but bioforming. The goal wasn't to recreate an Earth-compatible world, that was the last thing they wanted. Instead, they wanted a world of their own, one in which they could walk free beneath her skies, while standard humans remain restricted to carefully controlled habitats.

All of which made my first big case notable. A body had been found, outside, without an environmental suit. But that wasn't what had killed him. The rock hammer stuck in his forehead had done that.

It was murder, plainly.

Pohl Station got the call, being closest to a tributary of the Kasei Valles region where the body was found. And it was Ward Riddock that brought me in on the case. In the past five months since I'd left the antimatter ore ship to join the Martian colony, Ward had taken an interest in my case.

To look at him, Ward was a sterling example of a Martian colonist. Third generation, the little guy hardly came up to my chest. Even with that, I don't think anyone would mistake him for a child. Like the rest of the Martians he was small, petite, but on that petite frame, Ward had packed plenty of muscles. He wasn't bulky, but he was strong.

He filled out that standard black uniform they all wore.

We took a gossamer out to the crime scene. The gossamer is an almost transparent airplane, with wide polymer wings. It's not fast, but it is light and quiet. With the mostly transparent sides, there wasn't anything between me and a long drop to reddish rocks except a toy-like plastic frame and plastic sheeting.

Along for the ride, in addition to Ward and me, were two forensic specialists and the Pohl Station coroner, a lovely woman named Angela Zimmerman. We all wore tight environmental suits, with the helmets off. The gossamer was supposed to be safe after all, but the air inside was heated only as it compared to the outside. It was still nippy. I was glad of the suit, even though it meant I had had to leave my coat and hat back at the station.

Sitting in the seat beside me, Ward pointed down between his feet. "Imagine, all of that space down there, never touched by a single living thing. We've mapped it down to tiny details, but most of the surface of Mars is still untouched."

"It's all rocks and sand," I said. "Beautiful, if that's your thing."

Ward shrugged. "Maybe you have to have grown up here to really appreciate what it would be like to walk unaided out there."

"That won't be for generations yet, right? You aren't ever going to see it."

"Not the way my descendants will." Ward grinned. "We're building a symbiosis here between us and the planet. A whole new form of life. Can't expect that to happen easily."

"Call me selfish, I want to see things for myself." I swiped my tablet on. Images of the crime scene appeared on the tablet. Not taken by anyone on the scene, the pictures came from the satellite network over the planet, that had picked up and flagged the anomaly.

I flipped through to the zoomed in, blurry image of the body. The details weren't quite there, but enough that you could see the body and the glint of what they said was a rock hammer in his forehead. I don't know how they got rock hammer from a few pixels, but they had. Probably analyzed the spectrum of the reflection, something like that, and found a match to the murder weapon.

I pointed at the image. "What about our victim? How does someone end up out here? Anything close?"

Ward shook his head. "No, nothing out here. Nothing permanent, at least. There could be researchers, explorers, or nomads. When we get closer, we should be able to get some answers."

"There aren't any groups that have perfected walking around without environmental suits, are there?"

"No. Not yet. We keep trying. If that were the case, it would be a significant discovery."

"It sounds more likely that this is a case of a body being dumped, than someone going for a stroll outside."

"I agree. We're approaching the site in ten minutes."

I resumed watching the terrain passing by beneath my feet. The reddish color reminded me of Seabrook, but it wasn't the same. And it wasn't all the same color. This varied, between rusty brown reds and paler tan colors. I saw dunes and craters, gullies and deep valles. At some point in the planet's ancient history, a vast flood had erupted out of the planet's crust and had spilled through this region, carving out these valles and the tortured terrain.

A complicated world, one shaped entirely by non-living forces. An intriguing mystery, but not the one that I needed to solve.

The gossamer moved to sit down on a patch of relatively flat ground, covered in a scattering of rocks and small sand dunes, near the body. The speed of the aircraft dropped and dropped until it wasn't moving any faster than I might walk. The wings rotated, caught the air, and forward motion stopped.

Instead of crashing to the ground the gossamer dropped down, rocking slightly, landing as gently as a leaf falls on Earth. Of course, I've only seen recordings of leaves falling, that wasn't a trait of vegetation on Seabrook.

The gossamer's wing tips dropped to the ground, bracing the lightweight craft. Up front, the pilot twisted around in his seat.

"We've got a wind coming up from the South, kicking up some dust. We don't have long before we have to get out of here. Thirty minutes tops."

"We'll work fast," Ward said. He gestured to the others. "You heard him, let's get out there and get the job done."

The two forensic types had already put their helmets on. I grabbed mine and pulled it over my head. The bubble helmet snapped securely into the collar and a heads-up display projected itself on the curved inside of the helmet. Readouts on oxygen supply, temperature, environmental conditions, and biometrics. Everything that you needed to know, right there.

That was cool. And not as busy as the glasses that they'd shown me when I entered the colony. This much augmentation, I could deal with.

On their own, the suits had limited power and life-support capabilities. We all lined up at the gossamer's airlock, pulling survival packs from the rack. You slipped it on like a backpack, cinched the straps and plugged it in. A second for the systems to sync up with the suit and then you were good to go.

The techs went first, cycling through the

airlock together. Ward and I went next, and Angela brought up the rear.

On my readout, my heart rate ticked up over a hundred beats per second as the airlock brought us down to Martian pressure. I didn't feel any change. The tight suit clung to me like a second skin, one that kept me warm and comfortable while still allowing me to easily move. The joints were particularly clever that way.

The airlock status appeared as a small progress bar on my helmet. Several icons had also appeared, each representing the others with indicators on their condition. Apparently, the green heart icons in the corner indicated everything was good with them.

Stepping out onto the open Martian surface for the first time, that was a thrill. An alien world, but one with a rich connection to humanity in history and legend. It was never the world we imagined it to be, always surprising us.

I never saw any place this dry on Seabrook. The ground crunched slightly beneath my feet. A wind picked up dust from the techs walking ahead of us across the rocky surface.

From this vantage, the area looked flat

and unremarkable. A rocky plain. My eyes kept looking for a plant, for something, but everywhere I looked it was the same beautiful desolation.

Ward tapped my arm. "No time for sight-seeing."

I gestured. "Lead on. I'll follow."

Angela came out of the airlock and walked up beside me. She smiled at me through her helmet, the reverse heads-up display casting odd patterns across her fine features.

"Nothing like this back on Earth?"

I shook my head. "I'm not from Earth. I came from Seabrook. Definitely nothing like this there."

We followed in Ward's tracks. Each one of our steps, a step in a place where no one had walked before. Well, except for whoever had dumped the body. I didn't see any tracks, though, so whoever it was, they hadn't come this way.

"Seabrook, that's the water world, right?"

"It's called that, but it isn't really any more of a water world than the Earth. About seventy-two percent of the surface is under water. And it rains a lot over much of the continents, so it pretty much feels like you're always underwater."

Angela chuckled. "Hard to imagine that, water falling from the sky!"

"You were born here?"

"Fourth generation colonist," Angela said. She winked at me. "I could take off the helmet, as long as I held my breath, and could go for several minutes that way."

"Good to know."

The techs were getting farther ahead, and even Ward was putting distance on us. "We'd better hurry, or we're going to miss all the fun."

"Yes," Angela said. Her pace increased.

Give it to the Martians, they might be small, but they all moved quickly.

I walked past a crater. An actual crater! It wasn't big, a couple meters across, but it was an impact crater with sand drifting up along one side. Once I saw it, I saw others scattered across the landscape. When I hadn't been looking for them, my eyes skipped across, seeing them as dips and rises in the landscape, but now I saw them for what they were.

This world was pounded, at some point in its history. Was it related to the gap?

I was still thinking about the possibility, the scenarios around a large impact followed by a long period of secondary impacts as the debris rained down on the world, stopping the process of life forming before it could get started when we reached the body.

The techs had stopped before they reached it, at Ward's instructions. We caught up a second later.

The body lay out in the open, lying within a small gully that ran off ahead, down a gentle slope. In the distance, a line of what looked like distant hills must actually be the far wall of this portion of the valle.

I squinted at the body, wishing I had better eyesight. First impressions? Male, Martian, and no environmental suit. Bare feet that surprised me. A bright piece of tech next to the body looked like a set of the AR glasses.

And then there was the bright metal rock hammer, partially stained rusty red with dried blood. More blood had dried on the man's skin.

Ward's voice came over speakers in my

helmet. "Activating recordings. We need to do this quick. Let's move out and encircle the body at this distance and then work closer. Watch for any evidence left behind, particularly any tracks that could indicate how he got out here."

Acknowledgments came from the others. We turned and walked out, making our way around the body. An indicator on my helmet showed that it was recording everything I saw. Nice trick that.

The five us ended up spaced more or less evenly around the figure. Ward raised his hand.

"Okay, let's move straight in. Stay alert. A small thing might be enough to solve this."

We moved closer, and with each step, I became more and more uneasy. I hadn't gone more than three or four steps when I saw something on the ground and stopped. It was faint, easy to miss.

Sand, piled in a small dune against a chunk of volcanic rock. And in the sand, a bare footprint. Small, Martian sized. After I saw it, I picked up bits of others, a whole string of them. As if he had walked to the place where he died.

Chapter 34

2876, Terran Expedition ship Australia

A hundred years ago, except it wasn't a hundred years ago now, was it? Muriel rubbed her eyes and kept moving in the dark. Kept walking. Her finger traced invisible lines on the padded cell walls.

Messages. Invisible messages.

Messages that Brock could see with his scent-sight. She leaned into the wall, her finger tracing his name on the panels. If he came in here, with his scent-sight, he could see what she wrote.

Brock, my love.

No doubt the scientists were busy analyzing the video. Despite the darkness in the cell, they were watching. Infrared cameras, all sorts of sensors monitoring her respiration, heart rate and the rest of the signals her body gave off. They didn't need to touch her for any of that.

The panels might even suck in her sweat and oils, analyzing her hormone levels and the effects of the drugs that they had put in her food.

It sounded paranoid if you weren't the one that had lost consciousness and had woken up in a padded cell with no lights.

Brock. He wasn't coming. The last she'd seen of him was back on Hansel when they separated. And then he had ejected from the moon in an escape pod. Before they could intercept and retrieve him, an alien ship had intervened.

Had he been captured? Killed? She didn't know. He wasn't going to see her messages. Only the *Australia*'s scientists would see what she wrote.

Just let us go, she traced on the wall.

Muriel resumed walking. The floor was smooth beneath her bare feet. Not cold. Not hot, like the rest of the room. Comfortably warm even in the thin hospital gown she was wearing now.

All of it was in response to her escape attempt. They wanted answers, and now they obviously felt justified in doing whatever it took to get the answers. She was worried about Dyami, but worrying wasn't going to get them out of this situation. Brock wasn't going to come in and save them. Subha was back on Olinda along with Shanley Walsh. Who knew what had happened to them, or to all of their Moreau Society after Kelwyn's attempt to hold the planet ransom with his mutation-inducing ray? Hopefully, he had been stopped before he killed too many people.

Whatever had happened back home, none of the people they left behind knew what had happened to her and Dyami. Even Captain Kynan Brice, who knew that they had gone off looking for Kelwyn, wouldn't know where the trail had led them.

Somehow they'd gotten thrown back in time, a hundred years ago. Before, back before they lost contact with the Pilot and *Australia*'s expedition arrived, the Pilot had said something about the displacement drive. If the Tretan's Pilot was still functional, he might have figured out what had happened to the ship.

But what would the Pilot do? He was a

non-organic, a cybernetic mnemonic clone of the Tretan. And that wasn't even his name, the Tretans were outcasts from the Galactics. Once members of the Glittering Throng expelled for some reason. The one she knew operated Galactic DNA Suppliers on Olinda. He was known as the Tretan, no one she knew in the Moreau Society knew his name.

Would his cybernetic mnemonic clone do anything to help his passengers? If he figured out how to return to the future, it seemed more likely that he would do so to share the secret with his creator, leaving them stranded in the process.

Muriel couldn't count on the Pilot's help. If she was going to get out of this, she had to rely on her own abilities, and Dyami's if she could find him.

A hundred years ago, except a hundred years ago was now. A hundred years ago was walking in small circles around what was essentially a padded cell.

A hundred years ago the *Australia* under the command of Olivia Blackstone had —

No. She wasn't even going to think that, even though she never read anything about the people of a hundred years ago reading minds.

That's what they wanted. They wanted to know what she knew about the ship. About the mission. About what was going to happen because a hundred years ago was now. What was going to happen was happening soon.

Her fingers traced lines on the wall, erasing what she had written earlier. Over and over, parallel lines laid down like the mining on Olinda's moons.

A hundred years ago. What did that even mean? If she somehow got out of this, what would happen to her? To Dyami? Were they just supposed to go off and find a place to lay low for the rest of their lives? Start new lives? Ignore what she knew?

Muriel stopped walking. She crossed her arms, rubbing them. Blackstone had Helen Shaw doing this because Muriel had said too much. Blackstone knew that she was holding back from revealing what had happened, what was going to happen, with the *Australia*. The director was quick, she didn't miss much.

The darkness was absolute. Muriel's eyes

didn't find any light, anywhere. It was silent. Neither hot or cold. Nothing for her to fix on except her own thoughts and the feel of her own body. They hadn't taken that from her.

It anchored her enough. She couldn't look for Brock to save her. Or Dyami, or the Pilot, or anyone except herself.

And when she thought about it, the answer was as obvious as a burst of light in the darkness.

All she had to do was tell Helen the truth. Answer her questions. Reveal what she knew. Maybe it changed the future, maybe it didn't. Up until now, she hadn't believed that time travel was possible at all, so she really didn't know how it worked.

What if everything had already happened this way? If her actions changed the course of events, then wouldn't that be the history that she remembered growing up?

If her memories changed, would she even be aware of the change? Maybe it had already happened! Maybe there had been a future where the *Australia*'s fate was different, where the ship hadn't detected a small alien shuttle? Where they hadn't investigated and hadn't found Muriel and Dyami, wasn't that possible?

Except in changing the future, it had already altered her memories. She remembered a future now that existed because the Tretan's shuttle had come back in time. So anything she did, that was only what she had already done, like a recording being played out. She couldn't step outside the recording to see it, to compare it with the original, but was stuck forever doing exactly the same things again.

Another circuit of the black room had nearly convinced Muriel. Tears of relief stung her eyes. She could stop being afraid about the future and just tell them. History would be what it was going to be, and whatever it was, that's what she remembered.

Remembered. A hundred years ago, about the *Australia*. The story was told over and over.

Nothing she remembered mentioned an earlier encounter while on the way to CY-HC-2347. Nothing about an alien and a human woman discovered adrift in space in an alien spacecraft or about an encounter with time travelers.

Wouldn't that have been in there? The whole thing had to be in the records. It had to be logged. The entire crew knew about the encounter by now. Maybe not all the details, but rumors and those rumors would get recorded in journals and letters and reports.

And it would have been big news. Muriel would have remembered reading about mysterious encounters with time travelers claiming to be from a hundred years in the future.

Wouldn't that have been big news when the date finally rolled around?

No one was talking about the *Australia* in a hundred years except scholars and history buffs, and none of them mentioned time travelers either.

Muriel's fingers traced lines on the walls a hundred years ago. Oils, skin, bits of DNA proving that she was here, on the *Australia*. The longer they stayed, the more they became a part of this place. The more she was a part of the *Australia*, and Dyami, and even the Pilot.

All of that and she didn't remember anything about it in the stories told. Which meant that this hadn't happened before. If it had, she would have remembered reading about it.

A hundred years ago the *Australia* visited CY-HC-2347, a Terran exploration mission, designed for a long-term stay in the system.

A hundred years ago the *Australia* changed the fate of humanity.

All of this. Blackstone. Shaw. Constantine. The names trickled out of her memories. If she told them, then things changed. Nothing would ever be the same again.

A hundred years ago was now and now, she had a choice.

CHAPTER 35

Olinda

A pirate shuttle, yo ho, it's the pirate's life for me. I whistled, running my hands across seats covered in the finest leather I'd ever felt. The seats were black and smooth, with a subtle shine, warm to the touch as if living things. They glowed with a faint amber warmth that smelled of sun-warmed apples and a hint of salt.

Drac shrank back into one of the ring-shaped bench seats around a polished metal table on one side of the galley area. A large section of his wing was missing, the edges sealed with a hardened spray-on coagulant, pale green as if his wing was rotting.

Nosferans didn't regenerate, not from wounds like. He'd never fly again without extensive medical treatment, and that wasn't something that was generally available to the Nosferans. Not today, scattered as they were in isolated tribes.

"Drac, did Pike return the Mother Sack?"

With typical Nosferan evasiveness, Drac said, "The Mother Sack lives."

The tribes fiercely protected the identity of the male that carried the Mother Sack, relying on anonymity to protect the carrier. Drac only answered the question because of my standing.

It was still a relief. The tribe's survival depended on the safety of the Mother Sack. They never should have allowed Drac to come on this mission, but preventing it, treating him differently would have been the same in their minds as advertising that he carried their future. Paint a target on someone's back, it's only a matter of time before they get shot.

I wasn't going to ask anything more about it. I didn't have the same emotional wiring as Drac, but I knew better. Treating him differently would make things very difficult.

I moved forward past the galley, through the recreation sections, past the living quarters and forward into the control center at the nose of the craft. Drac followed me without asking.

The control center was small, designed for an intimate crew. Four sections of work areas and controls faced the broad windows that wrapped around the front of the craft. In between the four was a single station with two holographic screens. It wasn't my Cooperative shuttle that I kept back out at the spaceport. This was bigger and incorporated all sorts of galactic tech.

I settled into the main seat. Drac went to the forward station on my right and climbed onto the chair, squatting on it with his damaged wing wrapped around his legs.

At my touch, the systems came alive. Status displays popped up on the holographic screens. Obvious semi-autonomous controls. We could fly this, no doubt about that.

Activating the system tripped a message from Pike. A hologram projected itself from the screens, creating a very realistic version of Pike standing in front of the command chair.

"This shuttle, the *Wisteria*, will get you where you need to go. Review the inventory, I think you'll be impressed with the resources you have on board, including a complement of android enforcers, should you feel the need for some backup. All the files on your destination are at hand. You don't have far to go. I look forward to your return." Pike smiled. "And have sweet dreams, Brock."

The hologram vanished. Sweet dreams, *right*. I didn't think I would sleep easy until I had Pike's nanoweb out of my head, and him in custody. Or dead, if it came to that.

None of that changed the current situation. Drac was flipping through screens, obviously already reviewing information. I touched the first blinking packet indicator, and holographic documentation appeared in a ring around me. I spun the ring and flicked onto the information about the shuttle.

I whistled again. The pirate's life for sure, the *Wisteria* was fully equipped. It was sleek and covered with a chameleon skin that helped it blend into its surroundings. It wasn't invisibility, though it came close under the right conditions, mostly in the visible light spectrum. The keel of the ship held the STC drive and gravity generators. Above that was a long series of cargo holds, each capable of supporting a different environment in case they needed to hold living cargo or other sensitive materials.

Above the holds were the main decks. The galley, living quarters, recreation areas and the control center occupied only a small blister on top of the craft. Behind that were sections holding the promised android forces, a variety of vehicles and flitters suitable for different conditions. And throughout the whole shuttle, ample storage options, with several flagged as hidden storage areas, pockets set up as shielded and hidden for sensitive materials.

The shuttle was a smuggling ship, plain and simple. It supported up to a dozen crew, not counting the androids. Extensive data libraries were available at my fingertips. The ship was a worth a fortune. It didn't have the systems for interplanetary travel, but within a system, it was a fantastic craft.

In true pirate fashion, it also sported an impressive array of energy and kinetic weapons.

I preferred the Cooperative shuttle given to me by Felicity Strikes, but the *Wisteria* wasn't without its charms.

I spun the ring of documents and stopped

it when I saw the details about what happened to the Galactic tach field generator. It'd taken months of work on my part, and the Tretan's part to come up with a plan. The photo that Drac had brought me was enough to get the Tretan, an exiled member of the Glittering Throng, on board. I owed the Tretan. I was still paying off genetic samples the Tretan had provided, and I owed him for the loss of his shuttle. The fact that Muriel and Dyami were lost with the shuttle didn't matter to the Tretan, except that Muriel also owed him for genetic samples. It was the photo that Drac had provided, evidence that they had traveled back in time, that convinced him not to take what I owed him out of my hide.

I had to get the tach field generator. Without it, our plan couldn't move forward. Pike expected us to bring it back to him, but I had no intention of doing so. Maybe he could control me when I was within reach, but how far could his control extend?

His last trips down my memory lane hadn't taken him to my connection with the Nosferans. I'd managed to turn the wheel and send us off down my time at Pohl Station on Mars. It gave me hope that his control was limited. I was tempted to head back home, and go to my workshop now to try and remove the nanoweb, but there was no telling how long that might take. And as long as I was on Olinda, I wasn't far from Pike.

Better to go now, get the tach field generator, and deal with the rest later.

Scanning through the documents brought up detailed reports about the group that bought the tach field generator.

Enhancers, a group that grew out of the gene-sculpting that originated on Earth, had taken over an asteroid out by the third Jovian in the system. The asteroid tracked the Jovian's leading Lagrange point. Enhancers focused on creating original enhancements to their capabilities. In a way, it paralleled the work done by the Moreau Society, except the Enhancers didn't use the Moreau Pods. They relied on a variety of tech, Galactic, non-galactic or Terran to accomplish their goals which were loosely focused on expanding and exploring the human potential.

It reminded me of the Martians I knew back at Pohl Station, except their bioforming efforts were narrowly focused. The Enhancers didn't have the same focus.

The records didn't say what they wanted with the tach field generator. They'd paid a considerable sum to obtain it, and Pike hadn't asked questions.

His instructions, appended to the file, ordered me to retrieve it by any means necessary including offering them a full refund of the purchase.

I didn't think that they'd take the offer. I doubt Pike believed it either.

I didn't really care what he wanted, even if our purposes coincided. I had to get the tach field generator. I'd give the Enhancers a way out, but if they didn't take it, we'd go in with everything we had.

CHAPTER 36

Mars, Pohl Station

Barefoot tracks on the surface of Mars didn't make much sense. Worse, the victim had clearly died where the body was left. We'd gone out expecting a body dump, but he had bled out right there on the surface of Mars.

After a careful approach, the others stood with me, looking at the tracks in the Martian sand. One of the forensic techs had shared a view filter which highlighted the disturbed sand. Using the filter the footprints glowed red and yellow, leading off across the Martian surface, climbing up from the valles.

Barefoot. *On Mars.*

It looked like someone had actually managed to do what the colonists had been working toward for generations, a person capable of living outside without an environmental suit.

Except that it was a rock hammer to the forehead that had killed him. The hammer had impaled his forehead and had been left behind.

Only I didn't see any other signs of footprints near the body. The trail revealed by the filter showed the victim's footprints in the sand, leading right to his body. There was a cluster of prints around his feet as if he had been turning in a circle, staggering? And then he had fallen on his back.

The filter clearly showed our footprints. A ring of prints circled the body, showing where we had spread out and then like spokes from a wheel, radiating inward toward the body. Before reaching the body, the others turned and came over to my side to see the prints I'd found.

I turned toward Angela. "Could he have done this to himself?"

"A suicide?"

"Yes. There aren't any other tracks approaching the body. Thanks to," I checked the icons on my helmet. "Tiasha, we can see our tracks, his tracks, no others."

"We're down to fifteen minutes," Ward said.

Angela was facing the body. "I need to examine the body before I can give you an answer. If it was self-inflicted, I should be able to tell."

"We need to record the scene," Tiasha said.

"Go," Ward said.

"I'm going to follow his tracks," I said. "I want to see where he came from. It might give us answers."

"We don't have long," Ward said. "I'll come with you, but when that storm gets closer, we must leave."

For the first time, I really got the whole heads up, augmented reality display. Thanks to the real-time filter, the victim's footprints were visible. And aside from the various readouts, one of the indicators showed a faint map overlay marking our position and the leading front of the storm.

Ward and I set off following the prints. I quickly fell into a long, bounding stride that left Ward behind at first, until he picked up his pace and caught up. I slowed a bit, and we found a good compromise that kept us together. The lower gravity on Mars was especially noticeable coming from Seabrook, but in Pohl Station, there wasn't as much room to take advantage of the difference. Out here, even with the suit, it was exhilarating to run.

"He was moving fast," I said. The tracks showed the same sort of bounding stride that we were using.

The tracks led down the slope into the valle and stopped at an area with disturbed sand and rocks.

"Does that look like an aircraft landed?" I asked.

"Could be," Ward said. "If that's the case, then someone else was flying it."

I turned and looked back up the slope. The others were small in the distance, moving to bag the body. The storm readout showed it getting closer fast.

"So he gets out and runs barefoot away from the aircraft, then what? Drives a hammer into his own face? Why?"

Ward turned and pointed back to the others. "We have to get back. The storm is coming. We need to get the gossamer out of here."

I didn't like it. The situation didn't make

any sense, but maybe there'd be more answers when we got the body back to Pohl Station and got an identity on our victim or potential suicide.

"Sure. Let's go."

We bounded back up the slope to rejoin the rest of the team, already carrying the body back to the gossamer.

Δ

The next day, back at Pohl Station, Angela had her preliminary findings. Ward and I met her in the station morgue.

Three levels down, in the newer section of the station, the morgue was clean, Spartan and modern. I was back in my long coat, although I carried the hat. Both were unnecessary in the climate-controlled station, but it felt strange to go out without them. And even though technically the entire station was 'inside,' I only wore the hat on the upper levels beneath the domes. As close as I was going to get to walking around outside in my clothes.

Not, apparently, our victim.

"He wasn't specially adapted to conditions outside," Angela said.

We were all in the autopsy lab adjacent to the autopsy room itself. Through large windows, the victim's body lay beneath bright lights on a slab. The standard Martian uniform was gone, leaving him looking very naked, pale and small on the table. Almost childlike.

Angela pulled up close-up pictures of his feet on the lab screens. The images showed blackened tissues on the victim's feet.

"He was freezing even as he ran out across the surface."

The images changed. Some sort of cross-slices of tissues, red and purple on the screen. I didn't have a clue what it was. Instead of finding the images disgusting, I was fascinated by what I saw.

"His lungs show that oxygen was bleeding out of his blood, into his lungs. The process was slowed somewhat by generations of gene-sculpting, but no more so than any other second-generation colonist."

"Second generation?" Ward asked. "You have an identity then?"

"Yes."

More screens came up with portraits of the victim when he was alive, and information about him. Emrys Nash. Forty-six, a systems programmer, working for the Environmental Division. No one with any special connections to bioforming. Single, no family. Parents died in a depressurization accident when he was a child.

Ward said, "What about the wound? Was that self-inflicted as well?"

"Yes." Angela gestured, and more screens came up with her report. "Directionality, blood splatters, and prints all suggest that he ran out there, then took the rock hammer and brought it up with a two-handed grip into his own head."

Why commit suicide in such an odd manner? And it didn't answer the question about how he'd gotten there. "What about the tracks we found? Do we know what sort of vehicle it was?"

Angela shook her head. "It doesn't match patterns caused by a gossamer or any other vehicle in the station. And what's really strange, Nash wasn't from Pohl Station."

Ward flicked back to the profile on Nash.

"This says he worked in the Environmental Division."

Angela reached out and scrolled down in the document. The location block came up on the screen. I whistled.

"Amundsen Station? That's at the North Pole, right?"

"Yes," Angela said. More windows came up at her command, displaying images of domes resembling those of Pohl Station, although there were fewer domes. "Amundsen Station studies the climatic history on Mars, as well as providing easy access to the ice sheet for mining operations."

"So what was Nash doing down here?"

Angela shrugged. "I can't tell you that. There are no drugs in his system, no illness, nothing that suggests any injury or coercion."

Ward rubbed his chin. "As odd as it is, you're telling me that he killed himself and there's no evidence suggesting anything other than that?"

"No, I don't have any other evidence." Angela dragged down Nash's picture. "Without something else to go on, my preliminary ruling is suicide. One of the stranger ones we've seen, but suicide."

"Okay," Ward said. "Thank you for your work. Thank the rest of your team for me."

I stepped in front of Ward. "Wait a second. You're going to close the case, just like that?"

Both elfin Martians looked up at me as if I was the subject on display. Both their foreheads wrinkled with confusion.

"The evidence doesn't indicate any other explanation," Ward said. "You heard the report. I know I brought you in on this, Brock, and you'll get your fee. I thought maybe we had a murder and I thought having an outside perspective might offer some extra insight. Nothing left to do if it's only another suicide."

"I do have extra insight," I said. "Like this doesn't make sense. None of this tells us how Nash got all the way down here. Why did he come all this way to kill himself? Who else was with him?"

"Even if someone else piloted whatever vehicle they used, that's hardly their fault if he runs off and kills himself."

"And it doesn't bother you that whoever that was just left the scene?"

"Some," Ward said. "But if I tracked

down this other person, what could I charge them with? Leaving the scene? They didn't commit any crime. Maybe Nash wanted to die, maybe someone helped him, that's not a crime here. Was it back on Seabrook?"

"No. The constables wouldn't spend any time on a suicide."

"I understand," Ward said. "You're not from here, you wouldn't know. We're not suggesting that we don't care what happened, far from it."

Angela said, "That's right. Amundsen Station will get our reports. Their people will notify anyone that knew Nash, co-workers, and friends and see that they all get appropriate counseling. If they discover that one of them helped him, extra care will be given to help that person deal with any feelings of guilt or psychological issues from being used like that."

They didn't get it. It wasn't enough that the circumstances were so strange. It was just a suicide to them. Strange, but nothing that their procedures couldn't handle.

"I'm not convinced," I said. "Give me some time to check into it. If it still looks like a suicide in a couple days, I'll drop it."

Ward smiled up at me. "You really want to spend time on this?"

"I'm a private investigator. It's the sort of thing I do, and this one is weird. Let me take a crack at it."

"Fine," Ward said. "Two days, reasonable expenses. I can stretch the budget that much, mostly because I wouldn't mind a few more answers."

"Thanks, I'll get busy right away."

Both Martians beamed at me, making them look more child-like and elfin than ever. I raised my hat and hurried out of the morgue.

Next stop, Amundsen Station. I wanted to see where Nash lived and worked, track down his last day, and maybe discover how he'd gotten so far from home.

CHAPTER 37

Australia

When Helen had asked Blackstone to let her handle Muriel's interrogation she hadn't let herself think about what that meant.

Watching Muriel stumble around in the darkened chamber, her gut clenched tighter. Muriel couldn't see anything inside the cell. It wasn't a full sensory deprivation, but close enough. Two days in there and she still spent her time walking in circles, tracing lines on the walls.

Constantine was coming by later. He wanted answers, on Blackstone's behalf. If Helen couldn't get them, she knew that he would press the case with Blackstone to get a crack at Muriel and Dyami himself.

The cell was an isolation chamber off

lab 4. Lukas Zelenka sat at the second lab station, monitoring Muriel's vitals. Lab 4 was designed to handle all sorts of specimens from large to small with a full array of isolation cells, and other containment pods. This was the place where they planned to bring any life-forms discovered at Cyeechie as it would let them recreate the environment of each organism and monitor it in detail.

Helen couldn't sit. She sipped a coffee and paced the lab between Zelenka's station and station three, where Mina Lang and Ben Tol monitored Dyami in another isolation cell.

The screens revealed Dyami sitting placidly in the cell, long arms planted in between his shorter legs. His big wrinkled head hung down on his chest, eyes closed. A rumbling sound came from the speakers.

"What is that?" Helen asked.

Mina glanced up and back from her chair. Her bright orange lips quirked. "He's snoring."

Ben was busy on the desktop, flipping through screens of bright colors and lines. He didn't look up or offer anything.

"Ben?"

Ben turned his head, and his eyes focused

on Helen's breasts. Every time! It was so creepy, and how much could he really see with the workalls? It wasn't like she was all that busty.

"Ben?" She repeated.

He blinked and looked up at her face, finally. "Uh, what? What can I do for you?"

At the other station, Mina smirked and turned back to the screens monitoring Dyami.

Helen gestured at Ben's screens. "What are you doing?"

"Oh, this, I'm analyzing the recordings that we've made of his vocalizations. When I run them through the translation device with minor variations, it doesn't always produce the same translation. I'm trying to identify the specific word-sounds and the corresponding translation to help build our own translation matrix."

"Any progress?"

Ben nodded. "The alien's vocalizations are tremendously complex, almost musical. With the help of the translation device, I should be able to develop a detailed translation matrix."

Mina spun her chair around. "If we need answers from him, why don't we just give him back the translation device? Wouldn't that be faster? I mean, then he could actually answer our questions."

"And if he damaged it?" Ben retorted. "If he didn't want to answer our questions all he'd have to do is break it. Then we wouldn't have our answers, and no way to understand him if he did talk."

They both had good points, but none of them had time to waste anymore. "Ben, get the translation band. Mina, bring the chamber back up to standard conditions. I want to talk to him."

She'd made her decision. She'd try the alien first, and use them both to get answers.

Ben leaned forward, his face pinching tight. "Dr. Shaw —"

"No, Ben. Get the device. Now. We don't have time to discuss this anymore."

Mina was busy with the controls. On the screen the lights came up, spotlighting the big black and orange-striped back. It threw his muscles and bristles into sharp relief. The wrinkled head rose, eyes blinking. Dyami yawned wide, showing a massive set of teeth. He snorted and rose up, standing on his legs while stretching his arms up. His wrinkled knuckles brushed the ceiling.

When Ben saw that Helen wasn't paying any attention to him, he got up and left the station. Helen ignored him and stayed focused on the screen. Her heart hammered in her chest.

Dyami was big. She wasn't used to big animals. Not that he was an animal, she knew that, but in her gut, that's how it felt. Like seeing polar bears at the zoo as a kid. One of the bears stood right by the glass of the enclosure, not looking at all the kids and families, just standing there with its head turned to the side. Ignoring them. The only animal that she had at home was her pug named Bilbo. Used to have, up until a year ago.

This was different. Dyami was a person, an intelligent, tool-using, space-traveling person, who happened to look like something crossed between a gorilla, warthog, tiger, and something unknown. Monstrous, except that his eyes looked intelligent and thoughtful. Right then he was looking around the cell, obviously expecting something to happen since the lights had come on.

On one of the screens lines danced.

Helen pointed. "What's that?"

"He's saying something," Mina said. "Infrasounds, we're recording."

Helen twisted around. "Ben!"

He came back, cupping the armband in his hands as if it was a precious thing. For once he had eyes for something other than her breasts.

Helen took the metal ring. It was lighter than she expected, cool to the touch. The surface was dark, with a refractive shine to it.

"I don't think we should do this," Ben said.

"And I think we're running out of time to get answers." Helen went around the stations, heading to the cell's airlock.

"Shouldn't we get some guards up here?" Mina asked. "I mean, what if he attacks you?"

Helen opened the outer door and looked back. "What good would that do him? If he attacks me, takes me hostage, it won't get him out of there, will it?"

She didn't wait for an answer. Truth was, her throat was dry and scratchy. The airlock had transparent doors. The alien moved inside, walking on all fours over to stand in front of the inner door.

Wow, he was big. His arms were like tree trunks. Helen had seen the videos with Fiona, the way Dyami had grabbed her and picked her up with one arm as if she was nothing but a doll.

The door sealed behind her. Holding the translation device in her hands, she called out to Mina. "Open the inner door."

Mina's voice came over the comm. "I hope you know what you're doing."

Dyami could hear them, but Helen didn't comment. The door in front of her hissed open, faster than she expected.

The instant it opened Dyami came forward. His big fists smashed into the floor with loud thuds. He was right up in front of the doorway, his massive head above hers. A giant, by comparison.

Helen tried to swallow, couldn't with her dry throat, and instead made her trembling limbs move. She stepped into the cell with him even though that step put her within a foot of the alien.

Hot breath blasted her face. It didn't smell bad, a grassy sort of smell. Helen looked up, up right into his eyes. She lifted the translation device.

"We'll be able to talk easier if you put this on."

Wow, her voice sounded calm. Helen took a deep breath. This could work, she could do this.

Dyami reached out and two big fingers curled around the device. His skin was fascinating, thick, but flexible. Dark, thicker on the knuckles, small orange bristles in the spaces in between.

With a snort, he sat down and slid the armband up onto his left arm. A swirl of blue lights spiraled around the device.

A vibration ran through the floor. Was something happening to the ship?

"Where is Muriel?" The armband asked, the voice deep and sounding angry.

That vibration was the alien speaking. That was the infrasound passing through the floor.

Helen folded her hands. "I'm Helen Shaw, the —"

More vibrations and the device spoke again. "I remember you. You were on the shuttle."

"Yes, I was on the shuttle. I'm in charge of the science teams."

"Where is Muriel?"

"Safe. In a cell." Helen gestured at the cell. "Much like this one. In light of your escape attempt, the Director felt that such measures were necessary."

"Necessary." Dyami moved, quickly, swinging away from her. He walked on all fours, hitting the floor, to the corner and sat down again. "You imprison us. Violate our rights. What do you want now?"

Violate our rights. This wasn't an animal on display, no matter what her instincts screamed animal. A person, intelligent, emotional, and capable of reason.

"No one wanted this. You attacked our people. You claim you are from the future, something that we've considered impossible. What would you do in our situation?"

Dyami's head swung around, showing teeth. "On my planet, such disputes are handled directly, between those affected. You don't command here, Blackstone commands."

"In this case, I'm in charge. We need

answers, Dyami. You can help us, and help yourself and Muriel in the process."

"Let us go. That is all you need to do."

Helen forced herself to take a step closer. "I don't think you meant to hurt anyone. Work with me, and I will get you out of this cell."

"And Muriel?"

"Yes, her too. We don't want to keep you locked up."

The translation device didn't say anything. Dyami's head turned toward the wall as if he found something fascinating in the texture.

Helen took another step, then one more, which put her in the middle of the cell. "Help me get you out of here. It'll only get worse otherwise. If I don't get the answers that Blackstone wants, then she's going to let Constantine take over. You don't want that."

"It doesn't matter, you are all the same. All part of the same crew."

"It does matter," Helen insisted. "I'm trusting you, right now. If you wanted to hurt me, what could I do? Trust me. Give us some answers."

Dyami snorted. His hand punched the floor, and Helen tried very hard not to jump.

The floor vibrated. "We gave answers. Travel to the time that was, the universe should not allow. Caution is necessary."

"You mean that we have to be careful not to change the future?"

"Yes."

"In all cases?" Helen spread her hands. "What if your information saved lives? Suppose, for example, that there was a terrible accident, one which would kill many people, and you went back in time before the accident. Shouldn't you prevent it from happening?"

"Saving lives would change the course of events, with unknown consequences." Dyami thumped the floor lightly. "Outcome might be worse."

"But you wouldn't know," Helen said. "And realistically, I'm sure that the people that were saved, plus everyone that loved them, would find the future a better place with them in it. In the end, I have to think that saving lives is always the better choice, the higher calling!"

The big alien didn't respond, he gazed at her steadily, not looking away, giving every sense of considering what she had said.

Helen waited. Time was running out for them all. If he didn't come around...

The floor finally vibrated. "I want to speak with Muriel Reinhard," the translation device said.

"Will you try to convince her to help us?"

"I may. Let me see her."

Letting him out would put them all at risk. It was a gamble, hopefully, one that might pay off. Muriel had to be on edge already. If she saw Dyami, and he asked her to tell them what she knew, that might do it. That might be enough.

"Okay," Helen said. "I'm trusting you. Convince Muriel to help us, and we'll see about getting you both back into more comfortable quarters."

Dyami reached up and touched the translation band. "I keep this, and our other belongings returned."

That wasn't going to make some people happy, particularly Ben Tol. More worrisome, if Blackstone disagreed.

As prices went, however, it wasn't much. "I think we can do that. If you and Muriel cooperate, then you can answer more than we would ever get studying those items."

Dyami's head dropped down, coming forward as he shifted his bulk, looking right in her eyes. "Do not deceive me, Doctor Helen Shaw."

She swallowed. "I'm not. I want answers. You help us, you both help us, and things get much better for everyone. That's all there is to it."

And if you don't? Then Constantine will get the answers, and he won't ask nicely. He won't bargain. He'll demand, and she suspected that he was very persuasive. Helen didn't say any of that. The threat was there anyway, hanging like a shadow behind the politeness.

She gestured to the airlock. "Come with me."

Turning her back on him, that was hard. Her shoulders tensed. She breathed out and walked to the airlock. By his breathing, hot and animal against her neck, she knew that Dyami was following close behind. She resisted the urge to look.

Instead, she looked up where the hidden camera eyes were located above the door. "Open it up. We're coming out."

Ben's voice came over the comm. "I'm not

sure if we should, maybe we should check with director Blackstone first? Don't we need her authorization to take the prisoner out of the cell or something? And we can't—"

"Open the door now, Dr. Tol! I have authorization already from Blackstone to do as I see fit to get the answers she wants."

Mina's voice came on, all business. "Opening the door, Dr. Shaw."

That was better. The airlock door slid open. Helen walked inside, all the way to the front and turned halfway. Dyami squeezed in through the door. His lips pressed together as he scrunched in on himself. The space was so small that they could barely fit in together. His thick arm pressed up against her body, his forearm thicker than her waist. The bristles poking out bent and weren't as sharp as they looked.

The inner door closed and the air cycled.

A strong vibration from Dyami echoed through the space, running up her arm.

"Uncomfortable," his translation device said.

"Yes, it is." Helen looked up. "Can we get this moving?"

Finally, the outer door hissed open, and

Helen stumbled out. Dyami stalked out after her. At the monitoring stations, Ben and Mina rose from their seats, moving back to keep their distance. Dyami glowered at the two of them.

"Let's go talk to Muriel," Helen said.

She didn't wait for anyone, just set off around the corner back to where Lukas Zelenka monitored Muriel. Dyami walked beside her, taking advantage of the wide aisles. Seeing them coming, Lukas stood up.

"Dr. Shaw, what is going on?"

Helen gestured at the darkened cell door. "Bring her out of there. I'm taking them to the conference room. Bring their belongings, clothes, devices, all of it."

Behind her, Ben spoke up again. "Dr. Shaw —"

"Ben," Helen said. She turned halfway. "We're doing this. Dyami has offered his cooperation, with his help we'll convince Muriel to cooperate as well. Why don't you help Mina get the rest of their belongings?"

No one said anything. Dyami stood hulking over them all.

"Now," Helen said.

Ben scowled, opened his mouth and

Mina hit his arm. He closed his mouth and without another word followed Mina out of the lab.

Helen turned back to Lukas. "Lukas, would you mind?

"Of course, Dr. Shaw." Lukas sat back down at the station. "We need to ease her into it. It will take some time."

"That's fine."

"What did you do to her?" Dyami asked.

"She isn't hurt," Helen said. "We used a technique to damp down her sensory input. From her perspective, she's been in the dark, experiencing a mild form of sensory deprivation. We'll ease her back into the light, and then we can let her out."

And hope that she decided to cooperate. Her time in the cell was hopefully just enough to show her that the alternatives could get much worse.

CHAPTER 38

Australia, 2876

The first break in the darkness was so faint that at first Muriel wondered if she imagined seeing her hand against the wall.

No, it wasn't imagination. Muriel waved her hand in front of her face. It looked real.

She turned her face up. The ceiling panels above now had the faintest glow, like phosphorescence or bioluminescence. Very, very faint, but there, a real break in the darkness.

How long had she been in the dark? Days, at least. Fed in the dark. Provided with a seat on a bucket to take care of her business. All of it mysteriously appearing in the darkness without sound or warning, there for her to find as she stumbled across them.

The light grew brighter like the sun slowly

rising. Her eyes didn't hurt from the light, but it was a relief to see again.

The cell was much like she had imagined, covered in padded panels, but smaller than she had pictured. In the dark, the cell had felt larger. It wasn't more than four meters on a side, octagonal in shape. On one face were clear lines indicating a door.

Her clothes sat neatly folded in front of the door, along with her comm and tablet, plus a few personal items.

That was a welcome surprise, if suspicious. Muriel crossed the cell and picked up the tablet. Everything worked, although it didn't show any outside connections beyond her comm.

"Muriel?" That was Dr. Shaw's voice, coming over speakers hidden behind the panels. "Please change, and then you may come out to join me and Dyami."

"What's the price?" Muriel asked.

"Please, I'll explain everything when you're ready," Helen answered.

Obviously an attempt to get her cooperation. Muriel picked up her clothes. They were watching, they were always watching, but real clothes were still better than the hospital gown. She didn't really worry about nudity anyway, years on Olinda with Subha and the others saw to that.

It only took her a moment to dress, brush her hair, and pocket her belongings. She'd kill for a shower. Maybe Helen could do something about that.

"I'm ready," she called.

The panel door slid back and to the side, revealing an airlock. The outer door was transparent. Dr. Shaw stood there, wearing those green workalls so popular with the *Australia* crew, her narrow face pinched and worried.

More welcome was Dyami's giant head, hanging above Shaw. He shoved past the doctor, nearly knocking Shaw over in the process, to come to the door.

It was really, really good to see him. Brock was lost a hundred years in the future, but at least she wasn't alone here. Dyami's presence made it better. Muriel stepped into the airlock.

There were others out there, too. Mina and Ben stood behind Shaw, Ben with a sour look on his face. Dyami had on his translator!

No wonder Ben looked like he was going to be sick. Helen had taken away his toy.

Lukas Zelenka sat at some sort of control station, controlling this cell, probably. And behind them all, a door opened, and a young man with red hair and his arm in a sling walked in. He stopped, and his eyes grew big when he saw Dyami.

"Whoa! What's going on, doc?"

Without turning, Helen said, "We're having a conversation, Clay. This is Muriel Reinhard and Dyami. That's Clay Yeager, one of our eager researchers."

Clay lifted his good hand. Helen smiled at Muriel and gestured.

"If you'll come with me. We'll go to the conference room. Clay, can you see to refreshments?"

"Yeah, uh, sure. I can do that."

"I'll help," Mina said.

Days kept in darkness, and they were trying to act like they hadn't done anything. Muriel gritted her teeth. If she lost it now, what good would it do? What if they put her back in that cell?

Her stomach tightened at the thought. She'd fight, tooth and nail, if they tried to lock her up in the darkness again. She'd experienced darkness before, in deep dives, but then she felt the pressure difference. Her senses told her which way was up, which way to go to get back to the light.

This was different. And if Muriel ever got back home, back to the future with Brock, she'd research species that saw in dark conditions. Infrared, maybe. Sonar, definitely. That fit with her aquatic adaptations, so long as it also worked in the air.

Helen led the way through the labs to a conference room. The whole place was set up for studying organisms, but most of the equipment was still new and little used. All of it was familiar from what she knew about the *Australia*. It was amazing to see such an infamous place looking new and unsoiled, full of promise in the exploration of a new world.

It was a strange feeling, walking into the conference room with members of the *Australia*'s xenology department. Muriel watched them take their seats, taking a chair herself across the corner from Helen.

Ben Tol, the breast-obsessed linguist. Lukas Zelenka, one of the names Muriel remembered from the stories about the *Australia*. Helen Shaw, another familiar name.

These same people locked her in the dark for days. They hadn't physically injured her, but she still trembled inside. No one met her eyes as they sat. They looked at each other, or at Helen, or at the table top. Guilt? A few shot nervous glances at Dyami as his reassuring bulk settled behind her chair.

"Let's not wait for Clay and Mina," Helen said. "We'll get started, I'm sure he will be back soon with refreshments. Dr. Gordon won't be joining us, we will go ahead with him too."

"Fine with me," Muriel said, although her throat was dry. "What do you want?"

Helen folded her hands on the table. She looked up, past Muriel's head. At Dyami. The lines around her mouth tightened.

Her eyes dropped, finally meeting Muriel's without flinching. There was resolve in her brown eyes.

"Blackstone wants answers. If we don't provide them, she's going to assign Constantine to get the answers."

There was a threat there. Talk to us, or you get to talk to him. Constantine, every inch of him rock hard and focused on his job. Helen's implication was that Constantine would use any means to get Muriel to talk.

"I see." Muriel's mind spun. The darkness and abyss waited. This was all wrong. Illegal, but what could she do? "I want to be clear. After locking me in the dark for days, you're telling me that if I don't cooperate, it will get worse?"

Helen's gaze didn't waver. Not even when Dyami let a rumbling growl slip between his teeth. "Yes, I'm telling you that it will get worse. That's not a threat. It's simply the fact."

"You do realize that the sorts of answers that Blackstone wants could change the future?"

"Do you know that it will make the future worse? What if knowledge of events to come helps us make things better? Isn't that possible?"

Muriel leaned back in the chair. Hadn't she asked herself those same questions? Was it worth the risk?

"Maybe," she admitted. "Except you might not like the answers. And you'd have to trust us, without evidence."

Helen nodded. "Let's talk about that, it's a good place to start. Our analysis shows that you're a chimera, not entirely human, that you have DNA from other species. What can you tell us about that?"

The door opened as Helen was asking her question. Mina and Clay came in carrying trays with glasses and plates of food.

"Oh, wait, let me put this down. I have so many questions!"

Beneath the table, Muriel rubbed her hands on her pants. Answering those questions seemed harmless enough, although recalling her earlier conversation with Blackstone, nothing was ever simple.

Mina and Clay quickly passed out glasses of water, a couple pitchers on the table, an entire pitcher for Dyami, and platters full of sliced cheeses, meat, crackers, and fruit.

It looked delicious. Then Mina dropped into a chair next to Muriel and leaned forward eagerly, a tablet in her hand.

"Okay. Thanks! So, what's the scoop?"

Lukas leaned forward as well. Everyone was looking at her, no one was paying attention to the food. Except Dyami had picked up his pitcher and sipped the water.

"You'll hear about that soon enough. Another example of Galactic technology bestowed on certain Rim species. We call the device the Moreau Pod."

"Like in *Dr. Moreau*?" Clay asked.

"Yes," Muriel said. "The Moreau Pod essentially allows you to rewrite the DNA of an organism. Like much of Galactic tech, we don't know exactly how it manages to do everything that it does, but we know how to use it. Aside from numerous medical applications, it is used by some to incorporate traits of other species into our DNA."

"That sounds very dangerous," Lukas said. "What sort of safeguards are available?"

"It's limited," Muriel said. "And you're right, the technology is very dangerous. It is difficult to model all the potential outcomes of even what seems like a small change. The pod doesn't prevent non-viable, even fatal challenges. What we'd call a Dumpty."

Clay laughed. "Oh, that's great. As in, can't put them together again."

"It's not great," Muriel said. They couldn't know that she'd been hunting down someone who had corrupted the technology to murder by mutation, from a distance. "It's terrible.

You can't imagine the horror of someone you knew mutated into something like that. The lucky ones die."

Clay subsided. "Yeah, I guess that'd suck."

"How could such a device even work?" Mina asked. "Even creating chimeras among relatively closely related species has challenges, but to rewrite a complete organism, and incorporate traits from species not even related? It sounds impossible."

"Yet you've seen my DNA," Muriel said. "I'd think that that would be proof enough. How else do you explain my aquatic adaptations?"

"Breeding?" Mina shrugged. "Gene-sculpting?"

"Except you can tell, can't you, that there is coding that doesn't come from an artificial source?"

"It looks like," Mina admitted.

"Assuming what you say is true," Lukas said, voice rising. "Where could we get one of these devices? The benefits are incalculable. It could be more important than the STC drive or artificial gravity!"

Muriel shook her head. "In this time? The Galactics haven't released the pods. At least not to any species I know of. Unless you have direct contact, I think you're out of luck."

Muriel's chair vibrated.

"The life code should not be altered," Dyami's translator said.

Muriel leaned back and looked up. Dyami's big wrinkled head hung over her chair. She smiled.

"I know how you feel about it, Dyami." Muriel looked at the rest of them. "The Eyotans don't approve of genetic engineering, in any form."

Lukas blinked, opened his mouth, closed it.

Helen raised a hand. "This is good. Thank you, Muriel. This is what we want, an open conversation. I'm sure that our medical and biology departments will have many more questions about this technology."

"I can give you more detail," Muriel said. "Although, without a pod, it won't matter much."

"Even so, I'm sure they will find it fascinating. That said, I think we should move on to more pressing issues. Muriel, comments you've made have suggested that you're familiar with our mission. The implication is there is something of historical significance about our mission, for it to be remembered a hundred years later."

There was the abyss again. Back into the darkness. Muriel looked around the table. Everyone was interested, waiting for her response.

What could she say?

CHAPTER 39

Orlando Pike's Shuttle

Millions of kilometers away from Olinda and still Pike's nanoweb memory scan continued feeding on my past. On the control deck, I had located command subroutines in the system responsible for sending the collected data back to Pike.

I thought about deleting the routines. Now that I considered it, I willed my hand to move out and eliminate the offending technology. Nothing happened. Just like down on Olinda, facing Pike right before he kissed me. While he kissed me.

I didn't feel any compulsion, no outside force grabbed my hand and prevented it from moving. My muscles didn't shake, I didn't break into a sweat trying to overcome his control.

Simply nothing happened. My hand

stayed peacefully on the arm of the chair. Around me, the largely empty control deck monitors continued displaying information even though no one was looking. No one except Drac. He'd come to the galley a few times since we left Olinda. He took care of his needs. Then spent the rest of the time lurking around the bridge. Now that we were underway he didn't limit himself to a single station.

Right then he was on my left, sitting at the station there. As far as I could tell, all of the stations were configurable, swappable to take on different functions.

I wanted to call him over, ask him to delete the routines, and my mouth didn't so much as open. I sat calmly, without any external sign of the struggle going on for my mind, and did nothing.

I switched the console to monitor communications from the Enhancer's colony. No problem doing that, no hesitation from my hand to carry out what I wanted.

I pulled up our flight plan. "Ten hours until we arrive at the Enhancer's colony."

See? I could talk to Drac too if it weren't about deleting Pike's hold on me.

"There are many people in the colony," Drac said. "We need a plan to get the tach field generator."

"We have Pike's offer to refund what they paid."

Drac hissed. He limped away from the console, favoring his injured wing. "Humans rarely reason. They strike out."

"I'd like to do this without fighting anyone for once." I wanted to believe that violence wasn't always the answer, although I had found it effective at times.

"We have the units in the hold," Drac said. "Better to use them."

Yes, Pike's gift. The android shock troops he had provided. Add them to the *Wisteria*'s armaments, and it was conceivable that we could mount a precise attack on the facility.

Except that we had no knowledge of the asteroid's interior or where the tach field generator might be kept. We had to get inside and gather information. Going in for a frontal assault might not work, and it was even possible that we might destroy the tach field generator in the process.

"Let's try a less confrontational approach," I said. "Let's try not to create new enemies."

"I will stay here," Drac said. "I will secure the ship."

"Makes sense. If I get in trouble, you may have to come in to get me."

"I will send in the units to retrieve you." Drac's dark face wrinkled up. For a split-second, his pink tongue tasted the air. "Esteemed One."

"Great. Not unless I signal."

"And if they prevent that?"

He had a point. "I go in, if I don't check in within an hour, then you make our position known. Good enough?"

"It will suffice."

Hopefully, Drac was right. I pulled up the data on the Enhancers. "I'm going to familiarize myself with everything that Pike has on the Enhancers before we get there. I'll flag anything that might help you if you have to dig me out."

Pike was thorough. Over the years he had sold them quite a bit of acquired tech besides the tach field generator. Plus weapons. They had enough heavy armaments from Pike alone to hold off the *Wisteria*, not counting the probability that they had acquired more from other suppliers. I tagged the batch for

Drac. If we did end up attacking the asteroid, we'd need to get inside their defenses first.

I found the detailed dossiers on the Enhancers themselves more interesting.

Hypatia Meier, the absolute leader of the Enhancer colony. Severe looking woman, with a long narrow face. Metallic implants rose in intertwined rows over the back of her head. No idea what purpose those served. Above each eyebrow was a row of tiny, sparkling rods that pierced the skin. Ornamentation, or augmentation? From Pike's notes, her enhanced abilities included sensing the truth, superior reflexes and strength, and enhanced mental abilities.

Pretty standard stuff for the Enhancers. Something more than that had to make Hypatia special enough to rise to the head of this colony.

Her second-in-command, Jim Cook, was a good-looking guy with a cleft chin and an easy smile. Unruly dark hair covered his head. A metallic tattoo surrounded his eyes, which were artificial devices, black orbs that glistened wetly. Pike speculated that the eyes tied into the tattoos to give him abilities to see pretty much any spectrum. Two sea-shell like devices covered his ears, some sort of hearing enhancement. The notes included the usual comments about his strength and reflexes.

How had Pike gotten those details? The profiles didn't say, but both were marked as extremely lethal fighters. He must have sent someone against them and observed the result.

A risky gamble, but one that had provided information.

The files contained equally detailed profiles on other Enhancers that he had dealt with and notes on many more which had just been observed.

I tagged summaries on the key profiles and sent them to Drac.

Seeing the Enhancers, my opinion of our ability to take the tach field generator by force dropped even more. How could the two of us, even backed up by the weapons on the *Wisteria* and the android shock troops, really expect to take on the Enhancers?

Unlike his profiles on the key Enhancers, Pike's information on the asteroid was sketchy. Like the Enhancers, it had been drastically altered. Initial surveys showed it as an oblong shaped heavily cratered asteroid, a collection of rocks and ices and carbon compounds. Basic ingredients from the solar system formation, an excellent collection for someone wanting to create an independent colony.

That was then, now it didn't even look like the same body. The mass was slightly higher, and an artificial gravity field had pulled the materials into a spherical shape. A thin atmosphere surrounded the sphere, primarily nitrogen with a few trace elements. Not breathable, apparently an out-gassing from the contraction of the asteroid material.

A honey-comb of energy-collecting panels covered the surface, giving the asteroid an eerie similarity with the Gingerbread House. That ancient alien station was now a thriving hub of activity in orbit around Olinda. The design of the Enhancer's collectors suggested that they had borrowed technology designs from the Gingerbread House.

Pike had gathered that much detail on the Enhancer's home base. Just that, nothing on the interior. In itself, that was significant.

I sent the key points over to Drac's console. He hissed as he read the details. I waited for him to finish. When he finally turned his black eyes on me, I said what we both had to know.

"We can't go in there shooting. We won't get anywhere."

"Your plan does not suffice."

"No, it doesn't. But we need the tach field generator. Without it, we have no hope of getting Muriel and Dyami back."

"That is not our objective!" Drac hoped off his seat and lurched toward me. "Your obligation is to recover the stolen artifact for us! It is our salvation!"

Right. The Nosferans had somehow found the tach field generator a hundred years ago, and their plans had been disrupted by Muriel and Dyami. That was why they'd sought me out with a picture of the two of them taken a hundred years ago.

Up until then, I hadn't known what had happened to the Tretan's shuttle. Now everyone wanted to get their hands on that tech. The Nosferans, to resurrect whatever their plan was for the salvation of their species; the Tretan, as payment for his lost shuttle, the destroyed Moreau weapon Kelwyn had used, and what I owed him for genetic samples.

No telling what the Tretan wanted with the generator; Pike, who had his own agenda for the device; the Enhancers, I didn't have a clue about them; and me.

I needed the generator to find a way back to save my friend and the woman I loved. I didn't care about the rest of it. I'd help any of them if it got me closer to saving Muriel and Dyami.

I knew too well, better than anyone, what they were in for, and I wasn't going to leave them there. The Nosferans' picture was the only historical proof of their presence in the past. That gave me hope.

Drac's clawed fingers dug into my legs. The sharp tips dug into my flesh. I shoved him away with my foot. He stumbled and nearly fell. I stood up.

"I get it," I said. "We're on the same path. What you want, and what I want are the same thing."

"For now," Drac muttered.

"Yes, for right now. We work together. I keep my promise, and you keep yours."

"We still need a plan!"

I stepped around the chair. My C'lacktal

tentacles played along the seat back. "I have a plan. If you can't beat them, join them."

Let him figure it out. I was tired. I wanted to rest before we reached the Enhancer's asteroid. "I'm going to get some sleep before we get there. Wake me up if there's an emergency."

Drac hissed. I ignored it.

Join the Enhancers. It sounded simple, which probably meant it wasn't. I had no intention to become some sort of cyborg, but they might be able to help me with the nanowire's Pike had put in my brain.

And who knew? I might be able to work out a deal with them. If they'd listen.

Chapter 40

2876, Australia

Muriel nibbled a cracker, trying to think how to tell the scientists what they wanted to know. The words spun around in her head like a school of fish, slipping out of reach.

The break was almost over. They were looking at her, clearly wondering what she was going to say.

Dyami crouched beside her chair, bringing his orange-striped head down to her height. Muriel resisted the urge to reach out and scratch his chin. He wasn't a pet. He might be young for his species, but he was an intern with the Shanley Walsh agency.

Shanley. Her heart ached thinking of him left alone back on Olinda, no word on what happened to any of them. A mystery that he wasn't likely to solve, even as clever as he was. *Would be.* As old as he was, he wasn't even born yet!

"I don't know what to do," Muriel whispered to Dyami. "Whatever I do, it could change the future."

"For us, there is only now," Dyami's translator whispered back.

It *whispered.* Muriel had no idea that he could whisper with the device. Ben Tol had noticed too, he turned sharply, squinting at them suspiciously.

"Thank you," Muriel said. He was right. Everyone said that time travel was impossible, who knew what the consequences were? They had to be concerned with what was happening now.

Muriel nibbled another cracker.

The door opened, and Olivia Blackstone walked in, Constantine and the other security man, Dustin on her heels.

Muriel sucked air, and cracker crumbs into her throat. The cracker choked her, and she started coughing. Helen handed her a glass of water.

As she sipped the water, Lukas Zelenka rose and offered his seat to the director.

"Thank you," Blackstone said. She stepped in front of the seat but didn't sit. She leaned forward on the table, looking at Muriel. "Are you all right, Ms. Reinhard?"

Muriel nodded. Another sip of water cleared her throat. She breathed easier and put the glass down before her shaking hand could spill it.

The security men stayed standing behind Blackstone as she sat, her hands flat on the conference table.

"I realize the difficulty we've put you both under," Blackstone said. "I regret the necessity, but I must know what you know. Please proceed."

Proceed. Just like that. The please did nothing to soften it. Muriel looked back at Blackstone, heat rising in her chest. "You realize what you're asking may jeopardize the future? All of you here in this room are absolutely willing to violate our rights, to torture us, and you don't even know why? It doesn't matter, because in your view we don't count. I want some assurances before I get into details."

Blackstone shook her head. "I will not be blackmailed or held hostage. Constantine."

Without warning, everything around Muriel vanished. The room, gone. Blackness. No sound. No voices. She reached for the chair beneath her and found nothing. There wasn't even anything to tell her that her arm had moved. She thought it, but had it happened? She shouted, thought she did, and nothing happened. All of her senses were gone. She was nothing but thought in the abyss.

Like a wave crashing across her, it all came flooding back. Muriel gasped and jumped back. The chair hit her legs.

Dyami snorted, and his big hands caught her, steadied her on her feet.

Across the table, Constantine held a small black device.

It all made sense now. They'd done something to her, she'd read about it. Neural scramblers generated an interference pattern that prevented sensory input. It was first developed as a medical treatment, then strictly regulated when people abused the technology.

"She's cooperating!" Helen stood up, one hand reaching out to Muriel. "You didn't need to do that."

Blackstone settled into the seat, her flawless face expressionless. "That was two seconds. Take it as a clarification of the situation. Muriel, we can turn the neural scrambler on and leave you like that. After an hour, you'll think a day has gone past. Nothingness, not even the sound of your own heart to measure time. You will answer our questions fully, without reservation."

Dyami glowered at the director. Vibrations traveled through Muriel's arms, where his big hands still braced her.

"This is wrong," he said. "Laws exist against this."

"Human laws, applying to humans, and under current definitions neither of you are human. I believe I have made myself clear. Please sit, compose yourself, and begin answering our questions."

Muriel sat down in the chair, grateful for its solidity and Dyami's presence behind her. They could strip all that away, drop her back into that abyss of nothingness.

Maybe if she knew, absolutely the consequences, that might change things. Maybe she'd resist.

Not now. Not without knowing. Muriel

took a breath and then lifted her head, meeting Blackstone's gaze.

"I'm not answering because of the neural scrambler.

Despite whatever decisions the rest of you make, there are billions of lives at stake. Right now, and in the future. Dyami said that for us there is only now, and I think he's right. I can't pretend ignorance."

"I'm glad you've decided to cooperate," Blackstone said. "I'm sure there is a great deal for you to tell us."

"Yes, although if the future is mutable, then my knowledge of events will cease to be of any use as those events change." Muriel shook her head. "Unless by changing those events my own memories change to reflect the new future. I don't know what is going to happen."

Helen spoke up. "I feel like we're opening Pandora's box here."

"We are," Blackstone said. "And we will face the consequences. Given this opportunity, we can't turn back. We do the same thing we've always done, and make the best decisions we can based on available information."

Muriel laughed. "I've gone around and around on this. What if I say something that changes events and I'm never born in the future? Do I disappear here? If time travel is possible, don't we also have to deal with paradoxes?"

"Nature is full of paradoxes," Blackstone said. "If the Galactics have revealed anything of themselves, it is that our understanding of the universe only scratches the surface."

"That's true," Muriel said. "But you wanted to know what I know about your ship, what's going to happen to you and your crew, specifically?"

Blackstone nodded.

Time to take the plunge. "The scout ship that was destroyed in the CY-HC-2347 system was attacked by a species humanity calls Nosferans. That was an isolated incident until the *Australia* showed up and started humanity's first interstellar war."

Chapter 41

Amundsen station was even smaller in person than in the pictures I'd seen. Several of the domes were unfinished and unpressurized. After spending two days in a hopper, skipping across the Martian surface, I was ready to get out and stretch my legs. Instead, I was met by Amundsen security as soon as I disembarked.

There were three of them. A woman leading two men. All had that cute, diminutive Martian look, but in the woman, it came together with fine, perfect features and lovely almond-shaped eyes, a pale blue. Her yellow hair was tied back. She stepped forward smartly, cocking her head to the side. Red lips parted in a wide grin.

"My, you're big! You'll have to watch your

step. We get pretty tight out here." She stuck out her hand. Her grip was strong and lingered a second longer than was strictly necessary. "Riley Palmer, chief of security for Amundsen, such as it is. This is all of us. Chan Lee, and Ricky Palmer. My brother, if you can believe it."

Ricky grinned, and he did look like a masculinized version of Riley, except his hair and eyes were dark.

The third member, Chan Lee, had an olive complexion and a broader face, but he also smiled brightly. "We don't get many non-Martians out here."

Riley shook her head. "I can't remember the last time it happened. Pohl Station sent over the files on Emrys Nash, the coroner's report, and said you'd be coming out. I can't say I see the need, it looks pretty clear."

"Except we don't know how he got there, who he was with, or why he might kill himself like that."

"And you'd like a tidier package?"

I heard the suggestion in her voice, and it turned me cold. It wasn't the suggestion itself, but the circumstances, seeing as I was there to talk about a man who put a rock hammer into his brain.

"I like answers," I said. "Emrys Nash didn't get down to Pohl Station on his own. Some sort of vehicle took him there, he got out, ran away from it, and then bashed in his own head."

Riley's smile vanished. All brisk and business-like, she nodded. "Absolutely. We're here to help, give you anything you need."

She smiled brightly. "And when you're ready to call it for the day, give me a ring. I'll see that you get fed."

Then she winked.

Before my brain even finished processing that fact, she turned and bounced away, patting Ricky on the shoulder as she passed. "Give him the tour. I've got work in the office to do."

That left the three of us. Chan rubbed his hands together. "Yes, Mr. Marsden, what may we show you first?"

I looked at Ricky. "Is your sister always like that?"

Ricky shook his head. "Most of the time she's mean. She likes you."

"Great, thanks." I looked back at Chan. "Let's go see where Emrys lived."

Not only were there fewer domes at Amundsen Station, but it also had fewer levels. Emrys' apartment was on the first level, inherited according to Chan, from his parents.

It was a small suite carved into the rock, sealed and pressurized along with the rest of the base. The sealant left the rock visible, a nice touch if you enjoyed living in a cave. Scattered lights provided pockets of overlapping illumination, but on the whole, the place seemed dark. Tidy.

"He lived alone?"

"Yes," Chan said.

"Records don't show any living relatives," Ricky added. "Bachelor, no registered relationships."

And on Mars, any romantic relationship with the potential of creating offspring required registration and genetic compatibility testing.

Even so, unregistered men and women were rare and temporary. There wasn't enough of a population to take someone out of the genetic pool.

"Had he broken off a relationship recently?"

Ricky's hand swiped at the air. Apparently looking at augmented reality screens. "Nothing for two years, not since he left Barsoom to come here."

Barsoom was one of the oldest settlements on Mars, in the Southern polar region.

"He went clear around the planet? After a break-up? He must have really wanted to get away from her. Where is she now?"

Ricky's mouth opened. He closed it and looked at me with a look I've come to recognize. It reveals the person, their knowledge of the crime. His eyes flitted away. He swiped at the air carelessly.

"It doesn't say."

"I know better," I said. I stepped closer, looming over the smaller Martian. "A man died, Ricky. No one is calling it a crime, not yet at least, but if you're trying to cover for someone, it could get worse."

Chan said, "Here, let me look it up —"

Ricky waved his hands. "No!"

"Oh," Chan said. His eyes were focused on the air in between us, clearly seeing something I couldn't. Then he looked at Ricky. "We have to tell him."

Ricky's shoulder's sagged. "It was Riley. She never said I had no idea."

"Riley, your sister Riley?"

Ricky nodded.

"Okay," I said. "Let's go talk to her, see why she didn't mention that she had a connection to the victim."

Ricky stepped in front of me.

"What are you doing?" Chan asked. "Are you crazy?"

"No, Chan, stay out of this." Ricky pointed a finger at my chest. "You can't come in here and demand to interrogate my sister. You're nothing but a private detective!"

I took a step closer to Ricky. "You're right. I should file my complaint with the citizen's bureau and let them conduct their own investigation into Emrys' death. I would think they would want to do that anyway, standard procedure when someone dies."

"She didn't do anything," he insisted. "If you file that report, the accusations could ruin her. How can she do her job, if people think she murdered that man?"

"No one said she murdered him, but she

might be able to answer questions about the state of his mind."

"And if she cooperates?"

"I've got this, Ricky." It was Riley's voice in the doorway to Emrys' Nash's apartment.

Her cheeks were flushed pale red, it gave her more color, and with her blue eyes and golden hair, she looked like a dream. She stepped inside, shutting the door, and spread her hands.

"I like this better. Easier to read your thoughts, down here, away from the noise above."

"Read my thoughts?" I asked.

"Yes, sort of. It's a knack I have, thanks to engineering from our parents. A bit of gene-sculpting to enhance my senses, it gives me a clue what's going on in someone's mind."

Riley came closer, biting her lip. "Now you know my secret, want to tell me your secrets?"

"I don't know what you want to hear, I don't have any secrets."

"No? I find it hard to believe that a man from Seabrook came here to Mars and didn't bring along some secrets. You must have a few juicy tidbits."

I shook my head. "Sorry to disappoint. I'm more interested in your relationship with Emrys Nash. You followed him here after he broke off the relationship?"

Riley shook her head. "No. I wouldn't do that to him. The colonial board asked me to take over as chief of security here. I thought it'd be okay, we hadn't seen each other since the split."

"It wasn't okay."

"You're like an open book," Riley said. She moved closer, reaching out to run her hand up my chest. "You find me attractive, but our size difference makes you uncomfortable."

I took her hand and moved it away. "If you can read me, you know I'm more interested in answers than seduction."

Her smile widened. "We can't have both?"

Behind her Ricky looked away, so did Chan. She noticed. "Am I making you boys uncomfortable?"

Her lip pouted briefly, tempting me to kiss it. I ignored the urge.

"Fine." Riley stepped back and clasped her hands. "Answers, then. Not nearly as much fun. Emrys hadn't broken it off with me, it was the other way around. He couldn't take it and went as far away as he could get. Having me back in the same station was too much, I guess. He had wanted to get back together, and the day before he disappeared I turned him down. But I didn't have anything to do with his death."

Ricky stepped close to his sister and touched her arm. "You should have told me."

"I was dealing with it."

I was tempted to believe her. She sounded sincere. It answered some questions, but not all of them. We still had to find out who had helped Emrys, and why.

CHAPTER 42

Wisteria, at Enhancer's colony

I hadn't thought about Riley Palmer in a very long time. Pike's trip down my memory lane was digging up old cases.

At least while the scan was on that, it wasn't leading me down my connection with the Nosferans. I didn't want to go back to those memories. Even seeing Drac dredged them up, never letting me put it entirely behind me.

Back on the control deck, Drac back sitting at the right-hand station, I studied the image on the screens.

Right now the Enhancers presented a bigger problem. The asteroid had gone from a bright speck to a fully-realized world in front of us while I slept, dreaming of Mars. Behind it, Miranda, the Jovian that it led, was a large world of swirling orange, yellow, blue and red gasses. A storm in those cloud banks was bigger than Olinda. It was still far off, but the details were visible on the screen. The asteroid appeared bigger by virtue of being so close.

It reminded me even more of the Gingerbread House, but the panels were different. Solar panels that caught the light, each one composed of many small rectangles, each angling like the leaves on a plant to catch the most light possible. Nearly the entire surface was converted into one large collector, drinking in the light from the sun.

It was an ingenious way to power the colony, easily fabricated and simple to maintain. It would provide a constant source of power. Although many people relied on galactic tech for power, this was a very human system. It was fascinating that they had gone that route rather than a more exotic power supply.

"Any chatter?"

"Chatter?" Drac asked.

"Attempts to communicate? Any signals from the colony?"

"No. Systems detect only leakage from electrical activity within the colony."

They had to have detected the *Wisteria*. We weren't on an aggressive approach, just matching trajectories.

"Let's give them a call," I said.

I flipped the controls to open a wide broadcast to the station.

"This is the shuttle *Wisteria*, Brock Marsden speaking. Come in, colony."

If they had a name for their colony, it wasn't in Pike's files. It seemed like a strange thing for them to keep to themselves.

No reply on standard channels. I switched to quantum channels, leaving the standard channels monitored for a response.

"*Wisteria* to the colony, please respond."

This time I got a response. "*Wisteria*, access to this colony is restricted to authorized trading partners. Your shuttle matches one in our system, but not your identity. Please explain."

That was something at least.

"The shuttle belongs to Orlando Pike. We're..." I had to think about that for a second. "Partners. He knew of my interest in enhancements and suggested I come to speak with you. He said I should ask for Hypatia Meier."

"We require a full background, and genetic profile from you and all those on board before your request to speak with our Guide will be considered."

"Full background? Genetic profile? What for?"

"It is required," came the flat answer. "Comply, or vacate this region."

"It'll take me a little time to pull that together. Pike didn't say anything about this."

"You have five minutes."

"Okay," I said. "You'll have it."

Five minutes. I closed the link. "Drac, get working on your profile. Highlights only, they can't expect an exhaustive biography in five minutes. Just the basics."

"I dislike this," Drac hissed.

"Dislike it all you want." I pulled up a simple format and flicked over relevant details. "Do it. We have to get in there."

Drac hissed and went to work.

I populated the table with key details. I hesitated a second or two over my age, then included my birth date in standard time, and the planet. A hundred years, that had to impress even Enhancers. I didn't hide being a

Moreau. They might not use the technology, but they had to appreciate the results.

Thirty seconds before the deadline I opened the link and sent over my packet. "Here you go. One other following, there are only two of us on board."

Drac finished, and I passed his packet over the link without reviewing it. I had to trust that he wanted the mission to succeed as much as I did.

"Information received," answered the same voice as before. "You may enter an orbit 5,000 kilometers above the surface while your information is evaluated."

"Thank you —" Nothing but a dead channel. They hadn't stayed connected.

Drac hunched on his chair, wings wrapped around his skinny legs. "What now?"

"We wait," I said.

If they didn't let us come down, our chances of getting back the tach generator diminished greatly. The first priority had to be getting down on the ground. Legwork, the first rule of detective work, only worked if you had legs on the ground. If I got down there, there was a chance I could figure out a way to get to the generator. From up here? Not a chance.

The answer came back ten minutes later.

"Our Guide has granted you landing permission. Slave your controls to our signal. Our control will bring you in."

"Understood, thank you." I switched over the autopilot controls and kept my finger on the disconnect in case the Enhancers tried anything.

Although, if they fired on us while we were under their control, it was unlikely that I could disconnect fast enough. Even with my reflexes.

The projected course took us down into a crater among the panels, straight edges and dark, a pit in the side of the colony. Obviously some sort of docking facility, a full thirty kilometers across, covered by interlocking panels in the shadowed depth. Six panels near the center lifted upwards like a flower opening.

"Coherent energy beams have locked onto this vessel," Drac said.

"Lasers? What are they doing?"

"Guiding the vessel."

Of course, they were. On the screen, the

asteroid grew until it filled the view. The massive crater swallowed up the view, and then the opening began to glow. The light was faint, blue and pulsed along the edges of the panels.

Nothing threatened the *Wisteria*. After running into non-organics on the Gingerbread House, burn-addicts on Gretel, and Pike's own synchronized mercenaries, I was more accustomed to threats. Apparently, the Enhancers were willing to talk.

Their systems guided the shuttle through the opening, which immediately began closing once we passed inside. I noted that, but was more focused on the inside of the crater.

The *Wisteria* rotated, descending hull down into the crater. Local artificial gravity switched off in favor of the colony's gravity. Suddenly I felt ten pounds heavier.

Docking rings surrounded the sides of the chamber, connecting to thousands of ships. Many were no bigger than the *Wisteria*, sleek and cylindrical in shape. Others were larger, clusters of cylinders connected by spheres. The ships created a forest of shapes around us, like descending into a crystalline cavern.

Bluish lights from the docking rings

reflected off the clusters of the ships, and filled the place with a moonlit glow, reminding me of the light of Hansel and Gretel on the shimmer shells along Subha's beach back on Olinda. It was beautiful.

Although what did the Enhancers need with thousands of ships? All docked here, as if they were seeds, waiting for the moment when they would be cast adrift on the interstellar winds.

Maybe that was exactly what they were, seeds to spread the Enhancers far and wide across the galaxy.

The *Wisteria* was guided to dock in an empty space on one of the rings. I scanned through the images and found hundreds of other gaps. Either they hadn't built all their ships yet, or they had ships out now.

A dull echo rang through the *Wisteria* as clamps locked on.

A man appeared on the screen, a live feed. He was mostly human, with silvery eyes and a variety of piercings on his ears. No hair, his bald head glistened beneath blue lights. Too bad smells didn't translate over the transmission, it might have given me a clue to what he was thinking.

"Please remain in your ship until the inspection team arrives. Make no attempt to interfere with their inspection of the vessel. Is that understood?"

"Yes, we understand."

The connection closed. I settled back in the chair to wait. Drac spun his seat around.

"If they search the ship, they will discover the androids!"

I pointed at the main screens, showing the voluminous space outside, shinning with thousands of ships. "What chance do you think we have against that?"

That was one of the problems with Nosferans. They always thought they were better than anyone else that they encountered. Discovering the Galactics should have come as a big blow to them. Instead they treated the Galactics like gods.

Which probably had something to do with their reasons for wanting the tach field generator a century after it was taken.

Drac hissed at me and turned back to his console. "A party has arrived at the airlock."

"Open it. Let's be friendly and go meet them."

I slid off the chair, legs feeling heavy in

the stronger gravity field, and headed off the control deck. Once I was moving I put the gravity change out of my mind. It wasn't enough to make a big difference. Drac hadn't moved.

I paused in the doorway. "Drac, come on. Let's not keep them waiting."

Claws scratched over the controls, and then Drac flopped off the chair. His whole posture was slumped. I didn't think the gravity was the main cause, mostly he looked drawn in on himself, unhappy. Had to be stressful going into this with the Mother Sack, and with an injured wing. He couldn't take flight to escape.

It was almost enough to make me feel sorry for him. Except that the Nosferans didn't feel pity or remorse, so I didn't give them any in return.

We reached the airlock as the inner door opened. The Enhancers went in for dark colors, none of them black. Dark, dark reds, blues and the first two through the door wore a dark green that shimmered in the light. Those two, one a man and the other a woman, were masses of muscles piled on muscles beneath the leathery outfits. Each had a variety of piercings, and they entered holding out their hands. A metallic pattern was bonded to the skin of their hands, like a complicated circuit board imprinted on skin. They moved their hands around in motions that brought to mind martial arts, but I figured they were scanning the area with their implants.

To my scent-sight, the group glowed with bluish energy. They smelled of metal and health. They smelled eager, and yet calm. Anticipating something.

I didn't reach for my weapon. I didn't make any threatening move.

Behind the green-clad scanners, came three others. None of them Hypatia or anyone that I recognized. The man in the center was thin and tall, with pale skin and metallic eyes. Metal ridges ran back over his head in place of hair, but he did have a dark goatee. With his dark, almost black, red suit, he basically looked evil. On purpose? A way to intimidate visitors?

"Hello," I said, breaking the silence of their arrival. "Brock Marsden. That's Drac, a nickname. He can tell you his name in his language."

Drac made a bunch of whistling, squeaking noises. I recognized it, but there was no way that I could make those noises.

Behind the man with the goatee were two women in dark blue suits. Same height, same athletic build, but where the one was pale, the other was dark-skinned, a deep brown. Again, each had a variety of piercings in eyebrows and ears. The pale one had artificial eyes, although they resembled normal eyes with a metallic glint to them and a larger than normal iris.

The man with the goatee nodded. "Inspector Bueller. I am here to impound your vessel and take you and your companion into custody."

I took a step back, just one, and the two green-clad mountains of muscle reached for me from both sides.

I'm fast, faster than a normal human. I dropped and rolled beneath their arms. I came up standing in front of Bueller. I didn't want to fight them. I wanted to talk. I resisted the urge to grab him and use him as a hostage.

"Wait," I said.

The inspector held up a hand. Without

looking behind me, using my scent-sight, I saw both of the enforcers settle back into a relaxed pose. Drac huddled back against the bulkhead, glowing like a pearly angel. The rust and blood smell of him had increased, presumably from fear.

"This doesn't need to get out of hand. We came willingly, and were told that we could talk to Hypatia Meier, your Guide?"

Bueller nodded. "And you will have that opportunity, once we take you into custody and finish our investigation."

"How long is that going to take?"

"That entirely depends on what we discover. You will not have an opportunity to harm us."

If I wanted, I could crush his windpipe with one blow, faster than he could react. Or sting him with my C'lacktal tentacles and drop him to the deck convulsing with the poison. Unless, of course, his enhancements also included faster reflexes.

Bueller shook his head. "I suggest you put such thoughts from your mind."

"You're a mind reader, now?"

"No more than you are," Bueller smiled.

It did little to warm him. "Now, let's proceed without the dramatics?"

"I get jumpy with people try to grab me. If we're going to go, I can get there on my own two feet."

Inspector Bueller stepped to the side and gestured. "Let us proceed, then."

"Drac, come on."

In my scent-sight, Drac pushed away from the wall and hobbled forward, leaving ghostly trails behind him. Streamers of orange poured out of the wound in his wing, smelling sour. Infection? Pain? Maybe the Enhancers could help if we could get on their good side.

From them, I didn't get much of a reading. There was a general scent of ozone and a peachy odor of eagerness, even happiness. They enjoyed what they were doing. Why? Was that normal for them?

I waited for Drac to get in front of me, and let him lead the way. It kept us all to his pace. The muscle-bound enforcers followed right behind, to either side, the rest of the Enhancers stepped aside to let us pass.

"Take them to processing," the inspector said. "The Guide will want a full report."

Drac's stride faltered. I reached out with my human hand and touched his oily shoulder, nudging him on. He hissed and jerked away.

Yeah, I didn't like touching him either.

Chapter 43

2876, Terran Expedition, Australia

The mood in the conference room was like ice. No one moved, all frozen in place by Muriel's words. Helen breathed in, let it out, and breathed in again.

War.

Wasn't humanity past war by now? After the Diaspora, populating the worlds of the solar system, hadn't they moved past that sort of thing? The solar system offered so many worlds, so many resources, and then when contact was made, and the STC drive opened up the wider galaxy, what reason was there for conflict anymore?

Clay laughed, shattering the ice that held them all. "Interstellar war? You've got to be kidding! What's the sense in that?"

Blackstone held up a hand and Clay slumped back in his seat. "Muriel, go on."

Helen studied Muriel's face. She looked young, although with the changes to her DNA, who knew how old she really was, but the most chilling thing was the resolve that came over Muriel's features. She looked right back at them all and her mouth tightened before she spoke.

"Nosferans, we call them that because they look like giant bats, somewhat. They are smaller than us, lightly built, but very strong."

"They fly?" Mina asked.

"Yes. Very well. Carnivorous, curious, and technically advanced. As species go, they're our contemporaries, although they've had access to STC drives for at least two hundred years longer than humanity. Still, in the spans of time we're talking about, that isn't that much. They've colonized four other solar systems since then." Muriel leaned forward. "Nosferans believe themselves superior to most other species."

Clay spoke up again. "Even the Galactics?"

Muriel shook her head. "No, they worship the Galactics as gods, more or less. In this time, they aim to prove their worth to the Galactics, hoping to join the Glittering Throng themselves."

It was amazing. A whole new species, one that they hadn't had any contact with, and they were going to be the first. And, from what Muriel said, it would go horribly wrong.

"What happened?" Helen asked. "Why was the scout ship attacked?"

"Why not?" Muriel countered. "From the Nosferan viewpoint, it was intruding into their territory. They're aggressive. We only have their fragmented report, which you've seen."

Blackstone shook her head. "I haven't shared that at this time."

What? Helen looked at the director. "Why not?"

"It wasn't time." Blackstone nodded. "I will make it available, but I would rather continue right now."

Muriel shrugged. "You can watch it yourself. There isn't much there. Telemetry, data on CY-HC-2347, and crew logs before the attack. There's a mention of bringing something back, but no details. We don't really know what happened before the ship was destroyed."

Looking straight at Blackstone, Muriel continued. "Director Blackstone was briefed while the *Australia* expedition was being planned. Although the scout ship had been destroyed, the potential for contact was too irresistible. A small scout ship was one thing, but a full expedition vessel was another. A large enough show of force, it was thought, would provide an opportunity to make contact while offering a deterrent to another attack."

Constantine spoke up. "Are you saying they have no common sense?"

"Common sense?" Muriel asked. "Common sense for one species isn't the same as another species. It's possible to work with another species, to see them build ships and cities, have children, and fall into the trap of thinking that they think just like we do. They don't. Physics make some things the same, but when it comes to something like common sense, that's not at all the same. Ask Dyami, you've got another perspective right here."

Vibrations rumbled through the table.

Helen lifted her fingers from the surface. The Galactic translation device spoke up, except it didn't sound like a translator at all, but the alien's voice.

"Humans don't always make sense," the alien said. "You talk much and avoid much. You expect the universe to behave the way you want, and try to change it when it doesn't. You refuse to see what others see."

Voices raised around the table, Clay and Lukas and Mina, all trying to talk at once. Ben joined in too. Helen folded her hands in her lap.

Was he right? Was that humanity? It was, at least from his perspective. There was that truth to it. This whole ship embodied that, to some extent. They were going out in the universe, telling themselves that it was in friendship and peaceful exploration, with weapons on board. For defense. In case anyone they encountered didn't see things quite there way, going into a situation that had already gone wrong.

Without even telling most of the crew that they were going into that situation.

"Are you saying that we should turn back?" Helen said loudly, looking at Muriel, not at Blackstone. "Should we turn the expedition around?"

Muriel opened her mouth, but Blackstone spoke first.

"That isn't an option, Dr. Shaw. We have our mission. It hasn't changed. None of this changed our mission. We will assess CY-HC-2347. With Muriel's assistance, we will avoid whatever disagreement happened in her timeline between the Nosferans and us."

"If we go back, we can't be here to start a war," Helen said. "Maybe we should, it'd —"

"The company defines the parameters of our mission," Blackstone said. "The Board decides, and they've already ruled on this matter. We continue."

Blackstone stood up. "Muriel, thank you for your cooperation. I'm glad that there will be no more difficulty. We will return you and Dyami to your suites. Constantine will coordinate your briefings, with your help it sounds like we will advert a terrible misunderstanding and save many lives. Thank you both. If you'll excuse me."

With that Blackstone turned and left with Dustin following her. Constantine stayed at the table. It was unbelievable. Helen watched her leave, feeling numb. The others must be thinking the same thing, there was a silence around the room. Muriel was looking up at Dyami, holding onto one of his sausage-thick fingers.

After the director was gone, Constantine rubbed his jaw. "Alright. I think we've all got a lot to think about. Dr. Shaw, if you'll see to returning our guests to their quarters? I think we'll resume the briefing in an hour. We can hold it there, just us. I'll arrange a schedule so that everyone will get an opportunity to ask their questions."

Helen found her voice. "Yes. I'll take care of it."

"Thank you." Constantine nodded at Muriel. "Ms. Reinhard, I'll look forward to our conversation."

Muriel didn't say anything. Constantine left. Then Muriel looked at Helen.

"You might have been right, avoiding the system might have been the only chance to avoid this," Muriel said.

Everyone was watching them. Helen reached out and took Muriel's left hand and gave it a squeeze. "We'll all just have to make sure it doesn't happen, that's all."

"Everything I tell you won't matter if you don't listen," Muriel said.

"We'll listen, I promise," Helen said. The promise tasted empty on her tongue.

Chapter 44

Amundsen Station, Mars

After Riley's confession, we went back to work discovering who Emrys might have contacted for help. His communication records didn't show anything. The man had few contacts, and those recordings he had were unexceptional.

"I'm not finding anything here," Riley said, returning from searching through Emrys' belongings. "I had no idea he was so cut off from everyone."

I had discovered three recordings that Emrys had made to Riley. Each, asking her out to dinner, and in each she turned him down, gently, compassionately, encouraging him to see others. Even offering to help set him up with someone. Each time he refused.

I hadn't said anything, but there must

have been something in my body language that Riley read. She came over and placed a hand on my shoulder.

"What'd you find, Brock? Something about me?"

I didn't think I was that obvious, but if she did have a heightened awareness of people, I might have been an open book.

I tipped the tablet to show her the screen with the recordings Emrys had made. She looked and made no effort to take the tablet.

"I tried to let him down easy," she said. "I tried to help."

"You did." Her touch on my shoulder was light, but this close I could smell her, a faint, minty sort of scent. Clean, soap-like, not perfume. "What I didn't find is more interesting."

Ricky and Chan came back from searching the rest of the apartment.

"What didn't you find?" Ricky asked.

I looked at the three Martians. "I didn't find a suicide note. Any of you find one?"

Heads shook.

"See, that's what strikes me as so odd about this. I get that Emrys was heart-broken that he was rejected again."

Riley's hand dropped away, and she stepped back. "I was gentle."

"You were," I said. "I'm not saying otherwise. I can see how someone in that position might hurt themselves. But why that way? How did he get down there? Why do that?"

"We might not ever know," Riley said.

I stood up and pocketed my tablet. "Emrys didn't walk all that way. There was some sort of vehicle. We should be able to trace that. Let's go talk to his co-workers in your environmental division. They might know something."

"Of course," Riley said. "Let's go ask them. Ricky, Chan, why don't you get back to work? I think Brock and I can handle this, no sense tying up the whole department."

Ricky grinned. "I don't think we're too busy to help out."

"Maybe not, but we also don't want to scare people by having all of us tied up with this. You know how rumors get started. The last thing we need is a bunch of worried colonists. Get out there, patrol. Show them that everything is under control."

Riley stepped closer. I saw it, I knew Ricky saw it too. And got the message that she wanted time alone with me. The only one that looked confused was Chan. Ricky tapped Chan's arm.

"Come on, buddy. Do as the boss says, let's get out of here."

Chan shrugged. "Sure, whatever. Nice meeting you, Mr. Marsden."

"Yeah, you too."

The two of them left while we lingered behind. Riley grabbed the front of my coat, looking up at me, her face serious. "You don't mind, do you?"

If we hadn't been in the middle of a case, I wouldn't have minded at all. I smiled at Riley. "Let's get this case closed, and then maybe we can have dinner or something."

"Deal." Riley stepped back and held out her hand.

We shook hands, hers warm and small in mine, but with strength there. It was the fact that I was different, I figured. Instinctual reaction. If we got so far as genetic compatibility testing she'd probably back off. I doubted that my genes would contribute much to the Martian plans.

The environmental division was two domes over and required Riley to show her security authorization to get through the door.

"What is this place?" I asked as we entered an airlock.

Riley opened a cabinet in the side of the airlock. She took out a bottle and a mask and handed it to me. "Here, you'll need this. When we get inside, we can get a parka, if your coat isn't warm enough."

I took the bottle and slung it over my shoulder by the attached strap. I pulled the mask on when Riley did the same. It covered my face, elastic enough to settle into place, and sealed around my head, making almost a helmet. She stepped close and showed me the controls on the bottle, turning the valve a quarter turn. The mask stiffened as air hissed into the space.

"That should do it, but you can go another quarter turn if you need to. It's just oxygen. We keep the dome levels low, to help protect the samples."

"Samples?"

Riley gestured, interacting with virtual controls. The airlock started cycling. "From the ice cap. This is where we process samples before mining operations can happen.

They're responsible for drilling cores, studying them before we do mine the ice for water.

The airlock door swung open, and I followed Riley out onto the surface of Mars.

It was cold, and there was a road cut
through solid ice on the ground. I shoved
my hands deep into my pockets. I looked up,
and there was a dome, much like the others, but this one covered an ice field. A few
buildings stood near the center, but around
those structures, it was just pitted dirty ice.

"Welcome to Mars." Riley laughed. "This
is the closest that anyone gets to walking out
on the surface right now. The atmospheric
pressure is higher here, but lower than in the
main station. There's also free oxygen, but
most use the masks and supplemental oxygen
if they're going to spend any time in here."

"So this is like a testing ground for colonists that want to walk around unprotected?"

"Something like that. It's serious research,
testing how well we can acclimate to surface
conditions. The less we need to modify the
surface of Mars, the better."

Riley pointed at the buildings rising up
at the heart of the dome. It was a cluster of
industrial, silo-like buildings, with visible

walkways and pipes running around the structures.

"The main offices are in there," Riley said.

The more I studied the structures, the more uneasy I got. There wasn't anything to suggest any activity. It was quiet in the dome. No people moved on those walkways. No escaping water vapor in the air. It felt abandoned.

Or maybe that was my imagination.

"Shouldn't there be people working here? Is it usually this quiet?"

"Not usually." Riley studied the structure. "Maybe they're having a staff meeting or something."

I started walking toward the structure. Riley matched my pace. The cold was biting through the coat.

"Did you call ahead?" I asked.

"No. I'll try to reach them now."

Riley gestured, interacting with her augmented reality interface. I'd been around the Martians enough now, to recognize what she was doing, and enough to see that it wasn't working.

She swiped angrily at the air.

"They're not answering. I can't raise anyone in the environmental division."

"Call Chan and Ricky, we may need backup."

While she did that, I picked up the pace, watching my step on the pitted ice. The surface wasn't actually slick. Whether it was the grit or the conditions, it was like walking on gravel. The path descended slightly as we neared the structure, and branched out, other roads leading off around the dome. We stuck to the central line that ran right up to the front doors.

We were almost there when Riley grabbed my arm, squeezing. With her other hand, she pointed off to the side of the road.

A body lay in one of the crevices in the ice. Martian, from the size, frosted and nude.

"Wait here," I said. "Keep an eye out for your brother and Chan."

I stepped up off the road onto the ice field. Here the surface was more pitted and cracked, crunching beneath my feet. The body lay on its side in a wider crack about twenty meters from the road. As I got closer, I saw a trail of prints, stained red, on the ice. It led from the structures to the crevice.

I reached the body and crouched beside the crack to get a good look. Male. Unquestionably dead. Impossible to tell his age. Muscular, fit, the way the Martians tended to be and covered in a thin layer of frost crystals. His feet looked raw, scratched from walking on the rough ice in bare feet. His arms were drawn up against his chest, chin tucked down as if he had simply laid down shivering in the crack until conditions sucked all the life out of him.

I went back to Riley.

"He's dead. There's a trail leading from the structure. It looks like he walked out here naked, lay down in the crack there and went to sleep until he died."

"Why would he do that?" Riley asked. "What's going on?"

"I think we'd better get inside. Is our backup coming?"

"They'll be here soon. Do you want to wait for them?"

"They'll have to catch up. I think we need to get inside."

It didn't take us long to get to the doors. It was another airlock. Riley opened the doors and stepped back into me as they slid open.

Another body was in the airlock. A woman. Not nude, blood on her clothes, and on the floor around the body. Dressed in a white full-body outfit, like from a clean room, but there was nothing clean about the outfit now. The blood had come from a ragged cut across the left side of her neck. A sharp-toothed saw was in her right hand, blade coated with blood.

I didn't need much of an imagination to picture her drawing that blade across her own neck, the teeth cutting deep. The spray of blood across the wall and floor, and then running down her suit as the flow decreased.

"What is going on?" Riley asked, horror clear in her voice.

One suicide was odd, possibly nothing more than the product of a broken heart. Two more, here where Emrys worked? There was something else going on.

Riley took a step toward the body. I caught her arm and pulled her back.

"Wait. Let's take precautions before we go in there. Call Ricky, have him bring biohazard suits. And emergency personnel."

"Biohazard?"

"We've got three suicides, counting Emrys

and these two. Suicide isn't normally contagious, but it seems like we've got an outbreak here." I pulled her back further from the entrance. "Let's wait for the others."

The cold was really sinking in through my clothes. I didn't see how Riley could stand it, her uniform couldn't provide that much more warmth, but she looked fine. I tucked my hands deep into my pockets, pressed my arms against my sides and shivered. My teeth started chattering before a crowd of Martians came through the door in bright green hazard gear.

Green. It made perfect sense. A color that didn't occur naturally on Mars.

Ricky and Chan reached us first, handing us each an environmental suit. My hands shook as I pulled it on. While I did that, Riley dressed and explained the situation, since her teeth weren't chattering together.

Fortunately, the hazard suit had its own heater. Soon it puffed up around me with warm air. Sharp tingles spread through my hands, but it was a welcome change from freezing.

"We need to look for survivors," I said. "They may not be acting normally. And Pohl

Station needs to be contacted. Anyone that has had contact with Emrys Nash must be quarantined until we get some answers."

"Chan," Riley said.

"On it," he answered.

Another Martian joined us from the group that had followed Ricky and Chan in. He was older, with hair turning gray at his temples.

"Doctor Daniel Carroll, chief of medical services. When did this start?"

"We don't have a timeline yet," Riley said. "But three days ago Emrys Nash went south and committed suicide near Pohl Station. We came here to question his co-workers and found two bodies."

Riley pointed out at the ice. "A male, there, and this one in the airlock."

Dr. Carroll's mouth opened, closed, and then he nodded. "Thank you for acting so promptly. We need to proceed with caution. And we'll need to monitor the two of you since you were exposed without protective gear."

"We didn't touch anything," I said. "And we both were wearing our breathing masks. I doubt we picked up anything."

He looked up at me. "Had you any contact with Mr. Nash before his suicide?"

"Me? Why?"

"Well, you are from off-world. Maybe you brought a contagion with you? An alien disease of some sort?"

I shook my head. "Sorry, doc. This doesn't come from me. I've been living in Pohl Station. I didn't have any contact with Nash before he turned up dead."

"Very disturbing," he said.

"Yes." I pointed at the airlock. "We need to get in there and search for survivors."

"You're right," he said. "Teams of three, I think. I will go with you and Chief Palmer."

Dr. Carroll turned to face the waiting group. "We're dividing up into teams of three to search the facility for survivors. Approach with caution. If your suit integrity is damaged, an alert will flag it. Wait for help. If it is unsafe to approach someone, then call for help."

He turned back to us. "Let's go."

I didn't mind him taking control. I didn't like this situation, and I wasn't eager to go into the facility.

Riley and I followed Dr. Carroll into

the environmental division facility, walking carefully around the blood splatters around the body.

"We must cycle the airlock," Dr. Carroll said.

"Go ahead, Doc," Riley said.

The woman looked peaceful, almost like she was sleeping with her head down to the right side. Her eyes were closed.

The airlock cycled, and the inner doors opened. Inside was an open area with lockers and a couple vehicles plugged in on one side, like electric carts, with thick fat tires. No signs of anyone else.

We went on in, deeper into the facility. Behind us, were the sounds of the airlock opening again for the next team.

CHAPTER 45

Enhancer's asteroid

Unbelievable. I sat up on the bunk in the Enhancer's cell. Even here Pike's memory scan was dredging up memories that I didn't want to relive. Particularly not the gruesome aftermath at Amundsen Station.

It took four hours to complete our search of the facility. In addition to the two bodies that we had discovered on arrival, we found six others. Everyone in the facility had committed suicide. Hanging, drowning, with knives and pills, they all had found a way to kill themselves.

I spent two weeks in quarantine. The culprit? A proto-organism found in the ice, released into the atmosphere by evaporation, it affected the human brain, depressing the production of neurotransmitters which led to feelings of hopelessness and suicide.

Ultimately the scientific consensus came back that the Martian proto-organism was a fossil relic, evidence of the in-between stage between life and non-life, from early in the formation of the planet. Life had risen throughout the solar system, but the Martian gap always had perplexed scientists. This discovery showed that life had started to form until something interrupted the process. Cataclysmic impacts? An unlucky solar eruption? The exact cause was still unknown, although now at least we know of other dead worlds, in other systems, sterilized in the early formation stages when life first took hold.

And, of course, there are those worlds that died after life took hold, but usually, life still finds cracks and toe-holds, even on those worlds, waiting for a time to expand.

Unless it expands because of intelligence, like the Enhancers coming to this asteroid and reshaping it.

Somehow I'd managed to move from one cell to another cell. The Enhancers hadn't even asked me any questions yet, and Drac had been taken away. I assumed to his own cell.

As cells went, this was a step up from the empty sensie room where Pike had kept me. Plain hard walls with a bluish, hard feel to them. Not metal. Maybe some sort of carbon fiber. Most likely made from material extracted out of the asteroid. Like all those thousands of ships that they had out there.

There was a bunk, a solid piece of the same material as the walls, that came out as a slab with a thin mattress lying on top. A couple of warm blankets, a thin pillow. On the opposite side of the room were a toilet and a sink.

The room smelled of chemical cleansers. A thin trace still clung to the surfaces in places.

I flared my Euzebian neck slits wide and inhaled deeper, concentrating for human scents.

I picked them up. A melon-scented sweat. I closed my eyes and let the image from my scent-sight form. The cell was dimmer in my scent-sight, the cleansers outlined the dark materials. The toilet and sink were clearer, the odors stronger there.

A man moved around the room, the shape indistinct. An old scent. He moved around the room methodically. Cleaning. Then he left.

I opened my eyes.

Nothing there to help me. I got up from the bunk and paced. I don't like waiting, and I don't like being caged. Somehow I had to convince the Enhancers to give me the tach field generator. Either I joined them, or came up with another plan, but to get Muriel and Dyami back, there wasn't any other choice.

I was only on my second pass across the room when the door dissolved away. It didn't slide, swing, or drop, it simply evaporated like a spray of water on hot biocrete.

One of the Enhancers stood in the doorway, and she wasn't anyone that I had seen before. She was tall, my height, with long limbs. She wore a tight outfit that hugged all of her sleek curves, but it left most of her legs, her midriff, and arms bare, exposing flawless skin. And it was so low cut, that it barely fastened in front.

A network of metallic tattoos wrapped around her ribs and formed a complicated pattern around her pierced navel. Three rods pierced the skin around her navel, like bars on a prison.

Her hair was thick and black as space, but interwoven with glowing strands, like wisps of a nebula, and sparks of light like stars. Her ears, lips, eyebrows, and nose were all pierced with smaller piercings. A smile touched her red lips.

To my scent-sight, she smelled confident, aroused and human, with a touch of that bluish ozone smell that the Enhancers all seemed to have—an uncomfortable echo of the scent of synthetics, non-organic intelligences.

"Brock Marsden. Moreau, savior of Olinda, according to some, in the recent unpleasantness with rogue non-organics and Moreaus. Part of the problem, according to others." She walked into the cell, her stride confident as she looked me up and down, giving back as much scrutiny as I'd given her.

"The Esteemed One, according to your Nosferan companion. Ambassador between humans and Nosferans during that other unpleasantness. You like to get involved, don't you?"

"Who are you?" I asked. "You seem to know plenty about me."

She continued circling. "Born on Seabrook over a hundred years ago, and you don't look nearly that old! Known organic enhancements include longevity, regeneration, improved nerve transmission rates, heightened senses, including some rather radical changes to your sense of smell. Euzebians, right?"

"I'm here to talk to Hypatia Meier, I was under the impression that she was willing to talk to me."

"Grandmother does what she wants." Her index finger made a circular motion, pointing at my left hand, the C'lacktal tentacles. "Those don't fit the rest of the picture. C'lacktal, right? Poisonous, one suspects, but they don't fit. Why that change?"

I lifted the hand. I was getting used to them, and they had proven useful. "It wasn't by choice. A side-effect of the mutation beam that was used against Olinda."

"Ah, thank you. I appreciate new data. For that, I will tell you my name. I am Tabitha."

"Hypatia's grand-daughter?"

Tabitha waved a finger. "Tsk, tsk. That's more data than you paid for. I'll need something else now. Why did you come to Proving?"

Proving. That must be the name of the place. I filed it away. Another bit of data that I hadn't known, but Tabitha didn't need to realize that.

"I'd prefer to talk to your grandmother about that."

Tabitha came around again and put her hands on her hips. "You said that before, and she's willing, provided that I give her a reason to go along with it. She's very busy, after all."

Sooner or later I had to tell them. Playing the eager convert didn't feel right. I didn't know what all of Tabitha's enhancements and implants were, but if she were here, she would probably be able to tell if I was lying.

"I went to Orlando Pike first, with Drac, to recover a piece of galactic technology for the Nosferans. Something stolen from them decades ago. Pike loaned me the shuttle and sent me here, saying that he had sold the tech to you."

"So you are working for Pike now?"

"Our interests are the same on this," I said

carefully. Nothing stopped me from saying that much at least.

Tabitha moved again, resuming her circling. "We detected the nanowire implants. It is technology that he adapted from the techniques we traded with him, but he has modified it considerably. How does that fit into your deal with him?"

I didn't answer. I wanted to say that it wasn't my choice, that Pike had used the technology to enslave my mind, and nothing came out of my mouth. I wasn't paralyzed, the words just didn't come.

"No answer?" Tabitha stopped behind me, clearly visible to my scent-sight as she moved closer.

Her hand ran up my neck, moving through my hair, and I smelled sun-warmed peaches. Faint, but there, beneath everything else. The smell of her skin.

Her fingers tightened in my hair, taking a handful. She jerked my head back, the pain sharp and immediate.

CHAPTER 46

Australia

In the end, Muriel gave up fighting and told them everything. After that first conversation, no one showed her the neural scrambler, and they didn't need to. It was always there, out of sight, ready to plunge her back into senselessness. The abyss of nothing.

And she didn't want to go back there.

They'd broken her. Muriel paced the suite, unable to shake the sick feeling inside, watching the screen's display showing the progress of *Australia* into orbit around the gas giant that CY-HC-2347 orbited.

Despite the dates, names, and events that she had revealed to Constantine, that she had shouted at the others, Blackstone hadn't altered the mission. The *Australia* continued into the system as if unaware of the Nosferan presence.

Dyami lifted his big head up from the couch. "Must you walk back and forth? Is it an exercise?"

Muriel pressed her hands together and stopped in front of the screen. "Sorry. I'm feeling helpless. I gave up, Dyami! I let them have their way, and I told them what I know about the Human-Nosferan war."

"The ship didn't change course," Dyami said. "This troubles you?"

"Yes." Muriel pressed her hands to her face and took a deep breath. She ran her hands back through her hair and crossed the room to the couch. "We're all in danger if Blackstone doesn't back down. She's acting as if she has no idea of the danger."

"Is that her strategy?" Dyami asked, rising up to sit. "To lure out of the Nosferans, while planning some action against them?"

It was possible. Muriel looked at the screen. The big Jovian wasn't visible at the moment. Only Cyeechie, the habitable moon orbiting the giant.

The moon reminded her of Olinda. There were white clouds and blue oceans beneath the surface. The entire Jovian system orbited the star once every couple hundred standard years. Meanwhile, Cyeechie orbited around the gas giant in twenty standard days and revolved around its axis every thirty hours. The other moons in the system exerted even more tidal effects, making it a stormy, violent world with weeks of dusk light while the gas giant eclipsed the star.

And when Cyeechie was on the sun-side of the gas giant, even revolving, it didn't have a true night. The night side received enough reflected light from the gas giant that night was only somewhat dimmer, if less directly lit.

A fascinating world, worth study, if it wasn't already inhabited by a Nosferan colony.

Blackstone knew that, Muriel had told them. So what was her plan?

"Does Blackstone have other orders?" Dyami asked. "Hasn't she been in communication with her superiors?"

Muriel looked at Dyami. He gave her a level gaze back.

"You mean orders to confront the Nosferans?"

"The conflict between humans and Nos-ferans was settled with the destruction of the scout ship." Dyami shook his head. "Humans do not accept the resolution of a conflict. They feud, using one conflict as an excuse to create another. They war."

"That never happens on Eyota?"

Dyami rose up from the couch. He showed his teeth. "No."

"And you still came to us, to learn to be a detective?"

"Yes. I've learned that sometimes what appears as a justified resolution, is not what it seems. Such as murder."

Muriel nodded and turned back to the screen. "It looks like Blackstone is ignoring my warnings, but she may have other orders, you're right. I'm not an expert on the history. And she might want to test what I told her."

"What will you do?"

That was a good question. If Blackstone didn't alter history, if she didn't change the timeline, then life on this ship was going to turn very dark, very soon.

"We're locked up." Muriel walked over to Dyami and put a hand on his arm. "Right now we're stuck. If things go bad, stick with me. I'll get us out of this."

No one had asked yet about the Tretan's shuttle, about the Pilot. It was still a potential way off the *Australia* if they could reach it.

CHAPTER 47

Enhancer's Colony

Tabitha bared my neck like she meant to slit it. My Euzebian neck slits automatically opened as I inhaled. I didn't get any stink of malice from her, and I restrained myself from striking back.

"Good." Her breath filled my scent-sight, making her brighten as she moved directly behind me, still holding my hair. "Don't move. This might get ticklish."

She ran her fingers of her other hand through my hair, making plucking and twisting motions. My scalp tingled. I hadn't expected a massage, then sharp pain!

I almost moved. If I hadn't been able to see Tabitha in my scent-sight, to smell her raspberry concern, I might have moved. I might have jerked away.

Tabitha pulled her arm back, and the pain increased as if she was scalping me. I didn't smell blood, at least none exposed on the surface. A bluish, ozone glow built up around Tabitha's hand.

She plucked and pulled, and the pain continued burning through my head. My eyes watered. The pain bounced around my brain like a loose cannonball. My C'lacktal tentacles thrashed and snapped, biting at invisible enemies. My Euzebian neck slits flared and collapsed and flared again, drawing in air.

Then, with one last pull, Tabitha released me and stepped back. "You can move now."

There was still pain, but it ebbed like an outgoing tide. I turned around. The bluish glow that my scent-sight picked up wrapped around Tabitha's hand was silvery and cloud-like to my eyes as if she was holding smoke or vapor.

She winked at me. "One more sec..."

The cloud collapsed, drawing into her hand. The blue glow faded away. The process happened fast, almost too fast to follow. In the next second, Tabitha held a shiny metal sphere in the palm of her hand.

"There. All better now, Pike's hold on you is gone." She pointed at Brock. "You owe us, now, Moreau. Keep that in mind when you talk to my grandmother."

She had removed the nanoweb tech from my head. "I will. Thank you."

"You might not thank me later," Tabitha said. "Come with me."

Despite the warning, it was great not having Pike in my head. It also made it clear that the Enhancers wanted something from us.

Tabitha led the way out of the cell back into the cool corridors of the colony. As we left the cell block, the passage opened up with a high rocky ceiling, reinforced by metallic beams. The lighting was bright, but indirect, bouncing off the rocky ceilings and reflecting on the polished floor. There was a sense, walking behind her, that we had entered the regular population flow of a busy metropolis. All around us people moved about their business, quickly, politely, but with a very human chatter. There were shouted greetings, hands waved in the air, polite excuses and amicable nods.

We didn't talk. Tabitha didn't offer any

explanations for what I saw. She walked, and I followed.

Not only did the colony feel more human than I might have expected, they looked human too. Bright colors weren't the most common choices, although I saw some young teens wearing bright colors, making themselves look like exotic birds surrounded by the more muted colors of the adults.

Piercings, those were universal, and the metallic tattoos embedded in flesh. The smells covered a range from unpleasant, to exotic and alluring, but over it all was that bluish ozone haze of electronics. Some piercings might serve simply a cosmetic purpose, but from what I could pick up it looked like most were enhancements, serving a dual purpose. In some cases, as I'd already seen, eyes were replaced by artificial devices, yet always with an aesthetic design.

In all, the Enhancer culture was most shocking for its obvious humanity. They might look exotic to someone unmodified, but I was used to my fellow Moreaus, many of whom no longer looked human at all.

Following Tabitha through the corridors, I also got a sense of the size of this place. At times the corridor would open up, overlooking public spaces, like bubbles caught in the rock. In some the gravity field was reduced, allowing people to fly and mingle in the open air, using a variety of suits with wing membranes to maneuver around.

As we walked, I realized that her path was taking us deeper into the asteroid colony. We passed a few different train stations, but Tabitha never turned into any. We kept walking.

After nearly twenty minutes we reached a secure door. No guard, but it didn't open as we approached. It was also almost back in the same area as the cell block, except down a couple levels.

"That was a long way to go, just to go down a couple levels," I said. "Did you intend to confuse me, or show me around?"

Tabitha leaned close and ran a hand up my coat. She smirked. "Both, except I could tell you weren't lost. "

"I have a good sense of direction."

She moved away and the door opened before her, with that same evaporating into nothingness way the cell door had vanished. She beckoned with a single finger.

"Come on, then. Let's not keep the Guide waiting any longer."

I walked inside. As soon as I stepped through the door reformed out of nothing. I reached back and put my hand on the surface. It was thick, solid and just slightly warm to the touch.

"Does anyone ever get trapped inside when it reforms?"

"Only if we want that to happen." Tabitha turned and walked down the corridor.

This was obviously a place of business. Less foot traffic, more purpose in those walking through. The corridor opened into a lobby, with a wide, tall desk forming a half-circle barrier.

Two thickly built Enhancers, both women, quite muscular, and wearing what had to be some sort of body armor, with reinforced lenses over their eyes, stood behind the desk.

"I'm taking him to the Guide," Tabitha said.

One of the women said, in a husky voice. "She's expecting you."

I didn't see weapons and didn't doubt that they had them. Their heads didn't turn to watch us, probably some sort of augmented reality interface kept them informed of everything going on around them.

These people did remind me of the Martians I'd known after leaving Seabrook. Bigger, more exotic, with more tech and a closer relationship with the tech, true cyborgs, but there were similarities. Of course, the technology was a hundred years more advanced too.

Tabitha led me past the desk, through another evaporating door into a lift. It took us down deeper into the asteroid. Without indicators or controls, I didn't see any way for me to operate the lift. Maybe voice, although Tabitha hadn't issued any audible voice commands. Maybe unenhanced beings couldn't operate it. Simple, effective security.

At last the lift stopped and we walked out into yet another corridor, not too different than the ones we left above. This one was short before it opened into a wide circular room busy with activity. At its heart hung a giant holographic view of the galactic arm leading right into the core stars. People worked around the room, and a number were interacting with the hologram, studying additional overlays and details.

It was immense, impressive and magnificent in scope. I also didn't have any idea what it meant.

"This is our heart, our center of operations," Tabitha said. "You're the first unenhanced person I've known to see this."

"I'm honored," I said, entirely serious.

Tabitha escorted me around the edges of the room. I looked around amazed, without any idea of what it meant. Obviously, they were busy with something. Whatever it was, the scope wasn't limited to this asteroid.

She took me up a short flight of stairs to a glass-enclosed area overlooking the operations center below. I immediately recognized the woman standing in front of the glass wall, dragging holographic displays across the surface.

Hypatia Meier, the same severe-looking woman that I'd seen in Pike's files, but those holograms failed to capture the woman. Alive, she was animated and dynamic, as tall as her granddaughter, but not dressed in such a revealing outfit. Instead, she wore straight black pants and a loose, sleeveless shirt. Circuitry tattoos crawled up her arms. She was talking with two other Enhancers but dismissed them with a wave as Tabitha led me inside.

Hypatia's smile transformed her face. Not softening it, but humanizing it. I didn't pick up any sour malice smells from her. If anything, her scent was faint, flowery and curious. Interested, in me, apparently.

Her handshake was equally open and welcoming. She shook my hand. "You'll forgive us our paranoia, did Tabitha try to get you lost?"

Tabitha hadn't left and her mouth quirked as I nodded. Hypatia laughed, and gestured to a set of chairs, moving with the clear expectation that we'd both follow.

I settled into one chair, Tabitha took the one to my left, and Hypatia across from the two of us. As if we were somehow together in this.

"I told her it'd only give you a better idea of our home."

"Maybe that was my intent," Tabitha said.

"Right." Hypatia leaned back in her chair. The synthetic material squeaked slightly. She looked at me, her hand gesturing lazily at

Tabitha. "My granddaughter thought Pike sent you to infiltrate us or attack us, but your Nosferan friend tells us a different story."

"Is he okay?" I asked, keeping my voice even since she had brought him up.

"He's fine. We're repairing the damage to his wing, and providing treatment for the female, as best we can. He's quite protective."

"That's the continuation of his tribe."

Hypatia steepled her fingers. "He says that Pike sold us stolen goods, and he's offered us reimbursement for our cost, plus the pirate's shuttle if we give him the tech and provide him and his people passage away from this system."

So Drac had finally decide to sell me out. It made sense from his point-of-view, since I'd been compromised by Pike. My ambassador status didn't require him to protect me.

"I can understand why he'd do that," I said. "Thanks to you, however, Pike doesn't have a hold on me. I agree with Drac, Pike provided authorization to reimburse you for the device, and it would serve him right if we threw in the shuttle."

Tabitha leaned forward. "If this is so valuable, it sounds like we should hold onto it."

"Perhaps," Hypatia said. She was still looking at me. In my scent-sight, her peach-colored aura was calm, giving little away except that faint flowery scent.

"Brock," she said. "We know much about you. I even know that you and the Nosferan attempted to break into Pike's base on Olinda to steal this device from him. That doesn't suggest a great deal of trustworthiness."

"I can see why you'd think that, although you are also aware of Pike's occupation and reputation. The plan had been to obtain the device quietly, since it originally belonged to the Nosferans."

Hypatia waved a hand. "Long ago. It has traded hands many times, and no one has found any significant use for it. Now you and the Nosferan want it back. Why?"

Tell her that we wanted it to open up time travel? Even if she believed me, what then?

Hypatia leaned forward, bracing her elbows on her knees. "Be honest with me. I see your hesitation."

"Just cautious," I said. "I have no idea what your interest is in this. Why did you buy the tach field generator in the first place?"

"That's not your concern," Tabitha said. "Answer —"

Hypatia raised a hand. Tabitha stopped talking. Hypatia folded her fingers together. "We do studies in perception, opening humanity to the fullest range of possibilities. The generator provides a reliable source of test conditions. I don't think that's why you want it."

Tabitha's tour had made it clear to me that there was only one way I was getting out of here with the generator — if they decided to give it to me. I took the leap by telling them the truth.

It took some time. I explained what happened to the Tretan's shuttle, how it engaged the displacement drive as the herd ship had fired. I explained what the Cooperative ship Washington saw of the event, and then the Nosferans photo of Muriel and Dyami, a hundred years ago at the start of the Human-Nosferan war.

"I remember that time," I said. "I don't know how, but I believe that my friends were thrown back there. A lot of legwork went into tracking down what happened to the tach field generator after it was stolen from the Nosferans —"

"By your friends?" Tabitha interrupted.

"That's what the Nosferans claim. They've been looking for it since, without luck until they came to me."

Hypatia ran her hands along the chair. "And your trail led you to a pirate on the same world, and then to us. That sounds very convenient."

I shook my head. "I don't think so. I don't think that it is an accident at all. I think it was planned that way. To bring it and me together, so that I can get them back."

"You don't know that," Tabitha said. "How could that possibly work?"

"I don't know," I admitted. "But that's what I believe."

"You believe that other forces are guiding what happens here?" Hypatia said. She rose to her feet before I answered. "Come with me."

I rose.

"You can't, grandmother!" Tabitha was on her feet, a sour green smell of apprehension pouring off her.

Hypatia's calm never wavered. "I am our Guide, am I not?"

Tabitha settled back slightly with a wash of peppery regret. "Yes, of course."

Neither explained it to me. Hypatia walked back toward the glass wall surrounding the room, which was still covered in holographic displays. When she got closer, a gesture sent them scattering into smaller versions clustered on each side. She stood in front of the wall, and I joined her.

Hypatia pointed at the massive hologram in the central chamber below, showing our arm of the galaxy leading on into the core.

"The Rim is populated by species picking up technology from the Galactics that live among the core systems. Although they seem disinterested and above life in the Rim, we believe otherwise. Our focus is on exploring human potential, how far can we go in enhancing humanity while retaining our humanity? As far as joining the Glittering Throng ourselves?"

I shrugged. "I doubt I'll be around to see that."

Hypatia turned and regarded me. "Yet you believe that something has guided this device here, that somehow events have been orchestrated for this outcome. That time travel, something every species believes is impossible, does in fact exist."

"There are many things I don't understand," I said. "Does that mean the Galactics are behind it all? I don't know. It seems easy to point to them, but they aren't gods."

Tabitha stepped closer. "Are you a religious man? Do you believe in ancient superstitions?"

I shook my head. "No, but some people would worship the Galactics instead. I'll accept that they're smarter than us. Other species are stronger, faster, or weaker and dumber than us. Life isn't a neat and tidy ladder. It's opportunistic and blind, most of the time, to anything other than itself."

Hypatia smiled. "And yet you believe you are meant to get this device?"

"I also don't believe in coincidence. As you said, it's moved around over the years. That it is here, now, and I am, that doesn't sound like a coincidence."

"Then who is behind the curtain?" Hypatia asked. "Who is pulling our strings?"

"I don't know."

Hypatia looked back down at the galactic hologram. "This is just one portion of an immense galaxy, which is only one galaxy among countless others. We've barely begun. My role is to guide my people forward, to walk that line that enhances while preserving our humanity. I think that following you will help us find our path. I will give you the tach field generator."

"Grandmother!" Tabitha said.

Ignoring her, Hypatia continued. "I'm sending Tabitha with you since the device is ours currently. I need to know how this changes our path and she will serve as my eyes and ears."

Tabitha and I looked at each other, and I think we were both thinking the same thing. How could this possibly work? Her earlier attempts at seduction had been an obvious effort to distract, like the tour, and both had failed. Now her grandmother wanted to throw us together?

"What do you mean, with me? For how long?"

Hypatia answered without a flicker of emotion. "Until your quest to recover your lover and your friend succeed, one way or another."

"Grandmother, I've been training —"

"To follow in my footsteps." Hypatia laughed. "Don't worry, granddaughter, my path has a long way to go yet, and you're only starting. You chafe at the restrictions placed here. It is time for you to walk among the stars, and apparently through time itself. That should serve you well if you pick up after me as guide."

"Yes, grandmother," Tabitha said more humbly.

"About Drac?"

Hypatia's mouth tightened. "Yes, the Nosferan. Don't trust them." She raised a hand, forestalling any comment I might have offered. "I know your history with them. Even with that, you don't know enough to trust them."

"We just met, and you're trusting me with the device and your granddaughter."

She didn't say anything. She didn't need to, her silence made her point. I looked back down at the holographic piece of the galaxy below. All those stars. Sometimes I forgot how big it all was, and here was someone who was trying to comprehend it all. The only person I knew that was like her, with the same drive for the future was Subha, back on Olinda, and Subha's vision was focused inward.

Tabitha said, "So we hand over the generator, and then what? Where are we going? What happens?"

Both women looked at me. "At first, back to Olinda. I have a contact there that will help us take the next step."

"You're not going after Pike, are you?" Hypatia asked. "I think that would be a mistake right now."

I shook my head. "Once we get Drac, and go back, I'm all about finding Muriel and Dyami. Pike is a distant concern, thanks to you."

Hypatia pressed her hands together. "The patterns are shifting. Our path will become clearer." She looked at Tabitha. "And you, granddaughter, will light the way. Follow him, protect him, and do what you can to ensure that his mission succeeds."

"As you wish," Tabitha said.

Her voice carried her reservations and a

faint rancid smell of doubt leaked from her pores like tiny drops of sickly bile.

Time travel. I never would have imagined it possible, but that's just when the galaxy surprised you. I'd learned enough about that in the past hundred years.

Chapter 48

After months of boredom were broken by the discovery of the alien ship, and the time travelers, it would have been easy to forget why they had come. As Helen stood in the control center beside Blackstone, looking at the holographic world displayed before them, it was suddenly very real.

Her gut twisted as if she stood at the edge of a window into space. With just a step, it looked as if she could fly out down to the blue and white world below. Despite Muriel's repeated warnings about their course, Blackstone hadn't altered the *Australia*'s path.

Helen glanced at her boss. White hair pulled back, held with a shiny, polished wood clip, so dark that it looked black against the white hair. Her face was perfect, composed as always as she regarded Cyeechie's violent winds and tempestuous oceans. The moon was a storm-riddled world, with high winds and erratic conditions. Blackstone didn't show it, but was the same going on inside her head? How could it not?

If it was her, Helen knew, in charge, she might have turned the ship back. Or at least she would have taken more time to reach the Jovian and its target moon. The original system plan called for robotic launches on the way in system, probes to each of the major worlds, several to some, to gather data. A whole, system-wide plan while the ship continued directly on to Cyeechie, a potential harbor in this system.

Unless Blackstone hadn't changed their path because a part of her was concerned about changing the future. That was the flip side of Muriel's information. Did they believe her? If so, it begged the question if changing the future was a good plan or not.

"Status?" Blackstone's voice cut through the chatter.

"All stations reporting in ready," said Mark Gunderson, running control right now. "Orbit is nominal."

"Other activity?" Blackstone asked.

Meaning aliens, the Nosferans that had attacked the scout ship, according to Muriel.

Blackstone hadn't approved bringing Muriel and Dyami up to control for the orbital insertion. Constantine stood at Blackstone's elbow, ready as ever, to carry out her orders.

"No activity detected so far," Constantine said. His mouth quirked. "Maybe they've bugged out already if they were here."

He, Helen knew, had taken measures in anticipation of Nosferans attacking the ship. He might sound confident and bold, that didn't make him careless.

Even though the information hadn't been released to general knowledge, the crew knew something was up from the contact with Muriel's ship to now. Tense anticipation, awaiting whatever might happen, filled the gallery.

"Good," Blackstone finally said. "Let's hope it stays that way. We continue on mission, on plan. Launch orbitals and begin the detailed mapping phase. I want to know what's down there, to the smallest detail."

"Yes, ma'am," Helen said. She took her

tablet from her pocket and began addressing orders to the teams.

In the gallery, the orbitals group was audibly busy with the preparatory launch of a dozen satellites. Each one was a sophisticated device, networked together with the *Australia*, even more so.

"Teams on standby," Constantine said. "Still no contact."

Blackstone nodded. "Good. It looks like it is time for me to address the crew."

Blackstone turned, and Helen met her eyes. What are you doing? Helen wanted to ask. Constantine might think he and his security teams were ready for anything, that didn't make it so.

"Excuse me," Blackstone said. "It's time to make history."

The director stepped around Helen, walking around to the podium facing up into the gallery. That way her hologram image would include Cyeechie behind her. All according to plan.

But things weren't really according to plan, at least not the plan Helen knew about. It all begged the question. What plan was Blackstone following?

Chapter 49

CY-HC-2347 *"Cyeechie" Orbit, Australia*

Muriel stood in front of the holographic screen, her hand pressed hard against Dyami's solid arm. His bristles brushed her hand.

"It's really happening," Muriel said. "They haven't made any changes."

Dyami's big head swung around. "Maybe they want this conflict."

He was right. The realization was like a blown airlock—as if the room didn't contain enough air.

Blackstone stood before them, in holographic form, standing at a podium in front of CY-HC-2347, Cyeechie. No one had come to talk to them since yesterday, and even then the questions they had asked were perfunctory, or for small details that she couldn't remember.

She wasn't an expert. She had studied the war briefly while growing up. It was fascinating and terrifying. Brock had told her a bit more since they met and she had learned that, incredibly, he had lived during this time.

Which meant that somewhere, a much younger Brock was out there, right now. Not her Brock, not the Moreau that she knew. In this time he would have still been entirely human. It might be interesting to meet him—if what was happening right now wasn't so terrifying.

"We have to get off this ship," Muriel said. "Before it's too late."

"Ship security would resist any attempt."

"I know, but we need —"

Blackstone started speaking. The same speech that Muriel had heard in recordings.

"You've accomplished something amazing," Blackstone said. "All of you on this ship, this pocket of humanity, braving the abyss between the stars to visit a bright new world."

The abyss. Muriel bit her lip. She'd never thought about Blackstone's use of the word until now. Was it a reference to her? Had she said something in the interviews about the abyss?

Blackstone gestured at the hologram of Cyeechie behind her.

"Even now our orbital teams are deploying our satellite network to map the world you see, CY-HC-2347, Cyeechie. This world is our safe harbor after the vast crossing we've taken."

Blackstone leaned forward, her face intent. "In humanity's early history, brave men and women set out in tiny wooden crafts across immense oceans in order to reach distant lands and discover new futures for humanity. Those brave explorers were showing us the way forward, to expand the frontiers. In a way those early ships really are no different than our home, the *Australia*, that has carried us safely here."

Muriel turned, holding onto Dyami. "This is it, in just a moment, it will happen. When it does we have to go, head for the shuttle. That's our chance. We don't want to be on the ship after this."

He rose up, all bulk and power, wrinkled head hanging above her. "I will protect you."

Blackstone kept talking, her voice

powerful, and confident. "Our early information suggests unknown hazards, hidden dangers and challenges we can't imagine. I know this, whatever the future holds we will prevail —"

As if on cue the lights flickered and the great ship *Australia* shuddered. The holographic Blackstone looked up and the image cut out.

Was that the start of a smile on her face? Muriel had seen recordings of that speech, most kids saw it, but Muriel didn't remember seeing Blackstone start to smile before. Had she missed it, or was that a hint that the timeline had changed? There wasn't time to worry about it.

The ship shook again, hard enough to throw Muriel against Dyami. His rock-solid arm caught her and pulled her close. The lights flickered once more, and alarms began to sound.

A pulse of red appeared in the heart of each light and spread out in a ring to the edge, then repeated. A low tone sounded.

"All hands secure." That was Command on comm. "All hands secure stations. All hands secure stations. Lockdown conditions in force. Follow security instructions. We are under attack."

That was it. So far history hadn't changed. Blackstone hadn't altered her path. They had to get off the ship.

Muriel stood up on her own and headed for the door, Dyami at her side. Muriel pointed at the door. It was locked, as it always was locked.

"Can you open it?"

"Yes," he said.

It was a risk, going out into the corridors with hair-trigger security and worse, but this was their one chance to reach the shuttle and get away. Hopefully, the Pilot was back online and waiting.

They reached the door and Muriel stepped back, giving Dyami room.

He placed both hands on the door, his muscles bunched, and the door suddenly slid open. Dyami fell to the side, catching himself on his hands.

Helen Shaw gasped and stepped back from the door, lowering her hand from the access panel.

Dyami picked himself up, looming in the doorway. Muriel hurried past him, crowding

Helen, who stepped back. Muriel kept going, and Helen kept backing up. Dyami breathed down on Muriel's neck, his breath hot and yeasty. Comforting, like baked bread. Knowing that he was right behind her was also a comfort.

The ship shook again.

Helen didn't have any security with her. She held up a hand. "Wait, I was coming to let you out!"

Muriel unclenched her fists. "Why?"

"She didn't alter course. She stuck to the original approach plan. Why didn't she listen to you?"

No need to wonder who Helen was asking about. *Blackstone.*

"She wants this war," Dyami's translator said. The floor vibrated with his voice.

Helen nodded. "That's pretty much what I thought too. I don't understand it, why would she do that?"

"It's not just her," Muriel said. "The company, your Board, wants the war. Knowing its coming, they're busy preparing to profit from it."

Helen's mouth hung open for a second. Then the ship shook again. Helen beckoned.

"Come on. I'll get you to your shuttle, maybe you can get away."

"Why are you doing this?" Muriel asked.

"Because we shouldn't be doing this, you warned us. We had a choice. We could have turned around."

Muriel wasn't sure. Maybe the future had its own inertia. Little things maybe could slip through, but maybe not the big things. Most likely only the Galactics knew. In any case, she wasn't about to disagree with Helen.

"Okay, thank you. Let's go."

Helen nodded. "I can get us past security. Come on."

She turned and hurried down the corridor. The lights continued pulsing red. The ship shook hard. Helen stumbled into the wall. Muriel kept her balance and helped Helen up. Helen gave her a small smile and they continued.

No one paid much attention to them, as they passed other crew. Dyami got nervous looks, but with Helen waving them on, the crew had other priorities.

Right up until they reached the lifts, people came out running, and one of those people was Clay Yeager. He skidded to a stop.

"Whoa, doc? What's this?" Clay took a step back, pointing at Muriel and Dyami. "Another breakout?"

Helen stepped forward. "No! Clay, I'm helping them. We have to get them off the ship."

Clay stopped and rubbed his jaw with his good hand. "Oh, yeah. Okay. I get it. Alright, come on!"

He skipped back into the lift.

"Come on," Helen said. "He's okay. He'll help."

What choice did they have? Muriel followed them into the lift, and they all crowded to the side to make room for Dyami. Once in Clay swiped a card and entered a code on the control panel.

"I'm taking us straight down to the hangars," he said. "Nonstop. We don't have room in here anyway!"

The lift shot down into the ship. Another shake had them all bracing on the walls. Muriel braced her feet with her back to the wall. It was time to leave this place.

CHAPTER 50

Enhancer Ship Epsilon

Drac was back, his wing healed, his attitude worse, as we left the Enhancer's asteroid in one of their ships with Tabitha at the controls.

They were keeping Pike's shuttle. I got the feeling that they'd break it down into its basic components, even the androids, and reuse the materials.

This ship was one of the smaller ones among the thousands in the Enhancer's docking bay. It was fully equipped, I was told, to support a crew of six for a year. With the three of us, I guess that gave us two years. STC capable, with defensive weaponry, it was designed as a fast scout ship.

"Boys, sit back and enjoy the ride," Tabitha said. "I've got this."

We rose out of the Enhancer's asteroid, gaining apparent speed as the STC drive shifted us up faster and faster. In moments we cleared the petals covering the opening. I was at a station on Tabitha's left, Drac crouching in the next chair on my left. The bridge was small, cozy, even, with four chairs in the small space. Holographic screens floated at the front of the cabin, looking like windows except to my scent-sight which picked up the odors of the bulkhead behind them. In reality, I knew that the ship continued on ahead of us with equipment, sensors, and weapon systems. We were buried in a secure section back from the front of the craft even though the screens made it look as if we were perched out on the nose of the craft.

Familiar stars blazed across the heavens, drowned out as the craft swung around and the sun came into view. Small, at this distance, but bright. The screens masked its brilliance so that we could see it clearly. Data nodes appeared and drifted across the screens, details on distance and radiation measurements.

Guides appeared, bright green crosshair lines that moved across the screens and stopped, forming a circle around a bright spot to the right of the sun.

"There she is," Tabitha said. "Olinda, a whole planet in that tiny spec."

She did something with the controls, and the crosshair circle expanded, and with it, the view of the planet zoomed in as if we had jumped across the distance in seconds. We hadn't, not even with the STC drive. She'd simply zoomed in with the sensors. Olinda was a predominantly blue and white marble suspended in space.

Tabitha did something else with the controls, her hands gesturing and then she shoved the controls aside and rose. A new screen had appeared, a counter running.

A little over twenty-eight hours to reach Olinda. Faster than the *Wisteria*. "Is that as fast is this can go?"

Tabitha shook her head. "No, but any faster will attract attention. I'm assuming that we don't want to do that?"

"Right. Just curious."

Tabitha grinned. "You might as well relax, take a look around. This is going to be home for as long as the mission takes. I'm going to grab some coffee and go to my quarters.

Make yourselves at home, just don't touch the controls."

"Do you have any Torlian coffee down there?" I asked.

Tabitha raised an eyebrow. "We're interested in enhancement, not overdosing."

With that she slipped out past, us, swaying as she walked past.

She wasn't trying to seduce me, I think it was a habit more than anything.

I turned my chair toward Drac. The Nosferan had his nose in several screens, flipping through them with intense impatience. He smelled of mangos, and his normal pearly glow was streaked with green, pouring down his neck. The rust and blood smell of him was still there, it never seemed to fade.

"What're you looking for?" I asked.

Drac looked at me, his black face wrinkled, white teeth showing behind his lips. He hissed his annoyance. He was definitely back to his old self again, the restoration of his wing and the recovery of the tach field generator must have restored his confidence.

"I am searching for information," he finally answered.

"Information on?"

"The one who brought us the device. We must contact him at once."

The one? "Wait, who are you talking about? We just got the device back from the Enhancers. It's down in the hold."

Drac hissed. His claws tapped the console in front of him. "Long ago. The device was entrusted to us by a Galactic. It was a great honor."

A great chill went through me at his words. I was dying for a big cup of Torlian coffee. When we got back to Olinda, we'd have to take time to get this ship properly stocked. I wasn't going off into the past without a supply.

"You're looking for a Galactic? The same one that gave your people the device over a hundred years ago?"

"Yes." Drac flipped through screens, looking for what, I had no idea. "Now that we have the device back, we must find him."

"And you think you can find this Galactic through the Enhancer's databases?"

"No! I'm searching our records."

"Your records?" What was he talking about? "Nosferan records? How do you have those?"

"I opened a quantum signal to a secure data store."

Of course he did. "And if anyone is monitoring that data store, will they track it back to us?"

Drac slashed the air, discarding screens. He pulled up more. "No. It is secure."

"Right. Okay." Maybe it was, but it still made me uneasy. I hadn't contacted anyone back on Olinda. I didn't want to give Pike or anyone else with an interest in this device, any potential warning that we were coming back.

"I'm going to see about some food, and then I might take a nap. You should get some rest too."

"We don't require rest now," Drac said.

"Okay, but don't say I didn't suggest it when you get cranky."

His hiss followed me as I left the bridge. I wasn't sure about leaving Drac alone on the bridge, but Tabitha obviously wasn't that worried. The automatic systems were probably more than intelligent enough to get us to Olinda without any problem. It wasn't like we had to manually fly the ship anyway.

The galley was down past three work

levels, down in the habitation level which also housed our cabins. I didn't see Tabitha, but the smell of black coffee filled the air. I inhaled deeply, neck slits flaring and concentrated.

I picked up her faint peachy smell and saw her with my scent-sight, tinged with bluish ozone, moving around the galley before she disappeared heading toward the cabins.

So she wanted some privacy. Her grandmother had thrust her into taking this trip.

The galley was well-equipped, despite the lack of Torlian coffee. There was plenty of Terran coffee left in the pot, sitting inset into the wall, secure if the ship had to maneuver quickly. I followed traces of Tabitha's scent to the right cupboard for mugs and selected a tall mug with a lid.

I filled the mug with steaming hot coffee and inserted the pot back into the built-in maker. The galley, like much of the ship, was automated. I touched the screen of the maker, which lit up with faint white light.

"Yes?" It asked, the voice androgynous and friendly.

"Spring rolls? Can you make those?"

"Yes, in fifteen varieties. Do you have a preference?"

"Chicken, with vegetables and hot, spicy. Do you need more than that?"

"No, sir," the machine replied. "I believe I have what you want. One moment, please."

I'd recently had bad experiences with non-organic intelligences. I couldn't tell if this machine was actually sentient or not, which made me uneasy.

A couple of minutes passed, and a low tone sounded. The screen pulsed green. "Your food is prepared, sir."

The front of the machine dissolved away, and hot, spicy steam clouds rolled out. My stomach growled. That smelled perfect. I reached in and found a plate with a half-dozen spring rolls, and two small containers of dipping sauces.

"Thank you," I said, taking the plate.

"You're welcome." The door reformed. "Is there anything else you require?"

"Not right now, thanks."

I picked up one of the rolls and took a bite. A crunch and hot grease, spices, and chicken hit my tongue. Fantastic. If this was what the machine could provide, I'd leave aside the question of its sentience for now.

Still, that might be a question for Tabitha. What exactly was the Enhancers' stance on non-organics? Were they sympathetic toward synthetics since they incorporated cybernetic enhancements into themselves? I hadn't seen any non-organics during our time on their asteroid, but I could have missed them in the general electronic haze of the place.

Having the ability to see electrical and magnetic fields would be helpful not only in identifying non-organics but in analyzing all sorts of technology. In the wide galaxy, there were probably species that had those sorts of capabilities. It triggered the old familiar itch. I hadn't done any in-depth research since my work on the Euzebian scent-sight. Back home in my DNA collection were dozens of samples from different species. Many I had no idea how to incorporate into my own DNA. It was a complex, and sometimes deadly, puzzle.

I reached out with my C'lacktal tentacles and picked up another spring roll. For a second there was a bitter taste, but that came from the tentacles. Mostly I tried to ignore when they tasted something. The tentacles were unplanned, the remaining side-effect of Kelwyn's corrupted Moreau technology weapon. I'd been turned into a Dumpty, scrambled beyond any hope of being put back together again. The only thing that saved me was a backup program I had added to my Moreau Pod, an experimental test program with the potential to revert Dumpties back to their original DNA. It was a glaring flaw in the Moreau Pods, suggesting that the Galactics didn't intend the pods to be used the way the Moreau Society was using them.

Be that as it may, the backup program mostly reverted me back. The tentacles were useful, no doubt, but inhuman and disturbing. In addition to the sting they could deliver, they sometimes tasted things, and also were somewhat erogenous. It suggested that there might be other changes, deeper changes, that I hadn't yet realized. Until I managed an in-depth study of my own current DNA and physiology, I couldn't possibly consider incorporating any more alien DNA into my own. I needed to know absolutely what was going on inside, and right now I didn't. There hadn't been time since dealing with Kelwyn to even think about it. The only case I'd worked on was this one, tracking down the means to recover Muriel and Dyami.

The fountains of bright gasses from the spring rolls were ebbing as they cooled. I took a bite, crunching through the perfectly crisp exterior, unleashing a hot cascade of spicy flavors. Delicious.

Back home, in my DNA collection, I had a sample from a Neridian neocortex. The Neridians were extinct, wiped out long ago, but somehow the Tretan had managed to obtain the sample. Beautiful aliens, humanity had shocked some species when we emerged from our world for our resemblance to the extinct Neridians. They didn't look entirely human, but it was a striking example of convergent evolution at work. And they'd been one of the most intelligent Rim species to develop, considered potential additions to the Galactics' Glittering Throng.

If only they hadn't gotten themselves wiped out.

Just how had the Tretan managed to get the sample? The Tretans had once, so rumor said, been part of the Glittering Throng themselves before being kicked out. The one I knew ran Galactic DNA Suppliers, and I'd never learned if it even had a name of its own. It was the Tretan, that's it. I didn't know anything about how the rest of the species lived today. It wasn't a big stretch to suggest that the Tretan was behind everything that had happened. Muriel and Dyami had been in the Tretan's shuttle when it was thrown back in time. I would have been on it if we hadn't run into some problems with Crombie the zombie and local law enforcement on Hansel. I had promised the Tretan Kelwyn's technology, to cover what I owed him and the use of the shuttle, and hadn't been able to deliver.

What if the Tretan had intended for me to go back in time, not Muriel and Dyami? But why? When I'd gone to him with the photo of Muriel and Dyami, with proof that they had traveled in time, the Tretan had been eager to help. It had seemed genuinely unaware of the possibility of time travel, but even with my scent-sight, I couldn't read the truthfulness of a being so alien. People, sure, but not a super smart alien that resembled a giant spider.

I finished off the last spring roll before it cooled completely, and drained my coffee. I didn't know if the Tretan was behind any of this, it was all speculation. It might have played innocent to play along, planning to get me back in time. For what reason?

I smelled Drac coming before I saw him, fingers of pearly rust and blood smell reaching into the galley like faint questing fingers before he showed up. My scent-sight did make Nosferans appear somewhat more angelic than their wrinkled bat-like faces and bodies suggested.

I was still sitting when Drac, groomed, with his cross-chest belts and gear back in place, appeared in the doorway looking much more confident and formidable than he had been lately.

"We must kill the human cyborg," Drac announced. He drew a small gun, a glittering bit of dark metal that I knew well from my time with the Nosferans. "Given that you are the same species, I will claim the honor."

CHAPTER 51

Terran Expedition Ship Australia

History must be changing. Muriel clung to the walls of the lift as it shot down through the shaking ship, braced on one side by Dyami's solid bulk.

Wasn't history changing? Or had all of this happened before? Except, how could it be before when she didn't remember it happening yet? Before she was born, but in her immediate future.

There is only now, Dyami had said. For them. Future, past, he was right. None of that mattered more than right now.

Clay Yeager had braced himself by the controls with one arm and both legs, wedged into the corner, his broken arm tucked against his gut.

In the opposite corner, braced more or

less the same, except using both arms, was Helen Shaw. Their unlikely rescuer.

In all of the interrogations, Muriel hadn't revealed all of the details about what she knew about the *Australia*. Nothing of Zelenka's experiments, authorized by Helen. Or the crimes reportedly committed by Constantine.

Was that wrong? To bring it up would have felt like she was accusing them of something before it happened. From their frame of reference.

None of it mattered. When the lift reached the hangars, then they would get to the Tretan's shuttle, and hopefully get away from the ship. Find a way back to their own time.

The lift shook again, hard. Helen cried out, apparently in fright.

Muriel lost her footing and fell against Dyami. It was like hitting a firm mattress. His bulk remained rock-solid as she fought to her balance.

"What's happening?" Helen asked.

"Yeah, you know right?" Clay added.

"I told you about the initial attack. This is it." The Nosferans hit the ship with multiple vessels, puncturing the hull in several places, latching on and sending in shock troops. Other shots had crippled the *Australia*'s engines, making escape impossible.

The Nosferans aimed to completely take over the ship. It was only Constantine's security forces, effectively deployed across the entire ship, that prevented the immediate capture of the *Australia*.

Had it happened that way before? Before the trip back in time? That's how she remembered it from her lessons. The security deployment, fortunately in the right key places in the ship, had made resistence possible. But hadn't Constantine done that because she told him where the Nosferans would attack, more or less? As best she remembered? Had that changed history?

She had no way to know. Worrying about paradoxes now wasn't going to help them. The one thing that she did know was that there hadn't been any mention of her, or Dyami, or the Tretan shuttle, in anything that she had learned.

Odd, given the time they'd spent on the ship. Surely records, accounts from those that came into contact with them, something would have survived?

Of course the *Australia* was in bad shape when it was finally recovered, and the data found. Maybe those records were destroyed. At least their bodies weren't found, those would have been noticed, and remarked upon. Particularly since Dyami was an unknown alien, and she wasn't on the crew list on top of having DNA from multiple other species.

The lift slowed. Dyami leaned forward. A vibration that had nothing to do with the attack ran through the lift. "I will go first."

Helen pushed away from the wall. She reached up, hesitated, then touched his shoulder. "No. I should go. Security won't shoot me."

Dyami lowered his head down to human height. "It might not be human security out there."

Helen paled slightly. "They can't have gotten this far into the ship yet."

There wasn't time to argue the point. The lift stopped, and the doors opened. Helen marched out of the elevator, her voice rang out.

"Lower your weapons! Now! I've got civilians with me."

Dyami followed her, and there was more shouting. Muriel was on his heels, trying to see around him. Clay fell in beside her.

Once out of the lift, Muriel made it around Dyami, finding herself facing four security personnel. Dustin, from the team that took them from the shuttle, was at the center, his weapon pointed at Dyami.

Dustin lowered his weapon and motioned to the others. The splat guns dropped. "Dr. Shaw, you should be in your lab."

"We need to get them to the shuttle, there is technology there that can help us."

"That's a restricted area," Dustin said. He stepped closer to Helen and motioned. "Come here."

Dyami moved when Helen started forward. Dustin's splat gun rose. "Not you, big guy. This'll still take you down."

"It's okay," Helen said. She smiled up at Dyami. "I'll be fine.

A loud sizzling crack split the air and took off the top of Helen's head, her hair flipping around, her body falling. Her strings cut.

The body hit the floor, feet kicking in

quick, useless movements as if Helen was trying to get away.

Dyami roared and turned away from the security men.

Splat guns came up. Muriel lunged forward, in front of Dyami.

Another sizzling, electric-sounding crack like a thunderclap and one of the security guards, a woman, flew off her feet, folding in the middle. A red spot blossomed on the front of her workall, a fountain erupting from her back. She flew back, as if yanked, arms and legs trailing. Eyes wide with shock.

Dyami stepped right over Muriel. She ducked, unnecessarily, as he charged down the corridor.

"Dyami!"

Only then did Muriel see who was shooting. A cluster of small, black figures crouched in the corridor ahead. Inhuman figures. They wore suits, matte black, dully reflecting the pulsing red lights in the corridor. Helmets covered their heads and wide membranes stretched between their long arms and their short legs.

Nosferans. Here, clutching lethal-looking weapons, glittering bits of dark metal. She knew those weapons. Brock showed had her one, while training at the firing range. Magnetic rail pistols, they fired projectiles that turned molten as they were accelerated by intense magnetic fields. Essentially becoming a super-hot, super dense plasma.

Dustin's splat gun coughed. One of the Nosferans crumpled to the floor.

Dyami hadn't reached them yet. Dustin's shot distracted the Nosferans.

The remaining two security men moved up beside Dustin, splat guns firing past Dyami.

"Get back!" Dustin yelled.

Dyami obviously wasn't listening. He charged at the Nosferans. Another thunderclap as the Nosferans fired. Dyami jerked to the side, falling, crashing into the wall before he slid to a stop.

"No!" Muriel darted forward.

He couldn't be dead. He couldn't!

Sharp coughs behind her as the security fired back. Muriel threw herself to the side, ducking, hugging the wall, trying to stay out of the way as she ran to Dyami.

As she reached him, his head rose from the floor. *He wasn't dead!* Muriel dropped down and grabbed his left arm, fitting close against his body.

"Dyami, don't move! Where are you hit?"

More coughs from the splat guns and answering cracks from the Nosferans, and there was a high-pitched keening sound that went on and on.

A glance down the corridor showed three Nosferans backing around a door frame, dragging a fourth with them.

She turned her attention back to Dyami. His wrinkled Halloween face looked at her with wide eyes.

"My other arm. Hurts."

"Try not to move, I'll look at it." Muriel crawled around him.

No one was paying any attention to them. She got to his other side. He shifted his weight, not trying to rise, only make room for her.

The plasma bullet had left a crease across his thick hide, cutting through orange stripes and bristles on his right shoulder. It smelled like cooked meat. The wound was at least seven inches long, running from shallow to deeper where it cut through the outer layers of his arm. The plasma bullet had cauterized the wound, which oozed a clear fluid, but didn't appear to be bleeding excessively.

"The wound is sealed," she told him. "I think it will heal."

Dyami shuddered and planted his hands on the floor. "We must go, now."

He was right. Muriel didn't want him to move, but they had to take the chance. With Helen dead, they had to use the confusion to reach the shuttle. If they still could.

Dustin and one other guard were moving ahead down the corridor. No one was shooting at the moment. If the Nosferans had fled, Dustin would come back, and she didn't think he would take them to the shuttle, not after this.

In the other direction lay three bodies, two security, and Helen. Clay was still there, sitting next to Helen's body, tears running down his face.

"Can you make it?" Muriel said to Dyami.

"Yes."

"Let's go."

Dyami rose and turned, favoring his right arm, then moving with more confidence back the way they'd come. Muriel ran ahead.

Clay looked up tears in his eyes at them. "They killed her!"

"They did, I'm sorry." Muriel crouched next to Clay and touched his good arm. "Clay, we need to get to the shuttle. Now. Is there another way?"

Clay sniffled, wiped his nose on his arm. "Yes. Through the equipment rooms, you can get around to the other side of the hangars."

"Show us." Muriel stood. Clay looked up at her. She held out her hand. "Helen wanted to help, it's up to you."

He nodded, accepted her help, and she pulled him up onto his feet. He started to look down, but Muriel reached out and touched his face.

"Don't. Helen wouldn't want you to remember her like that. Let's go. Do what she wanted."

"Okay." Clay shuddered and launched into motion like a rusted robot.

He took them down the corridor in the other direction, to a side door. It opened at his touch on the panel. It was a small door. Human-sized, but narrower than some of the others. Clay was already inside when Muriel stopped and looked at Dyami.

"I don't know if he can fit in here."

The room was an equipment storage room, with racks of gear contained in secured plastic and metal crates on metal shelving. It was like entering a labyrinth. Muriel looked down the corridor, so far the security hadn't come back. That wasn't encouraging. They couldn't go that way and run into Nosferans, or security.

The floor vibrated beneath her feet, and the translator spoke. "I can fit. Go on."

"We can find another way," Muriel said.

Clay shook his head. "Not without going back up a level, and over through the connecting corridor."

"I can fit," Dyami insisted.

She wanted out of the corridor, away from the fighting, and to the shuttle. "Let's see."

Clay went on, and Muriel followed him in, stopping when she was far enough to give Dyami room. Dyami's shoulders were much bigger than the width of the doorway. He twisted sideways, his good left arm beneath him, supporting him and wriggled through the doorway. Even coming in sideways like that, his chest was nearly too wide to fit.

Muriel moved back more to make room. He kept coming, wedging himself in good.

"Go on, " he said. "I'm okay."

He didn't look okay. He was in a sideways posture, wedged between the crates. Wiggling forward, he came in far enough for the door to slide shut. It wasn't the sort of barrier that would stop a determined mob, but it gave them some security from the invaders.

"Come on," Clay said. "It's isn't far, and then I think it opens up in the next section."

Hopefully, he was right. If either Nosferans or security found them now, they were helpless.

And Dr. Helen Shaw had *died*. Her head blown clean off. That definitely changed history. In the original story of the *Australia* expedition, Shaw had survived and eventually faced charges for her actions. One of the few crew members to make it out of this alive. Proof now that the future could change. What did that mean? Except that Dyami was still right. There was only now. That's all that mattered.

Behind her, the Eyotan panted as he struggled sideways down the narrow aisle, dragging himself along between the shelves.

Muriel followed Clay but kept looking back at Dyami, making sure they weren't leaving him behind.

If the future wasn't set, then they could die. Their bodies could be found on the *Australia*, or worse.

They could get taken by the Nosferans.

CHAPTER 52

Enhancer Ship Epsilon

Physically, Drac wasn't any match for me. I out-massed him and had him on height, strength, reach and speed. There wasn't much room to move in the galley. However, even as fast as I am, I didn't think I was fast enough to get the weapon away from him before he fired.

I kept my hands in view above the table, the C'lacktal tentacles writhing as if agitated all on their own. "Put it down, Drac. We don't need anyone killed. For all you know that might punch a hole right through the hull and cause a major depressurization event. Or hit a drive-critical component. Why don't you tell me what this is about?"

If I could keep him talking, maybe I could get him settled down. The magnetic rail pistol shot high-density plasma ordinance. It'd do everything I said, causing severe damage to the ship if it hit the wrong part. Not to mention what it'd do to anyone in the path.

"She must die." Drac spread his arms. "She dies, we take the ship. Simple. She's unnecessary."

"And the first time I encountered Nosferans, they tried to board my ship. How did that work out? We can't kill her. We don't even know if we can fly the ship without her. It might use some cybernetic interface we don't have."

Drac hissed and motioned with the pistol. "You delay. I checked the interface. Easily bypassed lockouts. I can fly any ship!"

Probably true. Nosferans were natural flyers. I wasn't going to argue the point.

"Did you find the Galactic? Is that what this is about?"

"Yes! I found him, on the planet. Once we have the ship, we will contact him, and we can begin to restore my people to their rightful place in the galaxy!"

"Restore your people? You mean to change history?"

Drac laughed the high child-like laughter

that still haunted many of my nightmares. I knew that laugh—like I knew the casual cruelty of the Nosferans.

I pulled up my sleeve, revealing the underside of my right forearm, right below the elbow. There's a tattoo there, invisible in normal light but in infrared, it glowed like an ember in my skin. The Nosferans branded me with that mark, a high honor, marking me as the Esteemed One, a savior of their species. Drac's dark eyes glittered, and the weapon wavered.

"In darkness is security, life, and joy," I said.

"In light is jeopardy, death, and sadness," Drac answered. He turned his arm. "I too bare a mark. You have no rank over me!"

Damn. "Maybe not, but you still must listen to me. We need to get Muriel and Dyami back, that's the goal. We're not going back to change history."

More laughter from Drac. "Not change history!" His voice hit higher pitches. "Not change history! My people are scattered, weak! Thrown into the light! Many tribes perish! If this continues, we will all die! We face —"

A huge weight suddenly dragged me down. My arms smashed against the table. Gravity had increased. I fought against the pull, but Drac wasn't prepared to deal with higher gravity. He crumpled to the floor, his gun landing hard.

Gravity must have jumped to four or five gees. I braced my legs and rose. Each step was a challenge even for my improved muscles. I staggered around the table. My C'lacktal tentacles hung straight down, they couldn't fight against this gravity.

Drac lay on the floor, his chest barely moving. He only managed short gasps. Too much of this and he would suffocate.

As much as I didn't want to, I bent and picked up the gun. I was straightening when Tabitha appeared in the entry from the cabins.

"Kill me, will you?" She said, her gaze fixed on Drac. "I don't think so!"

"Restore the gravity," I said.

"Why should I? I can function in this just fine."

I didn't raise the gun. I didn't want to escalate things further. Plus, it was heavy. "Let him up. He won't be a problem."

"And have to look over my shoulder constantly? Or should I wait to get my throat cut in my sleep?"

"Release him, it won't happen. We stick to the plan. All of us are in this together."

Tabitha didn't do anything but the gravity suddenly lessened, reverting back to a standard gee. My tentacles writhed with relief. Drac sucked in a deep breath and let it out, before making a keening noise in his throat.

"Get up," I told him. "Swear on the tribe's honor that you will not harm anyone on this expedition, now or in the future."

Drac picked himself up slowly, rising up on his short legs. He stayed bent at the waist, sucking air for a second then straightened.

"On the tribe's honor, I swear."

Tabitha laughed. "That's it?"

"He won't break his word," I said. To prove the point I held out the gun to Drac.

Nosferans have very little these days. Honor was important. He took the gun from my hand, his black claws sharp but not scratching. He could have killed us right then. Even Tabitha's thought control of the ship might not have saved her.

Instead, the gun disappeared into a holster on his belts. "I have the location of the one."

"The one?" Tabitha asked.

"He is the one that gave us the device many years ago, before it was stolen." Black eyes fixed on me. "You know him as Shanley Walsh."

CHAPTER 53

Enhancer Ship Epsilon

There were three people in the Enhancer's small galley. Tabitha, stood in the doorway, her forehead wrinkled with confusion. She didn't have a clue why the name Drac had given was important.

Drac just stood in the doorway back to the bridge, waiting for my response. And there was me. This was a bigger surprise than Tabitha turning up the gravity and flattening Drac.

This time it was as if I'd been flattened by what Drac had just said, that Shanley Walsh, my boss and friend, was the Galactic that gave the Nosferans the tach field generator.

"He's not a Galactic," I said, finding my tongue. "He's human!"

"Who are you talking about?" Tabitha asked.

"My partner," I said. "We run the detective agency together. It started out with me working for him, but now we're equal partners. He goes in for the more routine cases, missing pets and divorces, things like that, while I deal with the harder cases."

I focused back on Drac. "He's human. Why would you say he is the one?"

"He doesn't remember it," Drac said. "I wasn't sure, at first. He's chosen to forget. He does that, becomes a species and forgets who he is for a time. Later, he returns to himself with the knowledge of what it was like to live as that species."

If anything that made my head spin more. Shanley was a Galactic, and he didn't know it?

"So we what? Show up and simply tell him what he is?"

"I believe I can trigger the knowledge," Drac said. "He will remember, and then he will help restore our people."

Tabitha came into the room, apparently convinced that Drac wasn't going to shoot her after all. "Just like that? How is he going to change history?"

"He will know," Drac insisted.

"Setting aside the question of whether or not you're right," I said. And I didn't believe that Shanley was a Galactic, he even smelled human. "We have other problems. The Tretan put resources into finding out that Pike had the generator. Plus I already owe him. He's not going to sit by while others use the technology. Plus there's Pike, he must have his own reasons for wanting to get the device back."

"I'm supposed to follow you," Tabitha said. "What do you think we need to do?"

The way forward looked obvious to me. Maybe I was missing something. I told Hypatia that I thought events had been orchestrated by a guiding agency. Hearing Drac's claim that Shanley was a Galactic, which I still didn't believe, opened one possibility.

"I'm not saying I believe Shanley is Galactic, but we need to talk to him. I'm not sure what the Tretan's end-game is, but I don't think that he wants to prevent us from going into the past. Drac, your plan also leads back in time. It seems like we're still all headed in the same direction— if we can consider something so crazy a direction."

"So back to Olinda?" Tabitha asked.

"Yes," Drac hissed. "Shanley Walsh will reveal the truth!"

"I can't say that stranger things haven't happened in my life." I stood up. "For now, it sounds like we agree. Back to Olinda."

Tabitha nodded and crossed the room. I tensed when she came within striking distance of Drac. The Nosferan didn't back down, he glared back at her with dark eyes. Tabitha looked down at him.

"I won't forget what you tried to do," she said, then smiled. "And if I wanted to lock out the ship's systems, I could do it with a thought, just like I did with the gravity. And if anything did happen to me? The ship would lock you out and power down so fast that you'd be sucking vacuum before my body cooled. Just so you know."

She went past him, leaving her back apparently open, not that I doubted her ability to defend herself.

Drac laughed. It was that chilling, high-pitched, child-like laughter that set my nerves on edge. Tabitha jerked around, but he didn't make any move toward her. The laughter died, and he stared at her with space-empty eyes.

I smelled the salty scent of Tabitha's apprehension, strands of it trickling off her into the air. She opened her mouth, closed it and went on ahead toward the bridge.

"Try to get along," I told Drac.

He looked back at me with that same gaze. Nosferans don't think like us. It takes a lot to get recognized by them as something other than food. If you're not a Galactic or a Nosferan, you're potential prey.

I returned his gaze. I've seen similar looks before. You don't back down with them. Hypatia said not to trust the Nosferans, saying that I didn't know enough about them.

Maybe not. What Hypatia didn't know was that I never trusted them, and never would. I had an idea of how they acted, and I used that model, but I was always ready to revise the model if I saw new behavior.

Without another word he turned around and headed back up to the bridge. Hopefully, he wouldn't break his word and try to kill Tabitha. I didn't think he would.

Drac was a Nosferan tribe all in himself,

among aliens. When we got back to Olinda, would he seek reinforcements? What would happen with Shanley Walsh?

And the real question on my mind, would we be able to use the tach field generator to find a way to go back and get Muriel and Dyami? If Shanley was just human, like I thought, then probably our only hope with the Tretan. It was his shuttle, after all, that had apparently carried Muriel and Dyami back in time in the first case. Intentionally or not, the Tretan might be the only chance to go back.

Back. If anything Pike's nanowire memory scanner had reminded me of things I had left long ago in the past. Remembering the past was one thing.

Did I really want to go back and relive it?

ΔΔΔ

Author's Note

I'm so pleased that you decided to join Brock Marsden on this trip in Past Lives. The adventure continues with Past Dark, find out more at MoreauSociety.com.

This book and the one that follows makes up the 'Past' duology. Writing these books gave me the chance to explore much more of Brock's past. They also gave me a chance to bring other characters to the foreground. I loved having an opportunity to spend time with Muriel, Dyami, Drac, and Helen Shaw.

I've especially enjoyed the opportunity to go back over this book to create this new edition. I know some writers who don't like to look at their older work. I'm not in that camp. For me, it's like rereading a book I've enjoyed. It's been years since I wrote this book. As I went through it, I didn't make major changes—this wasn't a rewrite. I approach these new editions with a light touch. Dust them off and give them some well-deserved attention.

Whether this was your first time reading *Past Lives* or your tenth, I hope you enjoyed this story and will continue to join Brock on his future (or is that past?) adventures. And if you did enjoy the book, leave a review. It is extremely helpful to other readers and to writers to have reviews.

Ryan M. Williams
September 2018

OTHER BOOKS

For information on these titles and to sign up for *Readinary*, my list with news, offers and more, visit my site at ryanwriter.link/novels

Like **science fiction mysteries**? Check out the **MOREAU SOCIETY** series. Private detective Brock Marsden investigates the toughest crimes, his alien-enhanced DNA giving him the edge he needs to save lives.

- Dark Matters
- The Gingerbread House
- Past Lives
- Past Dark
- Synthetic Pain *(writing)*

Do you like your **fantasy** dark and paranormal? Ravyn Washington isn't like other students. Her grandmother was called a witch and if the Inquisition discovers

Ravyn's abilities she could burn in the **DEAD THINGS** series.

- Waking Dead Things
- Dreaming Dead Things
- Killing Dead Things
- Burning Dead Things *(planned)*

Enjoy **adventure** and **fantasy**? Join Dalton Hicks on a cross-country race across two worlds in the **GOBLIN ALLEY** series.

- The Bloodied Fang
- The Eleven Lords
- Trow Forge
- The King's Runner

Not every high school student falls for the monster. Natalie is smarter than that in the **PIERCE, WA** series.

- Dirty Old Vampires
- Naughty Young Werewolves *(planned)*
- Pretty Dead Ghouls *(planned)*

Discover more **science fiction** with these books.

- Europan Holiday
- Stowaway to Eternity
- Time Retrievers

And if you like **romance** and **comedy**, the books by **KATE N. RYAN** will tickle your funny bone—and more.

- Watching You Sleep
- Waiting For Cake

Do you enjoy something a bit darker, like **horror**? Then check out these titles.

- Full Moon Nights
- Downland

Like **science fiction** with a dash of **steampunk** and enhanced sea creatures? The brothers Douglas and Brennan Dunne face an uncertain future with their Uncle Quigley's monstrous creations in the **LAND LUBBERS** series.

- Cabin Boys
- Sea Legs
- Murky Waters *(planned)*

Prefer something more **cozy** with your **mystery**? The **POEVILLE** series with feline detective C. Auguste Dupin and his human librarian Penny Copper might be just the thing.

- The Murders in the Reed Moore Library

- The Task of Auntie Dido

More books coming soon!

www.ingramcontent.com/pod-product-compliance
Lightning Source LLC
Chambersburg PA
CBHW032153180726
48284CB00001B/32